THE PAPER MAN DOSSIER

by

Minerva Taylor

TELEMACHUS PRESS

Cover designed by Telemachus Press, LLC

Cover art:
Copyright © iStock/172781640/davelogan
Copyright © iStock/182778825/Pgiam
Copyright © iStock/475426586/sdigital
Copyright © iStock/512218646/ABykov
Copyright © Stock/155277612/Savushkin
Copyright © iStock/157523118/ktmoffitt
Copyright © iStock/184090794/drbimages

Publishing Services by Telemachus Press, LLC
7652 Sawmill Road
Suite 304
Dublin, Ohio 43016
http://www.telemachuspress.com

ISBN: 978-1-956867-48-0 (eBook)
ISBN: 978-1-956867-49-7 (Paperback)

Version 2023.01.24

Also by Minerva Taylor

The Blood Stiller

The Blood Archive

Blood and Oil: The Devil's Tears

Children's Books

Alien Mom

The Mole Brothers' Magnificent Mission

James and the Mini

For John

With special thanks to Nancy Caparros

The New
Main
Building of
the KGB

Lubyanka
Building
ex-headquarters
of the KGB

1983   1948

Lubyanyki Facade

The place of
Dzerzhinsky
Monument

Children's
World

The
Solovetsky
Stone

Lubyanka Square

Trans-Siberian Railway

Caucasus Region

The Golem of Prague; a mythical monster created from clay and brought to life by a rabbi to save the Jews from a pogrom in 16th century Prague. According to legend, the giant creature could be reawakened if the Jewish people were in peril. At the beginning of WWII, some still believed he was chained up in the old synagogue.

Statisticians tell us that people underestimate the sheer number of coincidences that are bound to happen in a world governed by chance.

Steven Pinker

It is the narrow, hidden tracks that lead back to our lost homeland, what is the solution to the last mysteries is not the ugly scar that life's rasp leaves on us, but the fine, almost invisible writing that is engraved on our body.

The Golem by Gustav Meyrink

The Paper Man Dossier

Prologue
Germany: February 1945

Below Forest, Near *Sachsenhausen* Concentration Camp
22 Miles North of Berlin

The Boy

HE IMAGINES HE is the boy in the book, fleeing death, through the forest, a sinister place where dark fairy tales begin. It is night, and freezing cold. He struggles for breath in the rush of wind. The frost-covered trees shiver and claw at the sky. Crashing bombs, spouting fire and black smoke, pursue him.

He is twelve years old, but could be mistaken for an aged man, with hollow cheeks and skeletal limbs. His grown man's clothes—ragged trousers with broad red stripes down each leg, and a red cross on his coat—flap about his thin figure, and tear on the sharp bushes. Prison sirens pierce the darkness, sending terror through his body. He stumbles along on the frozen ground and the tangle of underbrush, in workman's boots much too large for his feet, frantically searching for a place to hide.

World War II is coming to an end. Allied bombs rain down near *Sachsenhausen* Concentration Camp. News has spread among the prisoners in cell block 19 that the Red Army is 60 miles east of

Berlin, but their hope of liberation fades when they learn that they will be evacuated to a place hidden from the Allied Forces. In these last days before the German surrender the guards have begun to kill political prisoners and those who are too ill to move into hiding.

Elijah, the steganographer, has chosen The Boy to break out of the camp, carrying Nazi classified intelligence, hidden in a pouch made of rags, and stitched inside his coat. It is a secret between him and Elijah, a belief that somehow these top-secret documents will save them.

Fredrich Bachman, an SS trainee, hoping that his good deed would rescue him from the invading Red Army, led The Boy through the soldiers' headquarters outside the camp. Shaking with fear of being caught and hung by the commandant, he shoved The Boy toward the edge of the forest, whispering, "Run."

The Boy is tall, his thin bones stretched by starvation. His hair, shaved at capture, has grown back in small tufts, and scabs of mange cover his scalp. But in this moment, he is convinced he is the character drawn in the book—sturdy with rosy cheeks, a mop of curls, and big, dark eyes.

He zigzags between the trees, slipping on patches of snow, clutching the pouch through his rough coat so hard his hand bleeds. The story flickers through his head, and there he is in print, traveling to the River Vltava with Rabbi Lowe. The Rabbi creates the Golem, a giant creature of clay, and brings him to life. In the story, The Boy has many adventures with the Golem who saves the Prague Jews on the very last page.

His escape into the safety of the story began at Terezin, a reception center and camp near Prague. There, he and his family and other Jews were herded by soldiers onto cattle cars, and transported by train, to a camp with a high tower.

His heart had beat hard with fear until he closed his eyes and pretended his book, with its smooth leather cover, vivid drawings, and elegant script was tucked under his arm, waiting for his tale to unfold.

The Boy ceased to care that he and the others were crushed together in the boxcar, without food or water, gasping for breath in the heat. An old man next to him died in silence, standing upright among the crowd. This was not real; it was not in his book, the place where he truly existed.

He had vanished completely inside the pages when the train arrived at *Auschwitz* gate passing the sign, *Arbeit Macht Frei*. He and the other prisoners were whipped and driven out of the railway car. Soldiers wielding blackjacks and guns and shouting *"Raus,"* inspected them. He was separated from his mother and sister and did not look up to say good bye, but closed his eyes and waited for the Golem to save them.

Now, as he flees in the dark winter from *Sachsenhausen*, the sirens, savage, insistent, seek him out. He dives into a copse of bushes, his heart banging against his weak chest. He hears the stomp of boots coming up behind him, and the command, *"Halt."* He darts in panic from his hiding place, his bone-thin legs pumping. The SS guard, close on his heels, grips his coat. A sudden thud against his head brings a rush of violent pain. The frozen ground, covered in twigs and roots of trees, springs up to meet him.

The guard stands over him, shouting and kicking without mercy, his boots crunching bone. The Boy will not let go of the pouch, even though he feels his body, a thin almost transparent membrane, shatter and slowly crumple like dry parchment. For one dazed moment, he is flying above the steeples of Prague, toward the starry sky.

Gunfire shatters the air; there is a scream, a grunt. The kicking stops.

The stars fade into black nothingness, and The Boy lies motionless in the dark silence. He gathers courage and opens his eyes. The guard is lifeless beside him. And just as he had imagined, the Golem has sprung from the pages of the book and stands by the trees in front of him. The giant carries a gun; he grins through a muddy face. He speaks a language The Boy doesn't know.

Moscow: December 2002

Borya, Major Boris Sergeyevich Piatikov

Chapter 1

AT 3 A.M. A car outside the Hotel National exploded in a fiery blast, lighting up the sky, sending the curtain of heavy snow leaping in a sizzling red glow, scattering the body parts of its short, stocky occupant over the street. Minutes after the dark rolling smoke cleared, a black van pulled out of the alley, and men in Hazmat suits jumped from its back door, extinguished the last of the fire, and scraped up the remains of the victim. A second crew towed away the black, smoldering car and cleaned the snow of blood and debris.

Two hours earlier Major Boris Sergeyevich Piatikov, Borya to his friends and family, had parked his old Lada on Mokhovaya Ulitza, in front of the Hotel National, a short distance from the giant walls and towers of the Kremlin. Dressed to be inconspicuous in a grey jacket and black trousers, he had walked several blocks around the empty streets and returned an hour later to his car, sure that no one had tailed him.

The Major, a serious history buff, had recently retired from the FSB, Russia's federal security service. From an early age he had been fascinated by tales of the Old Bolsheviks, the true heroes of the revolution. Until two weeks ago, he had been engrossed in writing a glorified history of their past, and spent most of his waking hours researching documents in the classified archive stored in the FSB headquarters in the Lubyanka building.

Borya possessed an unblemished, if undistinguished, service record, and was granted a security clearance to work in the one remaining, top-secret archive housed in the Lubyanka. This archive held only the classified files from the Russian Communist Party, the Central Committee, and the Politburo.

He was a man of routine, and when Eugenia, his wife, died shortly after his retirement, he had felt only annoyance at her demise, which upset his schedule for three weeks before and after her burial. His marriage to Eugenia, a fellow Komsomol member, had been impulsive, and he had soon regretted it. She became hostile and nagged him constantly. Any affection or love disappeared after the first two years of marriage. He retreated into his project; his true calling as historian and scholar.

Borya had joined the service as a young zealot thirty years earlier. A true believer in the virtues of the Soviet Union, he despised and feared the *glavny protivnik,* the main enemy, and was certain that even his humble work aided in the Soviet defense against the United States and the West.

He had been a desk officer, handling passports and other documents for First Directive intelligence operations in Soviet Bloc countries. He was not an original thinker, but was known for his meticulous attention to detail and ability to carry out orders without question. Consequently, he rose into the middle ranks of the vast organization. His gradual disillusionment with the government, aggravated by his meagre pension and dull lifestyle, had grown since he began his research.

The Lubyanka Archive held the closely-guarded personal records of the top Bolshevik and Communist leaders from 1917 to 1991. They included official papers, diaries, and letters from Lenin, Trotsky, and Stalin, and from more recent members of the Politburo and Central Committee.

The documents revealed all the dirty secrets from the time of Bolshevik rule to the Communist regime. In spite of public revelations after the downfall of the Soviet Union, Borya had been in denial, refusing to believe accusations levelled against former party leaders. But viewing this classified evidence for the first time had been a rude awakening.

The leaders he once idolized and vigorously defended were no different from the tsars—even worse—in their repression. Their pretense of living simply like the proletariat and being dedicated to the revolution was exposed in the files. They aped the aristocracy, living in mansions and driving luxurious cars confiscated from former owners. These documents revealed their secret perversions—the worst, Beria raping and murdering little girls; their love of luxury; their tables full of food and drink at banquets; their wild partying and orgies—while ordinary people lived in poverty. Their cruelty, casually brushing aside the indiscriminate murder and starvation of peasants in the famine during and after the Civil War was all-too evident. He discovered to his shock and dismay that top Bolsheviks stashed away false passports and money, to escape if the revolution failed.

He seethed with resentment at the enrichment of many of his FSB colleagues since the end of the Soviet Union. His anger surged over the success of his former colleague, Captain Oleg Mikhailovich Vasiliev, who had the right connections in the Kremlin, and had acquired a fortune under the new regime. Oleg owned mansions in the US and the South of France, a yacht and a private jet while the major, who was a rank above him and had given his all to his country, and struggled along on his pension in an apartment with a leaking roof and bad plumbing.

Now he waited impatiently, watching the snow piling up in drifts in the dark, empty street, in spite of the dvorniks' attempts earlier that evening to clear the walkway.

The chill that permeated his body was not from the freezing temperature, but from the warning impressed on him when he had joined the service: betrayal meant death. It could not dissuade him from this compulsion to change his life.

He mused on the strange twist of fate that had led him to this dangerous encounter. While searching in a special section for personal accounts of Old Bolsheviks who fought in the revolution, survived Stalin's purge in 1936–1938, and lived on into the 1970s, he had come upon a battered old folder, labeled: *1937–74 Misc.* This was very unusual, and aroused his curiosity. Blowing off the dust, he opened the folder and blinked. A gleam of amazement lit up his tiny, dark eyes. It contained one phrase: *To be entered: Misc.10B.*

He put the folder and brief contents back in place, intrigued by this strange file, obviously untouched for years. It could have been an oversight; perhaps the clerk had planned to come back to it and add documents and forgot, or thought it was unimportant. He combed through other folders in that section with corresponding dates, but found nothing relevant.

In the following days he continued his routine, rising before dawn in his drab apartment in a high-rise building in the Otradnoe District, and traveling from Dekabristov Street to the Lubyanka, arriving early at his desk inside the archive vault.

As always, before beginning his work, he set out the same lunch of buckwheat, sauerkraut and a tin of *shpotu,* the little fish he couldn't do without, along with the obligatory *bubliki* and strong sweet tea which he drank throughout the day until late at night.

It was preposterous, but he couldn't shrug off the fanciful notion that the missing contents of this folder might exist, could even be stored somewhere in the building. *10B* on the note could indicate room 10. Could B stand for basement? Could it be that simple?

On Friday of the second week after finding the folder, he drained the last of his tea, and waited, his heart battering against his chest, until Lidia Prescova, a brisk cheery woman in charge of security at check-in, hustled out the staff. She was accustomed to his working late at night. The archive room was protected by a heavy vault door. The major's rank entitled him to know the combinations of the locks and the alarm codes.

As soon as the staff voices faded, he walked quickly to the door at the rear of the file room. When he had first arrived at the archive, Lidia had explained that the steel door led to the old cellar, part of the former KGB prison. He had been astonished that it still existed because one section of the Lubyanka basement recently had been converted into a cafeteria and museum.

"But this," she whispered, shaking her head, "is the old prison." Her pleasant face contorted in a mask of fear. "No one goes there."

Chapter 2

BORYA OPENED THE steel door, surprised at his courage. He would never have imagined venturing near these cells, where victims of the secret police had been tortured and murdered.

"No one goes there." Lidia's whisper followed him down flights of metal steps into the dark cellar. He groped along the wall, found the rusty switch and clicked on the lights. The dim bulbs gave off a sinister glow and, with a stab of fear, Borya glanced over his shoulder into the dark hallway. He pulled up his jacket collar to conceal his face, a precaution against hidden cameras. His steps echoed in the heavy silence, bouncing off the steel-lined walls and cages, through the labyrinth of cavernous passageways stained with dark, scabrous, red patches. He flinched, recoiling, as a huge rat shrieking with fright, thumped over his shoes, hitting his legs. He moaned softly in disgust, but kept going.

Borya grew dizzy from peering out from his collar and searching for numbers on the heavy cell doors. He considered

retreating to the safety of the archive when he found a door marked
9B. The cell number next to it was hidden by a pile of empty crates
and boxes.

He pushed the jacket away from his face and tripping in his
haste, shoved the boxes away. The handle turned easily, and the
door to *10B* creaked open. He gasped for breath at the rush of stale
air. The sound of something dripping seemed to measure his own
fearful heartbeat. Was it the drip of blood? A fetid smell
overwhelmed him. He clicked on the light switch and stood in the
doorway. A leak from a broken pipe had deposited a moist slime on
the walls. Stepping cautiously over the threshold, he stared in
amazement.

This large room was like a junk shop, piled with furniture, old
posters, photographs and paintings. The mysterious collection,
probably stored from the revolution to the end of the previous
decade, was puzzling. Perhaps a discredited member of the
Politburo, attempting to curry favor, had assembled these artifacts
for an honorary museum which was later abandoned. A more
mundane explanation for the motley jumble could have been the
result of redecorating offices for new occupants, with the discards
forgotten or left when the First Directive moved to new
headquarters.

He struggled past photographs of Politburo members and
Army generals stacked against crumbling leather couches and tables.
Dozens of *Agitprop* posters exhorting workers to help with the war
effort were propped against the walls. Rummaging through the
room, he discovered an old desk buried under several WWII
helmets, and a set of pottery painted with muscular farmers driving
tractors.

He began to move the clutter to get to the desk, then froze at a faint noise in the hall. His pulse racing, he scrambled back through the junk to close the door and lock it. A white blur floated in front of him before the door swung shut.

He stood still and listened for long moments, but heard only drips from the leaking pipe. Satisfied that he had imagined the noise and the white blur, he turned back to the desk; it seemed only logical to search it first.

Pulling hard to open the warped top drawer, he found a frayed cardboard folder, labeled *1937–74,* with the same note as that in the archive: *To be entered: Misc. 10B.* Inside the folder was a sheaf of documents.

Distracted, listening for movement in the hallway, Borya stuffed the papers in his jacket, clambered through the piles of junk and closed the door. A faint tap, then another, echoed in the corridor. He crouched down among the boxes and waited, his mind blank with terror until the sound gradually faded into silence. He raced up the steps, pressing against the wall at each turning, and shut the cellar door. His hands trembled as he entered the archive alarm code, gathered up his belongings, and hurried out of the building. The tap of footsteps seemed to follow him as he crept along the street to his apartment, not waiting for the bus.

He sat at his kitchen table without taking off his coat and opened the folder. The documents, dated 1974, recorded the interrogation of a defector, Nicolae Andreyevich Platov (Agent cover name, Daniel Berger.) The defector Platov, a.k.a. Berger, had confessed to the existence of a classified file called the Paper Man Dossier, believed to have been destroyed or lost at the end of WWII.

The interrogators were positive the Paper Man Dossier contained high-risk intelligence, and that there would be grave consequences if the contents ever became public. Even after the torture, which made Borya's eyes water just reading of it, the defector claimed he had no knowledge of the dossier's contents or its location. Platov's signature on his confession, marred by dark red stains, seemed a threat to Borya, even though he was sure everyone involved was long dead. He stared, puzzled, at the back cover of the folder. A swastika, the Nazi symbol, was drawn in pen at the top.

Borya had thrown off his coat and now sat drinking vodka while questions ran through his head. Who had hidden this Platov interrogation and why? Was it placed there accidentally and forgotten? But then he realized it didn't matter. The risk he had taken had come to nothing. His disappointment was bitter.

This intelligence interrogation from the 1970s had to be outdated and not worth danger to his life; not worth anything. He contemplated the peril of returning the worthless material to the basement as he finished the vodka and drifted off to sleep.

In the following days, he gradually changed his mind about the importance of the strange interrogation. It might be a gift of fate and, if used correctly, could be his ticket to leave the country for a better life, something he often contemplated. He had been an insignificant figure in his intelligence organization, and until this point had no bargaining power to gain entry into any Western country. Now it seemed possible the West might welcome this information from the Lubyanka Archive, even if its value might only be for propaganda.

His thoughts became more ambitious. He might be able to use previous classified research to publish his book in the States; maybe become a famous professor at Harvard. His bitterness and jealousy grew as he compared his own existence to that of Oleg, whose connections had given him so many advantages.

He began to change his usual sober habits and no longer spent hours in the archive vault. He recklessly frequented nightclubs and bars, often drinking to oblivion. And then he met Marissa, so young and beautiful, at the Zima Club, and fell head over heels, surprised at his new depth of feeling.

One night after they had made love in a luxurious and costly room in the National, he held Marissa in his arms and, abandoning his usual caution, revealed his plan. She had regarded him fondly through her tangled hair, her lips in a pout. "Borya, you are a wonderful man, but remember, you promised. You must take me away, or I will find another lover," she said, pulling him on top of her.

Now, parked in front of the hotel waiting for his contact, he thought yes, he was a new man with courage. His head buzzed from the bottle of vodka he had drained, and he gazed up at the socialist realist mural at the top of the hotel. It resembled a *kokoshnik*, the traditional Russian headdress, with thick sheets of snow falling down like a veil over the National's art nouveau windows and columns.

He snorted with derision at the mural's idealistic depiction of workers and the industrial might of Russia. It seemed somehow fitting to his betrayal to be waiting in front of the Hotel National, Moscow's first Bolshevik headquarters.

Lenin, the Bolshevik leader and his wife, Krupsaya, had occupied Room 107 while damage to the Kremlin from revolutionary bullets was repaired. He had never seen this room, now a tourist attraction, and available only to the wealthy and famous.

Restless, he examined himself in the front mirror, and with stubby fingers nervously pressed down on his new hairpiece. The salesman had talked him into this shade, a little too bright and orange for his natural coloring, and not quite matching his greying moustache. He studied his thick features, disregarding his red bloated nose, imagined that he was still charming when he smiled and looked younger than his years. especially when he had the opportunity to wear his uniform. He dreamed of living with Marissa in California.

He checked his watch again and looked out the window. Beads of sweat popped out on his forehead. The contact from the U.S. Embassy was late, even though their compound in the Presnensky District was not far. Maybe he had decided not to show up, or had been caught by security.

That morning he had picked up his new papers and airline tickets and had a sudden urge to call Marissa, to hear her voice, but knew that they could be listening. Ah, Marissa; he thought of her long legs wrapped around him. He was to meet her later at the airport, escorted by someone from the embassy, for the flight to Nice and temporary accommodation there, before moving to the States.

From out of the heavily falling snow a dark figure appeared at the car window. Startled from his reverie, Borya jerked back against the seat, unlocked the door, and the man slid in next to him. In the dim shadows of the hotel lights the man, dressed in black jeans and a leather jacket, looked like a demon, with a shaggy beard and dark, sunken eyes. Borya stared at the small star tattooed on this demon's forehead. A jagged scar ran like lightning down the side of his face. His silence filled Borya with terror as the man extended his hand for the interrogation documents.

Borya tried to control his urge to vomit. He handed over the folder and waited, his legs quivering uncontrollably. The man leafed through the pages, looked up and grinned at him, opened the car door. and took off down the street, his phone in hand.

Panicked, blood rushing to his head, Borya struggled to get out of the car. His shrieks mingled with the roar of the blast.

The next afternoon a notice appeared in the Novaya Gazetta and other important Moscow newspapers. "Retired Major Boris Sergeyevich Piatikov was killed in a bomb attack. Two Chechens were arrested on terrorism charges."

The Major's hairpiece lay like a small, orange-colored animal—insignificant, forgotten in the snow.

Moscow: December 2002

Pasha, General Pavel Romanovich Mikhailov

Chapter 3

THE GENERAL, CALLED Pasha by close colleagues, stared absently at the photographs of military commanders displayed on his walls. His disciplined and stern appearance: short, iron-gray hair; and long thin face, accentuated with a large nose, hid his impatience in waiting for the new report.

He paced the length of his office, decorated in a semblance of Soviet style—plain and spare, in keeping with his well-cultivated image of puritanical dedication to his country. He stopped to warm himself at the huge fireplace at the far end of the room. His headquarters were on the third floor of the Lubyanka, a short distance from the office once occupied by secret police chiefs, from Lavrenty Beria to Yuri Andropov.

The location reflected his power as one of the *siloviki*, a high-ranking official from military and security services. He was Vladimir Putin's most trusted confidante, the only advisor permitted to call him Vova. But the true source of his power derived from his supervision and control of the President's vast fortune.

He was chief advisor to the Kremlin's Security Council with oversight of the country's major intelligence units, including the military-controlled GRU. Over the years he had successfully maneuvered into this powerful position, beginning under General Secretary Brezhnev. At times, he felt like a historical relic, and a miraculous example of how to survive at the top in Russia.

He paused at the window overlooking Lubyanka Square and watched the huge flakes of snow cover the Solevetsky Stone, a replacement for the giant statue of Cheka founder Dzerzhinsky, which had been removed after the dissolution of the Soviet Union. The enormous stone from the first gulag on Solevetsky Islands was erected in 1990 to honor victims of political suppression.

Frowning his disapproval of that substitution, he turned away from the window as his aide, Colonel Dima Korev, opened the large, wooden office door. Dima handed him the official report on Major Boris Piatikov's death and sat down on the leather couch, his feet not quite touching the floor.

Dima was a small man with boyish features and thick hair brushed neatly back from his face. He eerily resembled Nikolai Yezhov, Stalin's infamous interior minister who had conducted the deadly purges in 1937. Officers under Dima's command joked behind his back and called him by Yezhov's nickname—The Dwarf.

As he began to read the preliminary report he felt that he did not take the same pleasure as Dima in the Major's death, but it had been necessary. Violence always was the preferred choice to intimidate those who might be traitors.

Major Boris Piatikov, a non-entity but a trusted party functionary, had until recently spent his days toiling in the Lubyanka archives writing a Bolshevik history which probably no-one these days would ever read.

The *vyshaya mera*—'highest measure'—had been activated against Piatikov, and thus far, there had been no public relations fallout. The Russian press was tightly controlled, and there had been only the slight chance that some foreign reporter might investigate. He had not expected a leak but preferred not to take risks.

Major Piatikov had been under rigorous surveillance after his visit to the Lubyanka cellar. The General watched the tapes with disgust—plodding, fat Borya in the bar with a *pizda*, taking the whore to the hotel room; hopping naked like a rabbit while chasing her around the bed.

Next Borya was seen in a shop, getting fitted for a hairpiece. Why did he choose such a garish color? What a fool! His stupid antics had drawn even more serious attention when he had asked his dead wife's friend, Anya Petrovna, a maid at the US Embassy, to leave a note and one page of the stolen document on an official's desk.

After the third contact the maid was intercepted and forced to deliver a false time and place for the Major's defection. The whore and informer, Marissa Baracova, was arrested in the early morning hours after the explosion and found dead in her cell the next day.

He gave Dima a nod of approval, and opened the folder for his first look at the stolen documents. He was stunned at what Major Piatikov planned to hand over to the Americans and gazed out the window to the square, so that his aide would not see any shock that might be written on his face.

The folder contained the interrogation of Captain Nicolae Andreyevich Platov—Kolya, his greatest friend, arrested and executed in 1974 for attempting to defect to the West.

His grey eyes clouded into darkness and his mind broke into a wild storm of memory of the early days when he and Kolya were a team, closer than brothers.

They became friends the day they met at the Suvorov Military Academy, though they were opposites in every way. Kolya whose large, dark eyes sparkled with merriment, was strongly built and handsome with features like those of a Greek god.

While he, Pasha was thin and weedy with a sad narrow face; a beaklike nose; and pale, gray eyes. Kolya was the golden boy, handsome and brilliant; all that he was not. His friend could get away with almost anything. He was irreverent and foolhardy, full of jokes, and charming to all who met him, even to most of his superiors. Pasha sheltered behind Kolya, hoping others would see him in the same light. The bullying he suffered had stopped as soon as they became friends. Pasha, the less favored, always followed the rules, fearful that someone would ferret out his weakness and learn his secrets. This early decision was the reason for his survival and success.

The two boys became KGB officers and inspired by heroic legendary figures in Cheka history, had carried out several missions in Soviet Bloc countries. They called themselves "Chekisty," after the hard men of the past, and learned to kill without feeling, out of duty to the Motherland.

He anguished over why his friend had wanted to go over to the enemy. Kolya's attempted defection had never made sense, even though he had been involved in the Raven's failed plot in the 1970s to overthrow the Soviet government. Kolya, a true patriot, had once said that, whatever Russia's government, he despised the West and would never leave his homeland.

Kolya would throw back his noble head, his thick blond hair waving, and laugh as he applauded the success of the Prague Spring of 1968, which had crushed the Czech leaders fighting for independence from Moscow. He watched the US failing in Vietnam with great pleasure, believing it would be the end of their world dominance. And Kolya was the one most dedicated on their covert op in Prague, eager to pull the trigger on the dissident.

After Prague their careers had taken different directions. Pasha was on a mission to China, prior to being promoted to the interior ministry, when Kolya was arrested. His friend, always more adventurous, had become an illegal in Directorate S. Although still a minor player, a novice in that department, it was curious that he would be trusted with important information.

When he heard of his friend's arrest, he had lain in bed countless nights, shaking with sobs and went about his work with a deliberately bland face, attempting to disguise his grief. Aware that he, too, could be under suspicion, he distanced himself completely from the case, and purposely remained ignorant of any of the details.

It had been heartbreaking not to intervene and try to save his friend, but he had rationalized there was nothing he could do. Kolya was doomed, and he would have gone down with him. His laughing handsome face often appeared before him in unguarded moments, when he was shaving or drinking his morning tea.

He read through the interrogation quickly, searching for more detail. After enduring hours of torture, Kolya had confirmed the existence of the Paper Man Dossier, but insisted that was all he knew. The report gave no motive for his defection.

Then he discovered that there had been more to the interrogation, and that several pages had been redacted. This could mean the papers were removed after Kolya succumbed to torture, and might have revealed the dossier's location and contents. Sudden tears filled his eyes, and to avoid Dima's curious gaze, he returned to the surveillance tapes until he regained his composure. After he dismissed Dima, praising him for the successful operation, he reopened the folder.

He stared mystified at the swastika drawn on its back cover. The last page of the interrogation was signed by a Colonel Ivan Bokov. The name struck him as vaguely familiar, but was likely one of those faceless bureaucrats from their vast organization, long dead.

The fool, Borya, must have suspected this file contained valuable information but no one alive, even Dima with his vast knowledge of agency secrets, would be aware of this old incomplete interrogation. It was logical to think that the Paper Man Dossier no longer existed.

In spite of this self-assurance, he took a circuitous route to the archive vault. On the pretext of inspecting work efficiency, he had dived into the section where the major had found the folder, *1937– 74 Misc.*

Moving around in the dusty room he discovered in another old cabinet a subsection of folders drawn up by Yezhov during the Purge: One read: *Early revolutionary fighters—to be arrested under new law.* He felt a rush of blood to his head. His long-dead mentor, the old

Bolshevik spy, Peter Von Krantz, covert name, "The Raven," was first on the list.

He forced himself to control the barely discernible tic under his left eye, a sign of anxiety. Still, there was no logical reason for him to panic, to think he would be identified with this interrogation.

Before he left the archive room, he went back to the folder Borya had found: *1937–74 Misc.* and removed the note: *To be entered: Misc.10B.* He left the folder in place, aware that even though empty, it preserved its existence, recorded forever in the KGB secret registers.

Back in his office, he asked not to be disturbed, threw the *misc. file* note into the fireplace and watched it fall into ashes. Then he hesitated, picking up Kolya's interrogation, his friend's last words. For a moment, his taciturn features contorted in grief. He impulsively placed the documents in his private safe.

"Buried forever," he murmured. This would be the end of the episode. The only copy of Kolya's interrogation was safely in his hands.

Tecumseh County, Ohio: Winter 2003

Roo, Deputy Sheriff Reuben Yoder

Chapter 4

ROO CRUNCHED THROUGH heavy snow as he passed the boundary of the ancient Shawnee burial ground. Immersing himself in the landscape gave him some comfort, and he was grateful that his dad, crazy fuck that he was, had the sense to keep acres of his land in forest.

Groggy from a sleepless night, he pushed through thicker trees toward the top of the hill at the edge of his property. Taking deep breaths of cold, sharp air, he tried to shake off last night's dream, but the photograph of his cousin Lucy's face loomed above him, laced between dark branches.

Lucy, a victim of his last case, who was brutally murdered, poses in her driveway in Upper Arlington. Deep into his nightmare, her smiling face moves toward him. Her expression changes, her eyes bulge, her mouth opens wide in a silent scream. Her face twists in pain, as she is tortured for information on him. The dream shifts to her bedroom. A dark figure stands over her. Roo struggles in the dream to rescue her. He cannot see the killer's face.

He had sat up in bed, shouting, and rushed to the bathroom, splashing cold water over his pale and sweaty face. In the mirror, he saw fine lines, the scars left from a football injury, and a weird encounter with a raccoon. His sturdy, regular features and direct gaze remained the same, and did not reflect his doubts about himself, nor his anguish at failing to catch Lucy's killer.

He paused at the crest of the hill, lines from *Birches* running through his head.

> *And life is too much like a pathless wood*
> *Where your face burns and tickles with the cobwebs*
> *Broken across it, and one eye is weeping*
> *From a twig's having lashed across it open.*
> *I'd like to get away from earth awhile*
> *And then come back to it and begin over …*

The Robert Frost poem captured his feeling—that he could have been more expert and vigilant in his last case, and might have saved Lucy and the other murder victims.

He looked down on Amish farms, oases of calm securely wrapped in the bend of the hills. His dad had been born on the second farm over, but after Vietnam had severed any connection with the Amish community. Dark streams of smoke rose from farmhouse chimneys and slowly trailed off into the sky.

In the early-morning silence, broken only by the crack of tree branches blowing in the wind, he watched the men below in large black hats, herding the dairy cows into the white barns. A flock of sparrows soared overhead, following them in carefree abandon.

He searched for the wolf, the only survivor of the three cubs who had once given him solace. The solitary animal roamed this land as his last refuge. When he had returned from the hospital and was walking through the forest, the wolf had appeared on this ridge, his pale eyes staring directly at Roo, before he loped into the thick underbrush.

The poem's lines stayed with him; he also wanted "to begin over" his relationship with Katya, which once had promised so much for them. In spite of her urging, he had not returned to New York to take the job at his old boss, Devlin's security firm. His lame excuse: the head injury he had received from the killer Marat, at the oil field in Baku on his last case.

Katya had come to help him recuperate after he returned from his second visit to the local hospital. He felt indebted to her and loved her even more. She had been willing to give up her New York social life, and the Little Swan Gallery, to take care of him.

When he began to recover, she tried to convince him he needed counseling and should go back to New York for treatment. She couldn't understand why he refused, but there was no way to tell her about the fleeting, horrifying images which left him in despair. Her insistence had seemed to suggest that he was crazy. That got his back up, but maybe it was true. Ben Tyler, his high school friend and former football teammate, claimed that since his release from the hospital he looked pretty much the same on the outside, but sure was fucked-up on the inside.

Almost two months ago, though it seemed longer to him. Katya had returned to New York to help Geoffrey Banks, her partner and manager, set up a new exhibition at the Little Swan Gallery. Roo drove her to the airport, downhearted at the look of happiness on her face, believing that after her glittering social life in the city she could never live in the Midwest.

In an attempt to smooth over what neither of them wanted to believe was an end to their being together, he had promised to be in New York for the gallery show, and to consider working for Devlin, or at least have a conversation with him. She had said the job would be good for his career. Irritated at her words, he furiously brushed off the snow that had dropped from a tree onto his shoulder.

Her constant hints that he should do something prestigious or meaningful with his life were exasperating and had angered him, but couldn't dim his desire for her. Pictures flashed before him, of her laughing and running into his arms.

In his blackest moods he was haunted by the deceitful way she had left him last year, when he was wanted for murder and then had an affair with the Russian oligarch, Ostrikov. It was ugly, but he had to question her behavior. Was she naïve, attracted to men who were thugs and murderers, or was it something deeper, conspiratorial? Doubts about her remained like the wisp of chimney smoke smeared on the sky, stubbornly refusing to disappear.

He headed back toward the empty farmhouse, remembering her sudden fit of domesticity. She had tried to make the place homelike with pillows and new curtains. But her thoughtful attempt was a façade that couldn't cover the despair and fear that seemed to emanate from the walls. She became angry that he was so indifferent and didn't appreciate her efforts.

In the arguments that followed he told her that he hadn't wanted her to decorate, that he hated the house and never intended to live there permanently. He couldn't answer her questions about what he did want; he didn't know where he would live, or if they would be together. But now in her absence, a huge emptiness had opened in his chest. He wanted her back.

Last night he hurried into the house, turned on the lights, opened a beer, then sat in the kitchen. The TV was broadcasting the news from the Bush White House that the US might invade Iraq. He was thinking of his friend, Richie Grant, who had enlisted after 9/11 and was on his way to the Middle East. His buddies had said goodbye with drinks at Shorty's. It was the last time he had gone to the bar. The phone rang, cutting through the TV announcement. His heart leapt at her cut-glass, English accent, a world away from the kitchen.

"I might not be able to phone you for a few days. You know I've been having therapy. A session usually goes on for at least a week."

She had told him she had discovered a retreat called Solitude and Mind Peace, located in a luxurious town house in midtown. "I'm trying to cope with my anxiety, and the sessions have helped. It's a wonderful place."

He didn't get it and wondered what actually went on there. He guessed it was a kind of pampering for crazy rich people. But she had been traumatized by the discovery of her parents' true identities; their entanglement in a Russian plot; and their murders at the hands of Russian thugs, and was searching for help to recover.

"Roo, I miss you." Her voice hung in the air, but he couldn't think of anything more to say. Her experiences at that place were alien to him. Since she began attending these retreats she seemed distant, as though they were strangers and had never lived together.

He regretted their arguments, and his decision to persuade her to go on alone to New York. Had he thought she would refuse?

Thinking of it now as he made his way in the snow down the steep hill, he realized it was his own fault. He had driven her away. He had been fucking stupid. As he neared the house and was crossing the back yard, his phone buzzed, and thinking it might be Katya, fumbled in his pocket for it. He jumped at the sudden movement, a spray of snow from ruffled branches. The wolf came from between the trees, his ears upright, his body tense. The animal's pale gray eyes, the same color as his own stared back at him.

"Roo, you got to come in. I need you." Sheriff Stumpy Walker's voice was hoarse. The phone crackled with his last phrase, "butchery like hogs."

Chapter 5

IT WAS STILL early morning when Roo jumped in his truck and chugged down the lane past the forest to Route 25. Dolly Parton and Kenny Rogers were singing *Islands in the Stream* on the country radio station from Cincinnati. He had been a young kid when the song was popular, but the words seemed to echo his wishful thinking about his relationship with Katya.

He stepped on the gas in a rush to get into Paint Creek to help Stumpy, but he didn't feel up to investigating a murder in spite of his newly-acquired reputation. He had been praised in the newspapers and on TV for his detective work, but felt like he was a phony. He had failed to arrest the Brotherhood thugs from Little Odessa before they escaped to Russia and were safe from extradition. In spite of his protests, authorities had closed the case, refusing to believe his claim that a psychopath linked to the Brotherhood was at large.

It was true that he had only circumstantial evidence, but last year while searching in Devlin's files, he had discovered an anonymous note with a tip: a hunter in the forest outside of Paint Creek had come upon a wild-looking man who shot at him and then disappeared. He was later seen passing through one of the small towns in the area. There was no follow up.

The deceased Mikhail Borisov, who had claimed to be Katya's father, alleged that an agent called "The Priest" had saved their lives when Roo and Katya were being hunted down in Tecumseh County Forest.

He questioned the truth of anything the oligarch Borisov had said, but he did not have enough evidence to prove this psychopath was "The Priest," or even if he existed. At the time Stumpy had bluntly accused him of imagining the killer.

He drove carefully through the snow, which covered the road in thick drifts. At the crest of the hill he slowed to a crawl, glancing out his window at the adjacent rolling fields sparkling in the sun.

"What the fuck!" he yelled, hitting the brakes and sending the truck into a spin toward a deep irrigation ditch. He jerked the wheel in the same direction and landed back on the road.

In the distance, about four hundred feet from his truck, a dark figure had stepped out of the thick forest, and was slowly tramping over the bare hill. Shocked, he squinted at the phantom, silhouetted against the snow by the bright sun, and swinging something back and forth in rhythm. His pulse drummed. He was sure it was the blade of a long knife, reflected in the brightness. The dark figure seemed to grow larger even as it swept away from him and over the hill.

His hands froze on the steering wheel, but when he looked again, there was only the empty hill, framed by the forest. His face in the rearview mirror was constricted in terror, reflecting a maniacal stranger. The words of the song hung in the air until the radio went static, buzzing. He was coming apart; a mental case.

He did not know how long he sat with his fingers clutching the steering wheel before he realized the truck had stalled. His hands shook as he worked to restart the sputtering engine.

He shut off the radio noise and drove on unable to erase from his mind the image of the dark figure. It reminded him of other, strange visions he'd had; weird quirky hallucinations that he could never understand and kept to himself.

Stumpy's phone call rumbled in his head. The phantom that now rose like a shadow in his brain had been moving away from the road, deeper into the country, in the direction of the farm where an elderly couple, Joseph and Anna Knapp, had been tortured and murdered.

Shaken by the vision of the phantom, he drove slowly until he reached the edge of town and passed the new pain management clinic. It was located in the former Smith farmhouse, near a line of deserted shops on land once planted in corn fields. The old farmhouse had been repainted, white with a subtle gray trim. A professional-looking sign hung on a post at the entrance. *Dr. N Brewer, Pain Management Clinic, LLC.* Despite the early hour, several cars were parked outside the building, including a Jaguar he figured belonged to the doctor. A number of people were lined up at the entrance, waiting for the clinic to open.

As he came into Paint Creek, black clouds rapidly gathered, partly obscuring the sun. The New England-style buildings, rimmed in shadows looked glassy, distorted by occasional stabs of sunlight like a funhouse mirror. A few leftover Christmas ornaments hung outside Nelson's Restaurant. Roo was reminded of one of those picturesque American towns in horror movies where everyone, even the sheriff, is a zombie. His mood lifted for a moment, driving away his macabre vision. It was unlikely that there ever would be a zombie like Sheriff Stumpy Walker.

The parking lot was piled in mounds of dirt and abandoned machinery. Bad weather had stalled the renovation begun last summer, and the proposed forensic lab and offices remained only holes in the ground.

He waded through the heavy slush and opened the door, stamping his feet. A large map, marked with the areas that had been searched for the killers, hung on the wall beside the filing cabinets. The office was unusually quiet, as though absorbing the shock of the murders. No sounds came from behind the closed steel door, so he figured the two jail cells were empty.

The dispatch radios resting on the table beside the coffee pot were silent. He poured a cup, surprised at the unopened package of donuts; the sheriff usually devoured at least three by this hour in the morning.

Gracie, Stumpy's secretary, seemed subdued; her dried apple face was gloomy as she furiously typed a report. She looked up and frowned. "He's in there."

Stumpy was at his desk, his cigar unlit and his chin resting on his chest, as though he might be taking a nap or sneaking a look at one of his porn magazines. A massive rewiring job had recently been finished, leaving the office in chaos. Roo's photographs and newspaper clippings from his glory days as a high school football star, a constant embarrassment to him, had been removed—permanently, he hoped.

The sheriff looked up, his droopy features lined with shock. "You Ok?" He didn't ask why Roo hadn't answered his calls. Nor did he go on about his deputy's love life as he usually did, saying things like, "So are you still sleeping with Katya? What about that Russian she took up with?" He seemed to have temporarily lost his passion for gossip.

Roo said, "I didn't think you would call me. Don't you have two new men?" For years there had only been the need for a sheriff and one deputy in this sparsely populated rural area, but recently the growing drug problem had required more officers.

"I'm about to hire Irvin Radley and Pete Newsome, mainly to help with drug cases. You know, taking people who overdose to the hospital or the morgue. It involves new training. It's like being a fucking undertaker. We can't keep up."

"When I passed the clinic this morning people were waiting in line for it to open."

"Yeah, it's a great success. Dr. Brewer's qualifications seem good." Stumpy frowned. "I don't like some of the things I'm hearing about the place, but I'm too short-handed to go into that now. Anyhow, those two aren't equipped to handle a murder case like this. I need an expert. I want you to take over."

He opened his mouth to protest. He wanted to say he wasn't an expert, and had to get to New York, but he could never refuse this man who had given him support and a job when no one else would hire him.

"I'm deputizing you right now so you can get on with it. You know about this, this kind of butchery. No sign of the murder weapon. The bastards used a knife. Reminds me of 'Nam," he said in a low voice. Both Stumpy and his dad had been in Viet Nam as young men and never got over the trauma.

He reached in his drawer, and brought out Roo's badge and his glock. "If that's ok."

Roo nodded.

Stumpy said, "Right after I discovered the bodies I called in the State Police. They think druggies came in off the highway, even though it would be a fifty mile or so hike, and murdered the couple. But no traces of the killers have been found. May be the weather conditions. The only suspect so far is Matthew, the couple's grandson."

Roo had trouble believing this. He remembered Matthew as someone quiet who kept to himself, living on the fringes of high school life. He seemed an unlikely killer.

"You know he came back here. Sally Beatty reported seeing him in Kroger's about a month ago before the murders."

They had found the car Matthew had been using, and it was discovered that he had rented it from Sunnyside, the Mayor's company, much to his embarrassment.

"I've taken over the case. Anyhow, it's my responsibility. I have to handle this right here in my jurisdiction. I'm not asking for any more assistance from the State, or Columbus police except from the coroner's office, but if need be I can call them in at any time. The county prosecutor has been in, waiting for more evidence. Right now, Coroner Daly and his men are back at forensics in Columbus. Hell knows when our own new forensics lab will be ready," Stumpy burst out in irritation. "But we have photographs of the murder scene. More DNA samples and dental analysis are expected today.

The autopsies are taking longer than usual. Daley wants to study the methods used by the killers; thinks there might be something there."

He rambled on, a note of disbelief in his voice. "You know, the neighbors, Jimmy and Betty Lou Cochran, didn't see or hear a thing. They always get up before sunrise to start the milking and knew something was wrong when Joseph didn't come out to feed his chickens. The coop is a good distance from their farmhouse, but they can see the light go on every morning at 6:00 sharp, no matter what. Well, the Cochrans waited for an hour or so and then, thinking one of them might be ill, went over to the house. They knocked but no one answered, and then they saw a lot of blood had seeped out from under the door. Scared the bejesus out of them. They didn't go inside. Jimmy called emergency."

The sheriff picked up his cigar, made a half-hearted attempt to light it and threw it down on the floor. "We found Matthew's prints on one of his high school track medals dropped on the kitchen floor. They were in police records from when he was picked up for possession of marijuana, just after he left school. Judge Barker went easy on the kid and let him off with probation. As I said, we suspect that he's a druggie and may be dealing. Just was never caught with the goods."

He heaved a sigh. "We can't tell the age of the prints on the medal. It could have been dropped at the time of the murders or earlier. But I just can't think—" He interrupted himself. "And it looks like it might be more than one killer. I have to get results. That SOB, Swensen, is putting pressure on me, telling people I'm incompetent."

Mayor John Swensen, the only car dealer in town, was worried about being re-elected. Swenson's blond abundant hair was twirled in a smooth coif, and he usually wore a navy blazer over a shirt, unbuttoned nearly to his waist. The gold chain around his neck was designed to call attention to his body. He was a fitness fanatic and worked out at a gym in Columbus. Swenson was a bachelor, like Stumpy, and had a string of girlfriends. Roo suspected there had been a rivalry between the mayor and the sheriff over Nurse Masterson, and Swenson's abundant hair and muscular body had caused jealousy and hard feelings on Stumpy's part.

"There's a meeting at the town hall this evening. Folks are angry and worried about safety. Swenson's giving me a lot of shit. Wants me to take the blame; wants to rip my face off." His forehead creased with worry. "They're out for my blood."

Roo thought this was an exaggeration, since the only consequences were being hounded by the local news media, and not being re-elected. But re-election was Stumpy's reason to live.

Stumpy went on, turning morose.

"I'm pretty positive the killers are long gone, but folks won't take my word for it and are scared shitless. Swensen calls me every damn hour when he's not putting grease on his hair. Everyone's got their shotguns at the ready. Hell has broken loose. That fool, Sam Penfold, thought he heard something in his chicken coop and shot his own foot and three of his prize hens. Ha!" he said, in grim satisfaction.

"Yesterday at the mayor's press conference I tried to calm everyone down and announced that Tecumseh County and all bordering counties had been searched with a fine-toothed comb, more than once, I might add.

"Unless there are new developments, we'll put out a warrant at the end of the week for Matthew's arrest. Christ, killing your own grandparents." He shook his head in disbelief, the wattles of his jaw waving back and forth.

He handed Roo the most recent photograph of Matthew. "Found it taped to the front of the Knapps' refrigerator. Joseph probably took it."

"Matthew left here soon after he dropped out of school and was arrested for possession of marijuana. Most officers wouldn't blink an eye at the marijuana, compared to the drugs they see coming in now. There's no record of where he went, or exactly when he came back here."

His voice quavered. "The Knapp family lived on that farm for four generations. Good people; didn't deserve to die like this. They were my friends. Joseph was on my bowling team for years, before arthritis got him down."

There were tears in his eyes. "They had a real sad life. You know, something happened to Julia, their only daughter. She disappeared in the 70s; never found. People said she ran away and abandoned Matthew. He was raised by Joseph and Anna."

Roo studied the photograph of Matthew. who looked about sixteen, standing in front of the farmhouse. Tall and rangy with finely drawn features, his dark slanted eyes had a haunted look. His shaggy blond hair hung over his forehead.

"We have his yearbook photo and his mugshot from when he was arrested for possession, all taken about that same time," Stumpy went on, "He was a loner. We questioned guys in his class. They turned out to be just acquaintances. They weren't much help; didn't remember much about him. You know, sometimes these loners get queer and violent, especially if they're on drugs. As far as I can tell, only his girlfriend, Linny Brooks, seemed to know him well. She claims she has no idea where he is now."

"No reports so far of any other prints or other traces of DNA. Whoever did this cleaned up pretty well if Joe Daley, the coroner hasn't found anything yet. But you never know." Stumpy looked up at him.

"You Ok?" he asked again, although it seemed like he was asking himself. "Here, you'd better have a look at these. Daley sent them over this morning." He thrust a large brown envelope at Roo like it was a handful of hot coals.

"I'm skipping lunch at Nelson's. Someone's bound to yell at me. I'm going now to have a nap before the meeting. Feel like a piece of shit," he muttered.

Chapter 6

THE NEXT MORNING as he drove to the Knapp farm, gory images of body parts flashed by him in the truck window. Roo stopped on the road and waited for his mind to clear.

He had studied the forensic photographs last evening and a thought, like a hoarse whisper, crept into his head. Only a psychopath or someone drugged up could be capable of this evil. He could understand why the coroner was intrigued by the killers' technique, if the photographs were anything to go by. The bodies had been dissected with the precision of a surgeon.

He passed the edge of the forest, and turned onto the icy lane which stretched for miles toward the Knapp property, more isolated than his own farm.

The farmhouse was built in the 1860s and sat in a small yard surrounded by fields. It was square with no trimmings, and its flapping roof showed neglect. In the distance he could see the

Cochran farm. They were the only neighbors before the land spread out into the large forest.

He sat for a moment in the truck, staring at the house. Its faded color merged with the gray sky, giving it a bleak, slipshod look that reminded him of his own place.

He walked through the drifts, passing an old pick-up parked beside another rusty car and tractor, and opened the door. Coroner Daley's crew had cleaned up, but the house still smelled of blood.

Its bare ugliness seemed colder than the zero temperature outside. The scarred kitchen table and floor where the murders had taken place were clean, but there were some other traces of violence. The killers had searched the place with a thorough ruthlessness. Kitchen cupboards were emptied, and small pieces of broken china and glass had been swept up in a pile by the crew.

Melancholy, like the damp cold, crept over him. It seemed the couple had lived in poverty in their old age. He did not remember them that way.

The living room was equipped with a space heater, and an old couch and chair, slashed by the killers, their stuffed insides spilling out. The television, its screen smashed, had been parked on a homemade stand of wooden planks, and a radio from the fifties lay crushed beside it.

He pictured the couple sitting here, wrapped in blankets, peacefully watching their black and white television, before this inexplicable horror had taken them.

In a brutal reflection of the murders, the killers had gone upstairs to the three bedrooms, disemboweled the mattresses and tossed everything from the closets onto the floor. Roo walked outside to breathe in fresh air and then headed toward the Cochran farm.

Betty Lou Cochran answered the door. She was dressed in jeans and a plaid shirt that looked like it belonged to her husband. Her large brown eyes were rimmed in red; her short blond hair was uncombed and dulled with gray. Betty Lou had been a senior when he was in 6th. grade. He remembered her as the prettiest girl in high school; head cheerleader and homecoming queen. She married her high school sweetheart, Jimmy, a football star then; now a farmer on the edge of failure.

"I can't believe it. I just can't believe it. While we were sleeping, the killer—" She led him into the kitchen, and they sat down at the table. He noticed she retained traces of that popular cheerleader with lovely eyes, a small turned up nose, and curved cheeks, but her face was lined and coarse from sun after working in the fields, and maybe from great disappointment.

She dabbed at her eyes with a tissue. "Hey, you're famous. I saw you on TV."

Everyone had heard about his last case in Baku and his injury. After CNN he had refused more interviews, thinking that it might be one of the media's programs looking in on rural America to reinforce their opinions.

"A wonderful couple, good neighbors. They were frail and had no one to help them after Matthew left. They both suffered from arthritis, and I think they were selling their pain pills outside that clinic, just to stay alive. I heard a lot of people do that now. They were too proud to ask for help, although I tried." She sniffled.

Yesterday afternoon, he had checked with the couple's doctor and examined hospital records. Both had been prescribed

Oxycodone for arthritis pain. It didn't seem likely, but fit in with initial reports that drug money could have been the motive for the murders.

"You know, they had a real tragedy. This happened before we bought our place, sometime in the '70s. Anna told me that Julia left Matthew with them, and then she vanished. They never saw her again.

"She said no one ever talked about it or mentioned it anymore. Joseph ordered her never to speak about Julia. She said it was like Julia never existed. And then, after they raised Matthew, he didn't come around to help them when they needed it. That was disgraceful."

Roo looked around the kitchen. A greasy skillet floated in the sink, surrounded by stacks of dirty dishes. A stained curtain sagged over the window looking out on the fields.

She pushed back her hair. "I've been too upset to clean up," she said apologetically. The table was cluttered with the remains of breakfast; a half-eaten slice of toast, a plate smeared with egg, and coffee cups.

"Tell me more about Matthew. Something I might have missed."

"When we moved in here, he was a nice little boy, but in high school he turned wild and used drugs. He became a whole lot of trouble for them. He wasn't home much, and when he did show up, asked for money. Anna complained they never heard from him, never knew where he was. She was always anxious about him."

"When was the last time you saw him?"

"I remember now. It was more than a month ago. I was taking meatloaf and scalloped potatoes over to them when Matthew drove up in his car and went into the house without saying a word. He was in there a short time while we were talking. They were very upset but tried to hide it. I was just leaving when he ran out, shouting and swearing at them."

"Can you remember anything he said?"

"He took some things from the house. I couldn't see exactly what they were, but I think it was a bundle of stuff, maybe papers. Anna was begging him not to do it, not to take it."

"He accused them of hiding things that were his and said something about them keeping him from knowing his parents; his real father." She stopped and blew her nose.

"It seemed to me after that visit they became a little strange, kept to themselves more. They seemed afraid, almost as though they were hiding. But I never thought—poor things." She sniffled.

"Is it true that you've been planning to sell out and move? Stumpy checked at the bank." This was an abrupt change of topics, but he wanted to see her reaction. Stumpy had discovered that the Cochrans had money troubles and had missed their last two mortgage payments. Jimmy's parents finally agreed to help them out, but they were just plain scared after the murders and wanted to move away.

"So, you know." She glared at him. "Then, why are you asking me? How dare you check on us? It's none of your business. Anyhow, it doesn't matter now. I'm afraid to stay here." She shuddered and looked away from him.

He shrugged. "Part of my job. Just routine."

"Are you really accusing us? You'd better speak to Jimmy. He went into town but you can wait, if you want. I'll fix some coffee." She seemed to regret her outburst.

"Thanks. I think I have what I need now."

"I still can't believe it. I want to leave this place now." She was shaking with sobs.

Roo patted her on the shoulder, handed her his card, and said to call him if she or Jimmy thought of anything more that might help with the case.

He walked into the forest which bordered the rear of both houses for miles. He realized that, except for the Cochrans, the Knapps were so isolated that the killers had to have known their location before the attack. The idea crept into his head. Could the Cochrans have discovered the old couple were hiding money, and murdered them?

He dismissed the idea as farfetched, remembering the forensic photographs. Neither of the Cochrans seemed capable of such savagery. And, after a thorough search of their house and property, nothing incriminating was found.

Roo spent the next two hours tramping through the forest, hunting for footprints, broken branches, any signs of the killers; a hopeless task. Still, he didn't think stoners desperate for money would have had the precision to pull this off.

The sense that someone was watching made him feel for his gun, look around through the black limbs of swaying trees, and retrace his steps. The cold wind lashed his face. The specter swinging the knife was coming toward him. His head began to pound. For a moment he gazed, transfixed, into the thicket of bare trees. Knowing this was crazy, he moved quickly out of the forest.

The Knapp barn exuded the familiar smells of cows, grain, and fetid manure. Spiders and beetles hung from the timbers. He figured the stalls had not been cleaned since Knapp gave up farming several years ago.

He searched through the haystack and around the abandoned milking machines. Then he combed through the stalls, finding only loose pieces of wood and bits of straw. He stopped for a moment; unreasonable fear rushed through him, and the remembered pain of old wounds burned like fire on his back and legs.

He was back home, in the barn, and his old man loomed in front of him, holding his belt ready, furious that Roo had seen him hiding his money and whiskey bottles. Violent, always paranoid, even more so after years of drinking, his dad had picked an unlikely hiding place. He glanced over at the feed bin.

His hands shook as he skimmed off the congealed film on top of the bin and pawed his way through the grain, black and green with age, spilling it out on the floor. Halfway to the bottom, the edge of a tin lid appeared. He stopped. It seemed incredible. Was this a secret hiding place that some old farmers had told each other about?

He went on digging through the moldy grain, covering the floor around him, until a large Ball Mason jar, the kind bought at Baker's Hardware, emerged. He wiped the coated sides of the jar with his jacket and saw something inside the clouded glass.

He struggled with the corroded lid. Finally, yielding to his strength, it opened. A plastic folder was curled inside the jar.

Chapter 7

GRACIE LOGAN WAS alone in the office when Roo came in at 7 a.m. She glared at him, her forehead crumpled in a frown over her reading glasses. "Stumpy phoned. He'll be in late."

He nodded, guessing the town meeting had not gone well. He placed the material he had found in the Knapp's barn on his desk. Last night he had rushed home from the murder scene and opened the folder, labeled: *For my son Matthew from Julia Knapp.*

Its large size had been deceptive. The meager contents were disappointing: four sepia photographs, wrapped carefully in plastic layers. They were heavily damaged, and the dim figures were mere shadows, with no identification.

Julia's note for Matthew fixed his mind on her disappearance. It suddenly struck him that there had been no photographs of Julia, and no trace of her belongings, in the farmhouse.

He walked through the slush to the library, a small replica of Independence Hall; a reminder of when Paint Creek was a prosperous town. He always admired the solid bookshelves, the big clock hanging at the entrance, and the polished oak chairs and tables. It had been his refuge after football practice when he wasn't hanging out at Wagner's Drugstore. He would relax in one of the capacious, wooden seats, and read in contentment until the clock chimed seven and the place closed.

He had few books at home and hid those he borrowed, reading at night in bed, after his chores. His old man frowned on books and accused him of being lazy and a sissy, like a girl; sitting around reading, even though he had been the quarterback on the football team. He scorned Roo's grades and ridiculed him for being first in his class. "No use for studies if you're running a farm," he would say. His mother had been sympathetic but was so cowed that she never dared defend him. He adopted the library as his own, a haven, reading almost everything on the shelves by the time he left school.

Fiona Lindsay, his best friend Ben's fiancé, was behind the desk. Removing her large hornrims, she came out to greet him as he took his boots off at the door. She was wearing tights and a long white sweater. "Hi," she said, peering into his face with her beautiful green myopic eyes as though to make sure it was him. "Excuse my outfit. I'm on my way to ballet class at noon. Can I help?"

"Do you keep old Paint Creek High School yearbooks?"

She looked vague for a moment. "Yes, I think so, but don't know how far back."

She put on her glasses and led him through the fireproof door to the stacks and pointed to a lower shelf. "There they are. No one has looked at them for years."

He browsed through the yearbooks until he found the 1966 edition. "Can I borrow this?"

"Sure," she said.

Memories flooded over him as he returned to one of the chairs in the reading room and opened the yearbook. He found Julia Knapp, a serious-looking girl in the class photo. Then leafing through, he came to a page labelled *Fun Snaps.* Under *BEST FRIENDS,* Julia and another girl posed, arms entwined. He couldn't believe it, and at first hadn't recognized that Faye Reynolds, the girl with Julia, was Mrs. Weeks, the county clerk. He knew Faye had married Howard Weeks right after graduation. He snapped the book shut and said goodbye to Fiona while he pulled on his boots. She breezed by and said. "Come to supper. I'll call you."

When he returned to the office, Gracie's face was pressed against the window like an anxious spaniel, waiting for Stumpy to show up. She didn't move when he said he was going over to the courthouse and asked her to phone him if any important messages came in.

He crossed Shawnee Square, dodging the melting snow sliding in huge plops from enormous pine tree branches, and opened the courthouse heavy oak door. The entrance hall felt like the last ring of the Arctic Circle—cold enough to freeze his balls off. Shivering, he climbed the wide stairs to the county auditor's office. The place looked deserted, and he remembered that it closed Saturday afternoons. Maybe they hadn't bothered to open today, although a light was on in the auditor's office. The door was locked, but he heard someone moving around. He knocked several time, and rattled the doorknob.

"Who is it?" a high, quavering voice called out, followed by a shadow appearing behind the decorative glass panel, pointing a gun directly at him.

He yelled, "Hey, It's Reuben Yoder. No!" A deafening blast shook the hall. A shot ripped through the door pane. Dodging flying glass and splintered wood, Roo dove to the floor, his pulse racing, and waited for more bullets. After a long silence, he raised his head to peer through the shattered door. Holy shit! The shooter was Mrs. Faye Weeks. The kick from the shotgun had knocked her flat. Her stocking cap covered her eyes and her stubby legs stuffed into snow boots seemed permanently rooted to the spot, like small tree trunks.

He stumbled up and crunched through shards of glass to reach the lock through the hole in the door. Mrs. Weeks was crumpled in a motionless heap next to the gun. Her small, protruding teeth and round little body, bundled in a grey coat, reminded him of a furry woodchuck.

"Hey, it's Reuben Yoder. Are you ok?" He had taken out his phone to call an ambulance when she came to and began taking breaths in gulps. Relieved, he crouched down beside her and gently pulled off her stocking cap. Stunned, she opened her wide, brown eyes. Her hair, salted with gray, stood up in corkscrew ringlets.

"Are you all right?" he asked again, supporting her to a sitting position.

She shook her head back and forth, dazed by the knock on her head, and began to cry. "Yes, yes, I don't need an ambulance. I'm just a little shaky. Oh, Reuben, I'm so sorry. I didn't mean—What a relief I didn't hurt you. It's Howard's shotgun. I didn't have my glasses on, and couldn't see who it was," she gasped. "He gave it to me at breakfast this morning. No one else was in the office today, and he didn't like it that I would be alone here with killers on the loose. Are you going to press charges? Take me to jail?" Clouds of breath punctuated her sobs.

"Hey, don't worry. It's ok." His pulse slowly returned to normal. He picked up the shotgun and removed the cartridges, noting that the scattered shot had sliced through the entrance, destroying the entire wall. She could have killed him. He put the shotgun on a nearby table. "I think you should take this home and tell Howard it's too dangerous."

She nodded in agreement, then looked up at him. "Are you investigating the murders? They were such nice people. Why would this happen? Who would do such a horrible thing? It's terrifying. We're all so frightened." Her gaze flew sideways, as though the killers might burst through the door at any moment. "Sheriff Walker has to do something about this. Are they still out there?"

He put his arm around her and helped her to her feet, assuring her that the entire county had been searched thoroughly, more than once, and there was no sign of the killers.

After several minutes, she stopped shaking. "Reuben, I am so glad to see you. I know you came here for a reason and that you'll catch the evil monsters." Sniffling, unsteady on her feet, she took his arm for support and then dropped down in her chair like a sack of potatoes. She took a few minutes to control herself and put on her glasses before assuming some semblance of her normal voice.

"How can I help?"

He crunched through the broken glass and found the yearbook at the bottom of the steps. He opened to the page with the best friends' photograph.

"You and Julia Knapp were best friends in high school. Can you tell me something about her?"

Relief that she was safe and didn't have to use the gun again, and hadn't hurt Roo, made her talkative.

"Oh gosh." She looked up from the book. "I haven't seen this in years. Don't even know if I have one. Look at our long hair, and the beads. Yes, we were very best friends. I admired her so much. She was so beautiful, and slim. I was short and overweight and, to be honest, not that pretty. I was boy crazy then and hardly anyone ever asked me out. All the guys wanted to date Julia, but she was too serious and seldom went anywhere with anyone."

She sighed. "My grades were never as good as hers, and my dad would always say, 'Why can't you be more like Julia?' That year, I started to date Howard and already was in love with him forever, and that was a real distraction from schoolwork."

There was a sweetness in her chubby face that kept her from being ugly. Howard, a tall, lanky man with a large Adam's apple, towered above her. They were an odd-looking couple and always reminded him of the nursery rhyme about Jack Spratt and his wife who could eat no lean, but it was a love match and they were totally devoted to each other.

"Poor Julia. I was heartbroken when I heard that she'd disappeared. Sometimes I think bad things happen to the most beautiful and talented."

"When did you last see her?"

"We lost touch after she left for college. I read about her in the papers when she received a scholarship to study in London. Then, two years later, she returned to Paint Creek and came to see me, and brought Matthew."

"She was so thin, but then, she never had a weight problem like I do. She cried, and said she was leaving her baby with her parents for a short time but would return for him soon. I have regretted my words ever since, but I'm afraid I asked her outright who her husband was. Times were different then, and my dad was a strict Methodist minister who would have turned me out of the house if I had a baby out of wedlock. Julia admitted she wasn't married."

She squinted in a frown. "She wouldn't tell me the father's name. I suspected she didn't know. She was frightened. I just knew there was something awful going on in her life, but she wouldn't confide in me and only asked me to watch out for Matthew until she returned. Her parents were angry with her and had pleaded with her not to go to Europe. She was their only child. Her father tried to take her passport. They wouldn't give her any support. That was the only mean thing they ever did, and maybe they only wanted to protect her. I felt so sorry for her." She took a tissue from her coat pocket and wiped her eyes.

"After she disappeared, I tried to keep an eye on Matthew. It was easy at first, and his grandparents who were really nice, didn't mind, but when he became a teenager he quit coming around and didn't want to be friends with my kids. They said he didn't want to be friends with anyone. Even my chocolate chip cookies didn't tempt him. I think he was on drugs, and I didn't realize how troubled he must have been. I feel ashamed that I didn't do more for him." She stopped and became teary again, but composed herself. "You know, I am so upset that Matthew is a suspect. In spite of what everyone says, I can't believe he murdered Joseph and Anna."

She looked up at Roo, her face blotched from crying. "I know you'll find the killers. I saw you on TV. Goodness gracious, what you have been through, and so brave going to that strange foreign place, Baku. Oh my, you are such a hero. When can you come to dinner? You look thin. Your mother would want me to fatten you up." He remembered going to their house with his mom for Sunday lunch after church before she quit attending.

She patted him on the arm as though he were still a little boy. "Our place seems so empty now that both the kids live on the West Coast. It would be nice to have you. Howard would like it."

"Thanks. I will, soon." He smiled at this familiar refrain. She invited him to dinner every time he came to the office.

"Oh, I'm so sorry," she said again, her round chin trembling. "Please forgive me."

"Don't worry."

She walked him to the hall. Her eyes grew wide at the sight of the damage. "I guess I have to call a repairman."

When he returned to the office, Stumpy was leaning back in his chair, his eyes puffy and nearly closed. Gracie hurried in with aspirin and a cup of coffee, and patted him on the shoulder. As she left Roo noticed she was wearing lipstick. Astonished, he wondered if their rumored romance, weird as it seemed to him, was real, and on again after Stumpy's affair with Nurse Masterson. Or did Mayor Swenson, man about town, inspire the lipstick?

Before he could sit down, Stumpy burst out. "Christ, I thought these people were my friends. They fuckin' yelled at me. Bill Cooper said I needed to resign unless I found the killer." He grimaced. "And Swenson, the bastard, didn't stick up for me. In fact, said it was my fault there was no progress."

He gulped down some coffee. "It has to be the grandson, the only suspect we have. But he must have had an accomplice. Someone had to be with him to carry out that evil. Coroner

Daley called a few minutes ago. DNA from a drop of saliva was discovered at the scene. It's not Matthew Knapp's."

He showed Stumpy the photographs found in the jar in the barn. "These seem to be old pictures of strangers, not identified. And so far, I haven't found a real link to the murders."

The sheriff looked at each one for a moment and then waved him away. "So what? No matter. This crap isn't evidence. None of that has anything to do with those addicts butchering that poor old couple." Stumpy looked disappointed that Roo had nothing more to add. "Well, go to it," he growled. Roo left Stumpy nursing his head and began to organize all the evidence on the case.

He went back to the computer and logged into the missing persons data base, and found Julia's case in the dead files. She was reported missing in 1974, last seen in New York, leaving a Greenwich Village hotel. There was a description of Julia and a photograph of her standing in Washington Square.

Roo checked registered births in 1972 in both New York and Ohio in the Natality Data from the National Vital Statistics system and found no record of Matthew's birth under the name Knapp. Julia obviously gave birth to Matthew under a false name and address; it could be anywhere in the country. There seemed to be no good reason for this. Mrs. Weeks explained that it was a different time, but it was hard to believe that being pregnant and not having a husband could be that disgraceful.

Frustrated by the lack of clues, he called Joe Daley and asked him to check for a match of the unidentified DNA found at the farmhouse, with samples from two of the murder scenes from his last case.

Daley snapped, "Christ, do you think I'm an idiot? We're working on it."

He had been wasting time. There was nothing he had found on Julia Knapp that had any seeming relation to the case.

He remembered Mrs. Weeks' comment that there was talk in Paint Creek that no one knew who Matthew's father was, and that he was a bastard, the result of a one-night stand in that den of Satan, New York City.

Chapter 8

THE NEXT EVENING before leaving the sheriff's office, he phoned Katya. He tried to sound casual. "How are you?"

"I'm feeling so much better; not so depressed and anxious, now that I've going to the holistic well-being clinic. Sorry; can't talk long. I have an appointment for a massage in the next hour, and then a session with Gary, the psychologist."

He stirred in his chair. The idea of the clinic made him uncomfortable, but he knew she still grieved over the murder of her beloved guardian, Abigail. He remembered her shock at discovering the identity and fate of her parents and that her mother, Christina Gartner, had been forced to give her away to protect her. She always seemed to be searching for some reconciliation of the past. Maybe he was judging her too harshly, but he thought she used her trauma as an excuse for her erratic behavior.

"I'm on a case for Stumpy, and may not make the opening."

"Oh, I wanted you to be here." She did sound disappointed. "Is this one about the poor old couple in the farmhouse? I saw the news report. How terrible."

"Yes," he said.

"Be careful, Roo. I miss you."

Katya's voice stayed with him as he drove to the opposite edge of Paint Creek. He was in a black mood, thinking of her accusations that he lived in the past and was too conservative. He had to admit, he didn't enjoy the turmoil she generated in his life. He liked things to be regular; a kind of reassurance that he had missed growing up, when he never knew what he would find when he came home from school.

He parked in the driveway of Fiona's home, an old, Federal brick house, a gift from her parents when they moved to Florida. Ben had finally abandoned living on his farm and had moved in with her. Tamed from being a "good old boy," he even put up with an occasional attendance at her book club, and was still laboring over *War and Peace* because she had asked him to read it and wanted to discuss it with him.

His spirits rose when he was welcomed into the kitchen filled with the aroma of pork roasting in the oven and the sight of a freshly baked pie. The place was inviting, with a roaring fire; comfortable chintz-covered furniture; shelves filled with books; and some old primitive paintings from Fiona's family. It was an obvious improvement on Ben's farm which was cold and uncomfortable, and smelled like his hound dogs, who still lived there, and who he checked and fed once a day.

Roo had always been curious about their relationship, and supposed the old cliché, opposites attract, worked for them. She was delicate, bookish; the town librarian and ballet teacher. Ben was like a large, grumbling bear, and loved football, repairing cars, and hunting for wild game.

When he and Ben were high school football stars, the girls flocked around them. They enjoyed the attention, but he was going steady with Janey, and Ben was only interested in Fiona, which seemed like a hopeless cause. Fiona would sail past him in the school hall as though she didn't see him and had important things to do, and only occasionally said hello. Ben was entranced by her, and even her casual glance would make him happy. After Fiona graduated from Wellesley College, they got together. Roo was surprised that she hadn't married some corporate lawyer and stayed on the East coast, living a country club life.

They sat down at the kitchen table and Fiona served her special roast, mashed potatoes, and steamed broccoli. Roo poured gravy over his food, briefly musing on the couple's obvious contentment, which always caused a wrench of sadness and envy in him. It could never be as simple with him and Katya.

Before he picked up his fork Ben, ignoring Fiona's warning look, said, "I hear Katya's in New York?"

"She's been helping Geoffrey Banks, her manager at the Little Swan Gallery, with a new exhibition. I was scheduled to be there for the opening, before Stumpy asked me to take over the murder case. The way it's going I could miss it."

"What's the deal?" Ben dug into his mashed potatoes. "Are you two still together?"

"I don't know. It's my fault. Since the injury, and the last case, there are a lot of times when I want to be alone; to figure things out." He knew it sounded lame, but he couldn't overcome his nagging feelings of suspicion about her, which clouded his happiness.

"You know, you two should make up your minds. Either it's on, or off. This has gone on too long."

Fiona pushed back the red-gold curls cascading down her shoulders and said in a huff, "I didn't see you coming to a decision about us until I forced it."

"Hmm. Maybe." Ben frowned, concentrated on his dinner, and changed the subject. "So, what can you tell us about the murder case?"

Fiona shuddered and put her fork down. "You know, the funeral is Monday. Anna was such a wonderful person. She volunteered at the library. I loved her." She gulped, fighting back tears. "The casket will be closed. There are no relatives except Matthew, so it will be all their friends from grange and church, and everyone else in town."

Roo said, "A search warrant will be issued tomorrow for Matthew, even though there's not enough evidence to charge him. He was seen around town before the murders, but no one I talked to can be sure of the date."

"I remember him now. Very quiet guy. Sort of faded into the wallpaper," Ben said. "He used to date Linny Brooks. You probably didn't know her. She was a couple of years behind us."

"Stumpy brought her in for questioning, but got nowhere. They searched her apartment and found nothing. She said she hadn't seen Matthew for over a month, and had no idea where he'd gone."

Fiona said, "Linny comes into the library to check out books, and has been using our computer facilities to look for a job. It's hard for her because of her reputation. She was on drugs, and there were even rumors she was dealing." Her voice lowered. "This is gossip. Someone at the library told me Linny was desperate and would wait outside the new pain clinic to buy pain pills from old people on Medicare, then sell them for a profit to pay for her habit. I'm not sure that's true. Hard to believe if you know her.

"Linny told me she had entered the rehab program on her own. She's really a nice girl, very intelligent, and suffered from a terrible family life. People said her stepdad beat her, even when she was a little girl, but no one reported him or did anything about it. He skipped out, and her mother hung out in a beer joint on Rte. 12, looking for clients." She raised her eyebrows as she removed her uneaten dinner and the empty plates, returning with apple pie and a bowl of whipped cream.

"Last year her mother left town with someone she met at the bar, so Linny lives alone. I don't know how she survives, but she did mention once that her grandpa sends her a check every month. I've suggested to the library superintendent that they hire her. She's desperately poor. You know, she lives in one of those apartments in the Elite Living Complex, on the outskirts of town."

Chapter 9

ROO BELIEVED ANY place named Elite would be anything but, and saw that he was right when he pulled up near the abandoned railroad tracks and old depot in front of the shabby apartment building. Paint was peeling from its exterior in large scabs, and the area was surrounded by high, brown weeds sticking out of the snow, the bare branches of elderberry bushes and yellow weeping willows growing wild.

He climbed the steps up one floor to the apartment, and rang the bell several times. A pale young woman with long, blond hair opened the door to a room with only a table and one chair. It was cold, and he noticed the radiator was broken. She was huddled in a blanket.

"Linny Brooks?"

She saw the badge and stepped back, hunched up to protect herself, as though he might strike her. "What do you want? I haven't done anything."

She was very thin, with small childlike features. Her neck was twisted, which forced her into a sidelong gaze.

"I'm looking for Matthew Knapp."

"I told the sheriff everything. He is a suspect, I know." Her voice was a whisper. She shook her head. Her large, gray eyes filled with tears.

"He would never do anything like that. He had drug problems like me, but he was always a good person. He was the only one who ever cared about me."

"Do you know where he is?"

"No." She tried to close the door.

"Wait." He blocked the door with his foot. "It would be better if he turned himself in."

"Please go. You have no right." She shut the door in his face.

He was still parked outside Elite Living when Stumpy called, growling into the phone. "Can't fucking believe it."

The DNA Index System for State and National data base comparisons had yielded results. The unidentified DNA from the Knapp murders matched the samples found at the murder scenes in his last two cases. Stunned, he got out of the truck and stood, motionless, in the parking lot. Stumpy was still talking. Daley had discovered from the marks on the bodies that the killers had used a hunting knife, made to cut through bone. Stumpy went on talking, but Roo wasn't listening.

He was not crazy. The psychopath existed, and was still on the loose. He suspected the murders had been deliberately pinned on Matthew. But that didn't explain how the killers knew the way to get to the farmhouse. Matthew could have been followed, or forced to return with them.

He raced back to Linny's apartment and banged on the door. She answered, drawing back from him.

"I just got a call from the sheriff. I believe Matthew is innocent." He knew he was stretching the truth. "I have to find him. You have to help me."

There was a tremor in her voice. "I didn't mean to lie. I was only trying to keep him safe. I didn't tell the sheriff, but Matt had been dealing in drugs until a few months ago. We promised each other we would quit. He was only doing it to make enough money so we could have a new life somewhere else."

She stifled her sobs. "He left here days before his grandparents were killed. He was frightened. There was a letter at the post office for him. It came care of my address. My grandpa sends money to me, so I check every other day. After the letter arrived, he went to see his grandparents. There was also another letter. I don't know what was in it; he wouldn't say."

She went into her bedroom and came out carrying a bulky folder. "He took away some papers from his grandparent's house, but left his mother's notebook. He was frightened and in a hurry after he received another message sent from the post office. He went through everything until he found what he wanted, and asked me to keep this, and other papers until he returns. Maybe this will help."

She was silent for a few moments, as though deciding whether to tell him what else she knew. "He said there was someone he had to see in New York; someone who had information about his father. He is a good person, no matter what people think. We were outsiders at high school. It brought us together."

She looked away from him. "He didn't mind that I was on drugs and had a bad reputation. He said I was pretty, even though my neck is twisted. It was my stepdad who caused that"

Roo winced, almost feeling the blows striking her frail body. He wanted to put his arms around her to comfort her.

She reflected for a moment. "Matt didn't know who his father was. People said he was a bastard, that his mother never married and abandoned him when he was a baby. He didn't remember her. His grandparents wouldn't talk about her. It bothered him a lot."

"Do you know where he's staying in New York?"

She reached into her pocket and handed him a slip of paper. "He gave me money to buy a phone before he left and said he would call me if he had to move on."

"How did he get this address?"

"I don't know; maybe from the letters. He promised he would come back for me. He didn't say when he would return. Now I know he could be gone forever." Her small face composed in a picture of grief.

Auschwitz, Poland: March 1944

The Boy

Chapter 10

THE BOY SHIVERS in the cold; his striped, ragged prison uniform is soaked by rain pelting down. His ill-fitting wooden clogs fill with water and mud. He chokes on the stench that pervades the camp; the smell of decomposing flesh and feces, and the smoke rising from the furnace. He is standing in line in the early morning dark for the *Aufstehen*, the roll call. Each morning, he and the other prisoners wake to guards' shouts and are harried and beaten to line up in the *Appelplatz*, the central square. The guards run through the lines, shouting "*Raus*," carting off the dead and those too weak to stay on their feet.

He never dares to move, and some mornings is forced to stand for hours while the weak drop dead like vermin as one guard says with a laugh. The Boy wonders why he is called vermin and searches in his mind for something he has done wrong to deserve this hatred and punishment.

But this morning is different. Hope flows like a slipstream through the lines of prisoners. There are rumors that the lucky ones will be saved for a special task.

Major Bernhard Krueger walks slowly in front of the lines staring intently at their faces, then glances down to read prisoner registration cards. Krueger is a small man, only 5'8", shorter than The Boy who is tall for his age. He tries to stretch to a greater height as the SS officer stops for a moment in front of him. Major Krueger does not seem threatening, with his soft brown eyes and receding hair line. But the mild-looking officer, with a flick of his wrist, on a whim, can send him to death in white clouds of smoke and ash spouting from the chimneys.

The Boy tries not to tremble as Krueger smiles at him and studies his fake registration card. At Terezin, the Czech holding area for prisoners being sent east to the camps, his father, once owner of a print shop, had written the lie on the card. It stated that The Boy was 16, old enough for work; his occupation was printer's assistant.

He shivers, in terror of being discovered. He uses all his will to concentrate on standing upright, looking straight ahead at nothing. Starving, near collapse, his head swirls, as though spiraling toward the sky.

The Golem is there—rising from the pages of his book. He feels his presence. After the guard passes, he quickly glances up again. The Golem's giant shadow hovers in the dark sky, waiting to be freed from the book. His thundering, mammoth feet will crush the barracks, the guards, the camp, all the evil before him.

The Boy grows faint. His legs tremble, and he closes his eyes for only a moment as the Major walks slowly up and down the line and begins to choose, for each prisoner, life, or death.

New York: December 2002

Big, Francis Bigelow Stoddard III

Chapter 11

FRANCIS BIGELOW STODDARD III stood before the fireplace in his paneled office at Stoddard Investment Bank, clutching a folded letter in his hand. For one of the few times in his 62 years, his handsome, ruddy features twitched with worry as he muttered the cliché. He had "tempted fate" by running for office. The blackmail letter, enclosed in a plain envelope, postmarked from Grand Central Station, had arrived in his mail tray three days after he had announced that he would be a candidate for US Senator from New York in 2004.

Running in the Republican primary against Senator Henry Conrad should be a slam dunk. Conrad was an old fart, and had been in the Senate for years. Lately, the senator had angered his conservative supporters by voting against a tax cut beneficial to them. After Big won the primary, he would face the real challenge of beating the Democratic candidate in the general election. New

York always went democratic, but he had loads of popular support. His charisma would make the difference.

Lily Butler, his secretary, wearing extremely high heels and a tight skirt and sweater brought in some papers for him to sign, and lingered near him. Her sweep of blond hair hung seductively over the back of his chair. He gave her a pat on the bottom. Since he had cornered her in the hall on her first day, four years ago, and cupped his hands over her large breasts, these brief early-morning encounters in various inventive positions, behind the locked doors of his office, had become a ritual.

She was eager, always ready to please, and deluded into believing that one day she would replace the current Mrs. Stoddard. After the election he would get rid of Lily, for a younger, even sexier version. Stoddard had put a check on his libido since deciding to run for office and had hired Brady Medford as his personal assistant and future campaign manager. Medford watched Big's every move.

Impatient and irritated with this vexing threat, he had waved Lily away to her office in the adjoining room and stared out the window at the panoramic view of downtown New York. His luxurious office, which included a large apartment, was nestled in his giant bank building near One Wall Street.

The office, decorated in Georgian style, was furnished with expensive antiques. Inspired by dinner at the Prime Minister's residence at 10 Downing Street, he had purchased several pieces of furniture during this last trip to the UK. Like his father, he believed traditional surroundings gave customers a feeling of solidity, a safe haven for their investments.

Until this ominous note arrived, Big had everything going for him in his privileged life, and in this coming election. His patrician credentials would be marketed as noblesse oblige, the obligation of duty to the poor and disadvantaged. His mother Elizabeth, descended from one of the Mayflower families, had been a lovely person, but slightly removed and always in the shadow of her husband. She had died several years ago.

The wall behind him was lined with photographs of his father, Major General Francis Bigelow Stoddard II, war hero and founder of the bank, recording his triumphant return from Germany after WWII. The framed charter and newspaper clippings of the 1949 ceremony opening the Stoddard Investment Bank, graced the large reception room. His father, Frank, had been an imposing figure of influence, an economic advisor to many politicians until his sudden death last year.

Stoddard Bank had been small at its founding, but in a few years had mushroomed into one of the most successful firms on Wall Street, a rival of Goldman Sachs. It was now one of the largest banks in the world, with enormous financial clout.

After Big graduated from Harvard his father had slotted him into an influential position at the bank. He was a charmer, expert at personal relationships, and in his early career had been extremely successful doing lucrative deals, financing green mailers and the junk bond market. His reputation grew, and some wise-ass trader in the dealing room had shortened Bigelow to Big. What began as a joke became his name on the Street.

When the insider trading scandals broke in 1987, sending several moneymen to jail, Big had been implicated, but with the use of the most able lawyers, and family influence with politicians, he escaped prosecution. After the scandals, he took the firm private and until he decided to run for senator, had been in merger discussions with the giant Neptune Bank, a venture that would have made him a billionaire many times over.

He had been willing to give up the merger to run for office, a great public relations move for a politician. In these last few years he had not been satisfied with just financial success, and felt the need to make his mark for posterity, and to equal or surpass his father. Politics would mark him out as more than a businessman. His election to the Senate could lead to a run for President. He was convinced that giving up the merger showed his desire to serve his country, to give something back, which would only add to his reputation.

Earlier that morning he had told Medford to take the day off. He didn't want him nosing around or listening to his phone calls while he contemplated his next move.

Brady was a younger version of himself; a Harvard grad, smart with a killer instinct. He was irritating; like Big's looking into a mirror and spotting his own smug sense of privilege. There was room for only one patrician in this office. He needed Brady to connect with donors and manage the campaign so he forced himself to be congenial even though he suspected the aide was spying on him. Still, he was sure Brady was ignorant of his morning dalliances and the occasional threesomes at his private Ritz Carlton suite. They were now in the past anyway, and would be hard to prove.

He grimaced, and gingerly reopened the letter as though it contained Semtex. His pulse climbed to a dangerous rate as he reread the childlike message, printed in uneven block letters on a sheet of ordinary printing paper.

You murderers, you thieves thought you were safe. You believed the only remaining Paper Man Dossier was destroyed in Germany at the end of the war. You were mistaken. A copy of this dossier survives.

It is time for you to face the consequences for stealing wealth from the murder of others. I will make the public aware of the dossier. It will destroy you and your bank.

You have only one choice to prevent your downfall—withdraw from the Senate race. Time Limit—March 15. Week before primary election. If you comply, the dossier will be destroyed.

1996200

"Time limit: March 15," rang like an alarm. Big pressed his forehead to eliminate the grinding noise in his head. The message was creepy, disconcerting; an existential threat to his safe, cushy life. He was bewildered, and had no idea what this meant. He had thought at first this blackmailer had information on his extracurricular sexual adventures, but dismissed that as easy to overcome. This could be more serious.

He sat down in his large, leather chair, trying to think this out. A dossier somehow dangerous to him, believed to have been destroyed at the end of the war, was in this blackmailer's hands. What could be in this dossier that threatened to bring down the firm and ruin his reputation? If he did withdraw from the race, he could not trust the blackmailer to destroy the compromising evidence.

He shook his head in denial. This could not be true. There was no proof. This must be a hoax from some dirty trickster working for the opposition campaign. Still, if there were the slightest chance the threat was real—he closed his eyes. What should he do?

There would be only one way to defend his position and stop this threat: deny, deny, deny, and attack his accuser. If his men could discover the identity of the letter writer, they would eliminate the bastard, and anyone else who might be aware of this mysterious dossier.

Then he realized that this dossier was believed to have been destroyed during WWII, before he was born. Could the threatening letter have some connection to his father, a war hero? It couldn't be possible. But even as he doubted this terrible thought, he placed the letter in the desk drawer and locked it. Then he hurried to a large safe in the closet next to his bathroom and removed a thick folder labeled *Frank Stoddard 1940–1949*.

Big opened the folder, leafing quickly through the papers, not sure what he was looking for. His father's affairs had always been a mystery. He hadn't had time during the merger talks to go through the papers, but had some vague memory that the folder contained various old bank documents and some private correspondence. His father may have intended to destroy this material before his estate was settled, but he had died suddenly of a stroke this past year, and everything was left with Big.

Many of Frank Stoddard's papers had been removed after the war, marked classified and stored in CIA archives. He had been a young, dashing officer in the OSS, the Office of Strategic Services, the fabled intelligence unit, a precursor of the CIA, headed by Wild Bill Donovan.

There were several photographs of his father attending meetings as a US economic representative after the war. He had been a member of the Allied Tripartite Commission for the Restitution of Monetary Gold, and was pictured in a 1948 meeting in the *Reichsbank* in Germany.

He continued to skim through the plethora of documents and discovered several more pictures of a young Frank Stoddard, one labeled "Bern, Switzerland 1944, OSS headquarters." He sighed with relief. These seemed innocent enough, but another photograph had slipped between two documents. The word 'shred' was written across the picture in large black letters. Before his stroke his father had become frail, forgetful. He must have intended that this be destroyed.

Big grabbed a magnifying glass from his desk drawer. Through the dark smudge of letters, only his father was recognizable among the uniformed men sitting at a table in a bar. The face of the officer next to him was rubbed out by the dark pen. All he could see was the man's hand raised in a toast. He gasped as he looked closer at the large ring on the man's left hand. It was in the shape of a skull and marked on the sides with a swastika and strange symbols. It stirred a childhood memory. His father, home from one of his many trips to Europe, was showing him photographs of a Nazi trove of silver and rings found hidden in Nowy Sacz Royal Castle in Poland.

The skull seemed to come alive, grinning maliciously at him. He dropped the magnifying glass. It was a Nazi death head's ring, a *Totenkopf ring*, awarded to fanatical members of the SS.

Moscow: December 2002

Pasha, General Pavel Romanovich Mikhailov

Chapter 12

THE GENERAL NEEDED only a moment to read the bizarre message on the screen. Handwritten in uneven block letters like a child's composition, it had been copied from a bank office and termed "of interest" by one of his agents in the US.

The letter had been sent to Francis Bigelow Stoddard III, a prominent American banker, and a candidate for US Senator. It threatened to reveal a file called the Paper Man Dossier, containing damaging information on Stoddard, if he did not withdraw from the primary race. The blackmailer had given no hint of the dossier's contents, but claimed, that if disclosed it would bring ruin to Stoddard and his bank.

A wave of anxiety swept over him. He didn't give a shit about this stupid *mudak,* this privileged ass who fancied himself a US Senator, but Stoddard's possible exposure and the ensuing scandal could lead directly to him.

If there was a chance this blackmail note was genuine, it would bring on an investigation into the Stoddard Bank. His own illicit deals in the '80s with Frank Stoddard, the banker's father, could come to light in old bank records. Inevitably, this would lead to inquiries into his present hidden financial account, set up in secrecy after the collapse of the Soviet Union.

After securing Putin's private fortune in institutions around the world, he had taken his cue from Lenin's command during the Revolution: *Rob the robbers.* He secretly accumulated his own additional fortune on an enormous scale. His private account, Archangel, had been placed offshore in Cyprus, out of reach of Russian authorities, and the money deposited in shell companies, masking his ownership. Then the illicit fortune was transferred to the States and funneled into real estate, banks, and corporations.

The exposure of his Archangel account would be more than an embarrassment to the Russian government, exposing the Kremlin's financial espionage and triggering an international incident. The West, led by the United States, would impose ruinous sanctions on the inner circle of the Kremlin.

If his nightmare became real, *vyshaya mera*, the "highest measure" of punishment would await him for his betrayal. It was a crime against the state. He would be liquidated and could not choose his mode of death.

He lit his second cigarette, then locked his office door, opened his safe and took out Kolya's interrogation. The recent liquidation of Major Boris Piatikov by car bomb, while he was attempting to defect by handing over Kolya's file, seemed a fluke; a strange coincidence.

His hands shook in a mild tremor as he scrutinized the documents. The Paper Man dossier had been the main focus of Kolya's interrogation. Despite the torture his friend endured, he had denied knowledge of the contents and location of the dossier.

He was incredulous that this could be happening to him, one of the most powerful officials in the Russian Federation. Over the years he had planned carefully, plotted his every move, and now, in spite of his grueling effort, he could become a victim because of the actions of that stupid nonentity, Major Piatikov.

The General had been appointed chairman of the board of Ikon Inc. a giant, aluminum company, and became a multi-billionaire. Ever careful, he did not trust the vagaries of the leadership or his cronies, who had the power to take it all away.

He paced over to the window, fidgeting, feeling trapped, looking down on pedestrians struggling in the snow, crossing the square toward the Metro station, and wished he could escape and be one of them.

This nebulous threat from the past was a sinister reminder that he was not all powerful, but one of the chosen under the *krysha* "roof," protection provided by the Kremlin to those who prospered after the privatization of Russia's companies.

He took several drags on his cigarette, and was enveloped by the cloud of smoke. His doctor had warned him to quit, but death by nicotine seemed almost welcome, compared to what could be his downfall.

Visions of what had happened to Kolya filled him with remorse and terror. He could not understand why there were no details of his betrayal and arrest in the interrogation file. He closed his eyes, visualizing Kolya's capture by special operations, like those he had conducted in the past.

Kolya was drugged, wrapped in bandages by the Special Actions Department, and flown to headquarters in Moscow. He was dragged down to the cells of the Lubyanka; interrogated, tortured, and shot in the back of the head. A terrible rumor had floated around the organization that Kolya had not been shot but was fed, alive, into the crematorium. Rumors often proved to be true.

He steadied himself. He must take control of this situation and direct the actions of Stoddard without arousing the suspicion of his colleagues. The banker had connections with the powerful in the US, and would have access to inside information. He could be managed, kept under surveillance. and be forced to provide information leading to this Paper Man Dossier.

The blackmail letter set the deadline, March 15, for Stoddard's withdrawal. He foresaw with growing alarm that even if Stoddard withdrew, the dossier's contents could still be released, and eventually he would be exposed. He could take no chances, and came to a swift conclusion.

He must find and destroy the blackmailer and the dossier before the deadline.

Chapter 13

A SLOW BURNING panic rose inside the General, but he kept his discipline and remained as always, outwardly calm and deliberate. He realized that his hunt for the Paper Man Dossier and the mysterious blackmailer would force him to look into his past, conjuring painful memories.

Before he took any action, he would thoroughly search the archive files and those of other departments. This must be done without his aide Dima's knowledge. An exaggerated interest might be noticed and could lead to unwanted scrutiny of his own actions in the '70s and on into the present.

For several days, even as he attended important security meetings, he worked feverishly, digging up obscure files remotely associated with the Raven, desperate to find some scrap of information to lead him to the dossier. He soon discovered that the Raven's files, and those under his real identity, Peter von Krantz, were empty. He should not have been surprised. It was only logical that the old Bolshevik had destroyed or hidden documents when he knew he was doomed.

The Raven haunted his thoughts. He could see him, in his tailored black military tunic and high boots, visiting Kolya and him at school. Standing before them in rigid posture, with swept-back hair and thin, distinguished face, his hypnotic dark-blue eyes missed nothing.

They called him *Dyadya,* although the Raven was not an uncle or a benevolent relative, but had become, in a bizarre, unexpected way the only father they knew. Both he and Kolya cherished his rare visits, knowing they were considered important because the old Bolshevik was watching over them. He wanted to believe the Raven plucked them up out of nowhere, sensing their potential for greatness, and that he had no other motive. In the end, poor Kolya had not lived up to expectations.

Kolya and he were orphans, casualties of the war. Younger than the other students, they had arrived at the exclusive Suvorov Military School in Moscow from very different paths. Kolya was one of the last group of children to fall under Order No.00486 article 12 of the Criminal Code. The ruling was intended to reform the socially dangerous, and as an infant Kolya had been placed in an orphanage for the "politically unreliable" for correction. He had no idea who his parents and family were. They had disappeared like many others during the war.

There were no details of how or why Kolya had been placed at the orphanage, only that someone in his family was a suspected enemy of the people. After the end of the Soviet Union, it was discovered that these children were often subjected to humiliation and beatings. Kolya never spoke of his time there.

Pasha's father had been a hero, a tank commander who died in 1943, at the Battle of Kursk. His mother, pregnant after his father's short furlough, had died at his birth in 1942, and he had been adopted by Sofka, Aunt Sophia Petrovna Arapova.

He later learned that Sofka was not his aunt, but had been a great friend of his mother's. She was a mysterious, elegant figure, celebrated for her unparalleled beauty, and rumored to be the daughter of a Serbian nobleman from an ancient family. He remembered that when he was small and peeked into the dining room, she would be presiding at grand dinner parties among uniformed men and elegantly dressed women.

In 1948 when he was six, she vanished under mysterious circumstances. He was terrified at her sudden unexplained disappearance, and was left in the apartment with the disagreeable housekeeper, Varya, who took him to an orphanage for children of war heroes.

It was a seemingly more benevolent place than Kolya's, but he had only dark shifting memories; sitting alone at a table; mocked for his small size and large nose; beaten and chased by bullies. But the most soul-destroying was the furtive groping of Abramov, the orphanage director, who visited his bed each night and forced him into painful sexual acts, even though he begged and cried.

He smiled bitterly. He did not forget Abramov and took revenge after he joined the KGB. Even though Abramov was a frail old man, he and his entire family were arrested, tortured, and died in one of the prisons near the Arctic Circle.

Always frightened by Abramov and forlorn at the orphanage, Pasha had no friends and withdrew into himself, a timid, lonely figure until the Raven rescued him. The boys were never certain why they were the chosen ones. Pasha suspected he was selected because of Sofka's mysterious connections with those in high places. Kolya, who had no connections, perhaps was favored because of his physical attractiveness, intelligence, and strength.

Both boys felt pride that this legendary spy, a powerful member of the Collegium, the body that controlled the KGB, had taken an interest in them. As a young revolutionary, the Raven, a colleague of both Lenin and Stalin, was one of the great leaders of the revolution, and risked his life traveling out of the country on clandestine missions. In the early 1970s, he remained a top operative and confidant to KGB chief, Yuri Andropov.

The Raven continued to direct their lives, sending them on to the elite Moscow State Institute of International Relations, then to School 101, the Andropov Red Banner Institute for trainee KGB officers. They were ordered to achieve, to be ranked among the first in the class. They did everything together; Pasha ever grateful for the protective shield of Kolya's friendship.

Drained from hours of going over papers, he took a deep drag on his cigarette and lay on his couch. Before drifting off to sleep, his mind travelled back through the long corridor of his past.

He and Kolya are on maneuvers in a Siberian forest. The sun shines through the trees, making a dappled pattern on Kolya's face. He raises the dagger, given to him by an old warrior from the Caucasus, stabs his arm, and then Pasha's. Kneeling, they grip arms, mingling their blood, and take the brotherhood vow. He stirs, and still feels the exhilaration in the sting of the cut. They are inseparable, tied to each other, and the Raven, by their loneliness, and their longing for a father.

He was awakened the next morning by Valentina, his plump, motherly secretary with the beautiful, large eyes of a Georgian, who fussed over him and brought his tea. He drank two glasses with honey before checking his reports.

Evidence found in the Russian consulate in New York. Notes are from one of our operatives, name redacted, active in the States in 1969–1975. He turned to the details thinking it strange that the operative's name was redacted.

The words seemed to jump from the screen and cascade around him. He dropped his tea, shattering the glass, and collapsed back in his chair. He didn't move for some minutes. A growing pain scraped across his chest, and he wondered if his heart was giving out from shock and grief. It was unbearable to learn that love could have been the major reason for Kolya's attempted defection. He sat with his eyes closed, slowly recovering from the pain and apologized to Valentina for being clumsy. She had rushed in, alarmed at the noise and his condition, and was cleaning up the glass.

The General's pale eyes darkened to black, a look that always brought nervous trepidation to his assistants. Now he knew where to begin the search for the Paper Man Dossier. He spent the morning planning the operation in precise detail, then picked up the phone and gave the order.

Two weeks after he set the plan in motion, he had to accept its failure. The op had been messy and bloody, a risk. His agent reported that there had been no information on the dossier. His men had not come close to identifying the blackmailer. Matthew Knapp, the major suspect in the murders of his grandparents, had disappeared somewhere in New York.

He sent a message to Stoddard.

New York: Winter 2003

Big

Chapter 14

BIG RETURNED TO his office from an overnight visit attending upstate meetings with farmers' groups, small town party workers, and prospective voters. The seductive twinkle of his dark eyes had transformed into a hostile, glacial stare. He ripped off the denim jacket, plaid flannel shirt, and work boots, and stomped into his bathroom to peel the tight jeans from his plump body. He had looked ridiculous, and cursed Brady who had convinced him the costume would help upstate voters identify with him.

He showered and shaved; then plunged his face into a bowl of ice cubes to firm his skin; applied collagen cream; combed and sprayed his hair; and dressed in a suit and tie. Brady knocked, and crept in to go over the latest polls.

Senator Conrad, his primary opponent, had turned out to be more formidable than he had expected. Conrad was a conservative, millionaire farmer who owned acres of land, and was very popular upstate. He was opposed to almost all social programs, and was chairman of the powerful Senate Appropriations Committee.

Brady, lounging in a confident manner on the couch, said there were some indications that Conrad's support was waning. "Slightly," he sniffed.

That was bullshit. Brady was protecting his job. Big noticed that Brady's handsome face was marred by huge jug-handle ears. The campaign manager had turned his head to one side, and was peering out the window. One large ear was visible, reminding him of one of the Toby mugs from his mother's collection. He controlled the urge to grab that protruding ear and pull the bastard to the floor.

Unaware of Big's violent thoughts, Brady's eyes rested on the latest polls. He looked up, smiling. "I think we might be in reach; even overtake the Senator. I heard their campaign staff is panicking. But we have a lot of work to do."

With a self-important smirk on his smooth face, he told Big he had to identify with ordinary people, keep on message, and generate more social program ideas. He wasn't doing enough to show compassion.

His other piece of advice was to strongly project family values. Big shifted uncomfortably in his chair. For over two years he had attempted to cover his tracks as far as his exploits with women were concerned. He wasn't always discreet in his sexual encounters, but no one would imagine he, a pillar of respectability, would be indulging in a "morning bonk" in his office. And, he had heard that Sissy, his wife, was having an affair with one of the family lawyers and did not want any scrutiny.

He had been married to Sissy for 25 years, but seldom saw her or his two daughters, Charlotte and Clarissa, until, at Brady's insistence, they joined in a meeting and photo op for the campaign. For a few moments at the meeting, he hadn't recognized Sissy with her new hairstyle. Brady said he couldn't stress enough how important it was to have the family involved, so it was agreed that Sissy and the girls would appear at more important campaign events.

He was relieved when the strategy meeting was over and his manager left the room. He found it rather amazing how much he detested Brady, and sensed the feeling was mutual. The prick believed he had attached himself to a winner, which would make his own career in politics. Everyone on the campaign thought Brady was doing a great job. Big knew his own awesome charisma was the real vote-getter.

New York was having a cold spell, but he had planned on going out to the Hamptons for the weekend. Brady, the spoiler, always seemed pleased to deny him any rest, and had scheduled several events with city officials and the State Republican Committee. He sighed, feeling a bit sorry for himself.

Campaigning was harder than he ever had imagined. It was much easier to run your own company than to try to win votes from the great unwashed. He shuddered with distaste at the greasy dinners, the men with paunches, and overweight women in polyester who looked at him adoringly.

Still, he was content that all seemed to be going in the right direction, with his slight rise in the polls. He had nothing on until later tonight, and relaxed, pulling off his tie and removing his jacket. He opened his Georgian drinks cabinet, poured himself a scotch, and began to check his email. A message popped up on the screen:

I know about the blackmail letter. You will survive this if you cooperate and obey my directives. You have no choice You must locate Matthew Knapp.

Chekhov, Чехов.

Blinking, he read it again, through a panicked blur. Someone who identified himself as Chekhov knew about the blackmail letter. How did he get his private email address and what did he mean by "survive?" And who the fuck was Matthew Knapp?

He remembered from his college lit. class that Chekhov was a Russian writer. The message was signed in English, and in what he assumed was Russian. Could this Chekhov be a Russian, and how did he know about the blackmail note? Frightening thoughts whirled in his head. He realized he had enemies who knew as much or more than he did about this threatening dossier.

Until now, he had managed to put the blackmail letter at the back of his mind. Two days after he received it, he had asked his traditional contact (or, to put it less delicately, his fixer,) Joey Burns, to hire members of the Odessa *Bratva,* a Russian mafia group in Little Odessa, Brooklyn, to investigate. On several occasions Big had employed the Odessa Brotherhood to find dirt on business rivals, paying them from an untraceable offshore account.

In spite of their usual efficiency, the group had failed to find any trace of this Paper Man Dossier or discover the identity of the blackmailer. Even the attempt to decipher the number at the end of the letter, using different telephone exchanges, had yielded no clues.

The Odessa group so far had found nothing connected to the Conrad campaign or to any other possible enemy. This must mean there was nothing to it. There was not even the expected request for money. It must be a crazy. Still, he squirmed nervously in his chair.

If need be there was more than enough money to pay off the blackmailer, even if it was a Russian. He would not withdraw from the senate primary simply because of wild threats. He would press on with his agenda.

He suddenly thought again of the photograph he had found in his father's papers. It had been a shock to see the Nazi death's head ring, with the grinning skull, on the officer's hand, but he had found nothing more, nothing really to be concerned about.

Big did not answer the message immediately, but pondered over it for almost a week. Should he engage with this nutter? He had considered ordering the head of the bank's IT department to look into his personal encrypted emails and try to find the identity of Chekhov, but he would have to sacrifice his own privacy—not wise to do at this time.

He took a wide berth on Matthew Knapp after discovering, to his horror, that Knapp was a fugitive wanted for brutally murdering his grandparents. Why is this Russian asking him? Any connection to Knapp would be political suicide.

He finally answered the email. *"Who the fuck are you? The blackmail letter is a hoax. There is no reason to deal with you. I have no information."* He ended with *"Fuck You."*

Then another dire thought occurred to him. Even if fake, the blackmail letter and the contents in the dossier could be out there, floating around as rumor in some political enemy's hands. The press might get hold of it. He asked Lily to phone his wife and warn her not to talk to any reporters until she heard from him.

That evening, he directed his driver to the Little Swan Gallery on Mercer Street. He was on his way to dinner at Nobu with Katya Marston, the gallery owner and a very attractive, socially prominent woman, whom he had met recently at a cocktail party and benefit at the Museum of Modern Art. She was one of those amazing-looking women he called his "party girls." He prided himself on presenting a glamorous virile image with this collection of wealthy society women who enthusiastically supported him for senator. It seemed to be working for him.

The Marston woman was an aristocrat, rumored to somehow be related to the Russian Royal family, although she refused to answer any questions about her background. Even if it wasn't true, it was good publicity; valuable to his campaign to have the support of a beautiful, white Russian aristocrat who moved in the right circles.

As the car wound downtown through the village to Soho, he reviewed his plans to persuade her to raise funds for his campaign, and maybe to have a discreet affair. Her exotic background and wild reputation intrigued him. He frowned, realizing that an affair was impossible with Brady watching him, and the press constantly on his tail.

Still, he was an optimist for good reason. He had never been forced to face the consequences of his often dubious, illegal behavior. When his driver pulled up to the gallery, he had convinced himself that the blackmail letter and the Chekhov email were phony, and would soon disappear. He was looking forward to the encounter with this glamorous woman.

Prague: 1944

The Boy

Chapter 15

THE BOY RIDES on a train, not like the cattle car that took him to *Auschwitz*, but a real train with seats and windows looking out at the world. He is traveling away from the camp, with Elijah and other lucky prisoners. He does not know where they are going, but feels a rush of joy and relief that he was chosen, his fate determined by the SS officer, Bernhard Krueger.

After his father collapsed and died during the camp roll call, Elijah had appeared beside him, comforting him and giving him scraps of food to keep him alive. The old man had tried to still his fear by joking; if they go up in the chimney smoke, they will be taken to heaven in a chariot of fire.

The Boy watches from the window as the Prague train station rolls by. A giant, black shadow slowly forms in the sky. His heart leaps. It is the Golem, hovering, following him as the train rumbles on. When will the Golem crash down, destroying all the evil in his path? Will he break free? Why is he waiting?

Tecumseh County, Ohio: Winter 2003

Roo

Chapter 16

ROO WAS IN the sheriff's office going through the large, pink scrapbook Matthew had left with Linny. It was filled with a collection of awards, photographs, and newspaper clippings of Julia Knapp's scholastic achievements. He made duplicates and gave them to Gracie, who put them in the Knapp murder file along with copies of the photographs he had found in the corn crib.

The sheriff glared at the file. "I don't see the connection here. This is just past stuff about the family, all of whom are gone. Don't see it. This isn't about the murders. This isn't evidence. We aren't any closer to arresting Matthew."

Roo believed Linny's claim that Matthew was frightened and in danger, and said he had a lead, a hotel address in New York.

Stumpy sat back in his chair. "So far we have zero since the main suspect has disappeared. There are no other leads and I'm counting on you to find him. Go to it. I'll continue the investigation here so folks will know we're working on the case. That will keep Swenson out of my hair."

Roo phoned Katya to tell her he was on his way to New York, following up a lead in a murder case.

"I'm so happy you're coming for whatever reason. I can't wait to see you. So much has happened. A few weeks ago, I met this nice man at a Museum of Modern Art benefit. His name is Big Stoddard. He's running for the US Senate. You may have heard of him. Everyone says he's like one of the Kennedys; very charismatic. I've had dinner with him a couple of times to discuss the charities I sponsor. I think you would like him. Maybe you could volunteer to work on his campaign; a kind of therapy to take your mind off things."

He hung up, muttering, "Fuck that," and threw the phone across the room. Gracie jumped at the noise and glared at him. What did Katya mean by "things?" How could she be involved with this guy? He drove back to the farm, packed a bag and called Ben to take him to the airport.

Ben was making his way through traffic, driving just over the speed limit. "I guess this means you're going to make it up with Katya, but you're looking for Matthew, aren't you? You think he might be in New York?"

Roo didn't answer. Stumpy had not announced publicly that he was on the case.

"I don't believe he did it, but a lot of folks here think he was involved; part of a drug robbery." Ben glanced over at his friend.

Roo told him about the coroner's report. The Knapp murders were similar to contract killings, and a Russian hunting knife could be the murder weapon. But this was not conclusive, and didn't eliminate drugs as a motive.

Ben said, "You don't honestly think a Russian killer was hired to knock off the Knapps. That's just fuckin' nuts." He stared over at him as though he should be locked up. "And just who do you think would have hired them? And why the Knapps? Senior citizens involved in a drug ring?" Ben hunched over the wheel, swerving to avoid a truck.

"I know. It doesn't make sense."

"And you're going after Matthew on your own? If there are thugs involved, that could be dangerous. Hey, don't do anything crazy. The bastards could whack you. Anyway, I'm around if you need me." Ben said.

"Thanks"

Roo was quiet the rest of the trip, his mind going back to the damaged photographs. There seemed to be nothing to connect them to the case, but the fact that they had been hidden in the corncrib meant they were important to someone.

New York: Winter 2003

Roo

Chapter 17

IT WAS LATE afternoon and growing dark when Roo arrived in Times Square, its myriad lights and giant signs blinking and distorted in the cold rain. The square's illusory promise of fun and gaiety always seemed forlorn to him.

He hurried through the crowd on Broadway, past Times Square to the 50th Street subway near the Gotham Souvenir Shop, permanently closed, a *Gone out of Business* sign pasted on the front window. Behind the shop he came to a small. unpaved alley which dead-ended at a door opening to a set of stairs. A handmade sign, *Green Mountain Hotel*, was tacked to the outside wall.

The door at the top of the steps opened into a small cramped room with three tattered, crimson arm chairs, and a reception counter. The dark brown walls were stained with a mysterious substance, and a makeshift bar filled the small space at the opposite end of the room.

Near the door, a woman with a name tag *Dot Briscoe, Manager* pinned to her lowcut top stared at him. A cigarette hung from the corner of her thin lips. Above her ax-handle features, her hair, dyed a glow-in-the-dark bright pink, towered in a bouffant arrangement like cotton candy sold at the county fair.

She studied him with inquisitive black eyes shaded with pink eye shadow, eyeliner, and thick mascara.

"What are you staring at?"

He was startled by the hostile question delivered in the refined, melodious voice of someone who had gone to a girls' finishing school.

He realized he had been gawking at her eccentric appearance, and flustered, lowered his eyes.

"Reuben Yoder, Deputy Sheriff." He handed her his badge. "I'm investigating a murder case and want a look at your register."

She studied the badge for a long moment, then hissed with indignation and stomped in high heels over to a shelf above the staircase, pulled out a dusty book, and shoved it over to him. "I don't require anyone to sign if they prefer not to."

He saw that the last guest registration was in 1998.

"Who are you hunting?" She blew out the smoke from her last puff and stabbed the cigarette into an ashtray.

He took Matthew's photograph from his wallet, struggling to keep his eyes off her bizarre appearance. "Have you seen him? His name is Matthew Knapp."

She hesitated before answering. "There was a guy staying here who looked like him." She lit another cigarette and let the smoke flow through her nose. "He said a friend recommended my hotel, but didn't give his name."

"Is he here now?" Roo looked up the stairs.

"He went out somewhere this morning. When he returned, he was very disturbed after I told him two men came asking for him. This afternoon, a few hours ago, he paid in cash and left." She flicked a long pink nail at the *Cash Only* sign.

"Today? Did he say where he was going?" She shook her head.

"Can you describe the two men?" He took out his phone.

"They were in their forties, dark hair; one had a beard and the other man had a star tattooed on his hand. They were pretty ugly. Both about 6 feet, but overweight. Too much beer. They wore black leather and one of them was packing a strange-looking, foreign gun."

"Anything else?"

"They spoke some foreign language; rough guys, not the kind of men you'd want to anger." She smiled. "I don't mind a bit of rough, uglies like that, but unfortunately, they rushed off."

"I need to have a look at the room," Roo said.

Her constant glances toward the stairs had made him uneasy, and he put his hand on the glock in his shoulder holster.

She tottered out from behind the counter, wobbling in the tight leather skirt, and led him upstairs into a long hall with two rooms on either side, and one community toilet. He quickly searched the rooms, his stomach rolling over at the combined smell of vomit and piss hanging in the air.

Back downstairs, she leaned forward in her neon pink top, revealing a wrinkled bony neck and shoulders, "You're a bit too wholesome, but I can cope with that. Stay around and have a drink. You look like you could use one."

"Maybe another time." He handed her his card. "Thanks for your help. Let me know if the men come back or if Knapp shows up."

"Funny, that fellow had only a backpack with him. He seemed scared. Didn't look like a killer. Definitely not a match for those thugs."

Her glacial features melted for a moment. "He seemed lost. I asked him where he was going. He didn't answer. As he was leaving, he asked directions to the nearest uptown subway. I warned him to be careful."

Chapter 18

ROO WOKE IN the sunlight with Katya lying next to him, her head on his chest, sleeping peacefully. He thought of Auden's poem *Lullaby*, his way to define her.

> *Lay your sleeping head, my love,*
> *Human on my faithless arm;*
> *Time and fevers burn away*
> *Individual beauty from*
> *Thoughtful children, and the grave*
> *Proves the child ephemeral:*
> *But in my arms till break of day*
> *Let the living creature lie,*
> *Mortal, guilty, but to me*
> *The entirely beautiful.*

He knew it was a cliché, but his heart skipped a beat as he looked at her, seeming so innocent and beautiful. He reluctantly held an underlying suspicion that she could be devious, somehow using him and plotting against him. But he could never be through with her. Last evening after he left the Green Mountain Hotel, he hurried to find a taxi in the driving rain, and then phoned Linny.

"Oh, wasn't Matthew at the hotel? I haven't heard from him." She sounded scared, her voice a tiny squeak. "He said he was going to see a friend—someone who knew his father's family."

Christ! Where was Matthew? Who had given him the hotel address? Dot, who looked like she had popped up from an amusement park funhouse, said he had asked directions for uptown.

He arrived late to the Little Swan Gallery opening. Distracted, looking for Katya, he walked into the packed exhibition, an elegant affair with men in evening suits and women in long gowns. Waiters dressed like Russian peasants in long shirts and balloon trousers, were passing caviar and champagne. Musicians playing balalaikas wandered through the crowd. He stood at the back of the room, soaked from the rain.

Katya had said this exhibition was one of the social events of the season featuring the 19th century Russian artists called *Peredvizhniki*, the Wanderers. Their realistic landscapes were very popular with monied Russians. Some of the paintings were for sale, others on loan for the exhibition.

There was a stir from the crowd gathered near the exhibition entrance. Katya had entered the room and he lost his breath; like having the wind knocked out of him on the football field. She wore a shimmering silver gown, and her silky hair, the color of wheat, flowed down her back. He was making his way toward her and then stopped.

She was gazing up at an older man, handsome in an overblown way. His regular square face was framed by thick blond hair, gray at the temples and coifed fashionably, like a news broadcaster's.

Enthusiastic clapping and cheering filled the gallery after Katya introduced Francis Bigelow Stoddard III, a candidate for the US Senate in the coming election, running in the Republican primary. "You all know him as Big, and he has big ideas for the good of New York and the country."

Stoddard nodded, putting his arm around her in a proprietary manner, and announced with a flash of perfect white teeth that he believed the state and the country needed him, and he could lead the Senate in a new direction.

Roo watched this display, with the sick feeling that he had brought this on himself. He had been unsure about their relationship and in their argument before she left, had rashly told her there were no ties. It was hard to take that she had become involved with this man so quickly, when she had declared two months ago that she loved only him.

Geoffrey Banks, partner and manager of the gallery, came across the room to greet him. Immaculately dressed in an evening suit, he took two glasses of champagne from a passing waiter and handed one to Roo.

"Am I glad to see you, even if you are a little damp. Beats the company of some of our clients," he said, glancing down at the puddle of rain water from Roo's clothes dripping on the floor. With a rare look of disgust on his normally pleasant face, he watched

Stoddard and Katya, arm in arm, continue through the crowd of enthusiastic supporters, hugging and shaking hands.

"We worked so hard to obtain some of these masterpieces on loan. But since she's met him, it's not about the gallery show. It's all about this prick who calls himself Big. What a jerk. He's using us to get contributions for his campaign. He's fed Katya a bunch of bullshit. I told her that, but she doesn't listen to reason."

"Do you know him?" Roo said, surprised at the outburst.

"Only what I've read in a recent profile. He's from a prominent family and owns the Stoddard Bank. He's someone new in her life; a novelty. Sorry." He looked at Roo with meaning.

Geoffrey waved to an attractive woman swathed in a tight black gown, with diamonds circling her low neckline and dripping from her coifed hair. "That's Maybelle Hughes. Her family owns a large pharmaceutical company. She's one of his enthusiastic supporters. I know what you're thinking. Big has a wife and two grown children, but women flock after him. Word is they're separated, but they'll certainly appear as a happily married couple on the campaign trail."

Alarm spread through Roo. He felt a chasm open in his chest. An overwhelming urge to pull her away from this pompous ass welled up inside him. He stepped farther back into the room to avoid meeting him. It was ridiculous, but he feared he would lose it and punch him, and make a scene. And then they were coming toward him.

Katya rushed up and gave him a hug. "How wonderful that you're here. I want you to meet Big Stoddard." The banker seemed to smirk as he reluctantly shook hands.

"Katya has told me so much about you." Big gingerly stepped away from the puddle of water forming around Roo.

He was conscious of his wet jeans and ski jacket, and that he had forgotten to get a haircut. His hair steamed with moisture, and flopped down his forehead.

Stoddard looked past him and waved to someone, then said in a dismissive voice, "Come 'round to see me. Maybe we can find a place for you on the campaign."

Like hell, you bastard, he thought, and moved away from the crowded room into the lobby. He waited in the reception room, trying to control his fury.

After everyone had gone and the waiters were cleaning up, she ran to him. He scooped her up in his arms, unzipped her gown in the elevator, opened the door to the apartment and carried her to bed. He moved over her and sank into her softness, a haven. He wanted to believe they had reclaimed their relationship and were lovers again.

The next morning, as he gathered up his damp clothes, a sudden flash brought back the scene of Katya calling the police to turn him in, when he was a murder suspect on the run. He could rationalize that she had not believed he was a murderer, but that surrendering to the police would help him. But he couldn't dismiss her connections to Russian men and her attraction to the oligarch, Ostrikov. It was as though there was some mysterious thread that tied her to these Russian thugs.

In retrospect, her background story seemed vague. He wasn't sure he believed any longer that she was a descendant of the Romanovs. Although there was some evidence in the Blood Archive that this story was true, it could have been planted. Why did she refuse to take a DNA test to settle the question? He didn't buy her excuse of wanting to avoid publicity, since she was often in the gossip columns.

She was always mysteriously present at the edge of the action, and much of her past life in London remained obscure. He tried to dismiss the absurd thought that she could be an agent, or innocently working in some way for the Russians. While he was on his last case he had read that Lenin, the Bolshevik leader, had described those unwitting helpers as "useful idiots."

When she woke, he had dressed and was pulling on his boots still damp from the rain. "I spoke to Geoffrey about your new friend, Big Stoddard." Sarcasm crept into his voice. "He says Stoddard is married and has grown children." He wanted to ask her if she was sleeping with him, but said, "Are you committed to his campaign, or is there something more?"

"Big is a good man, working for the poor and disadvantaged. I'm sorry you didn't have a chance to talk with him last night, but there are a number of events coming up to raise money for his campaign."

He concentrated on his boots to hide his anger, regretting that he hadn't punched the bastard. "I'm meeting Devlin this morning. Stumpy wants me to consult him on the investigation."

This was true, but the real reason for his visit had nothing to do with the Knapp case. He felt compelled to discover the truth about the photograph of his cousin, Lucy.

"Does this mean you're going to work for him; come back to New York?" Her face lit up.

"I don't know." He did not want to discuss it and went into the kitchen to make a pot of coffee, reassured that at least she had not thrown out the old machine for a new one.

He was carrying a cup into the bedroom and startled her. She quickly hung up her phone, but he had heard her say she was meeting Stoddard that evening.

Fuming, he left for Devlin's. Was he making too much of her meeting with Stoddard? It could be innocent. He couldn't give up on her, after last night.

Chapter 19

ROO TOOK THE Line Subway from Spring Street to Devlin's office, smashed between schoolkids thumping each other with bookbags, and sleepy office workers juggling plastic cups of coffee. The car rattled on, rocking on the tracks and screeching around curves.

Faint images of Lucy and the Knapps flashed by in the dirty windows. He was haunted by what he believed he had seen on Devlin's phone; that glimpse of Lucy before her murder drove him into a dark place, tormenting him. He questioned his sanity. Was he delusional? That same day he had suffered from a brain seizure brought on by his concussion, and was taken, unconscious, to the emergency room.

He signed in at the vast lobby desk and was directed to the third floor. Devlin's new office in midtown was sleek and modern, with black leather sofas and photographs of Manhattan scenes on the walls. Devlin said the décor was part of the lease. Like his apartment, there was little reflection of his personality. The place was spacious compared to his previous office, when he had been a terrorism specialist for the NYPD, but it was still small with no receptionist or secretary.

He waited in the reception room for over twenty minutes, thinking with some relief that this was his chance to leave, but then Devlin rushed through the door.

"So great to see you. Are you here for good? Your place is waiting." He pointed to the desk opposite his own, facing the window.

Devlin appeared to have lost weight, but Roo noticed how fit and strong he seemed. His gray hair was cut short, and he looked professional in an expensive designer suit. Roo felt a sense of loss over his suspicion, remembering wistfully how they had become trusted friends. When he arrived in New York to investigate the murder of Katya's guardian, Devlin had realized that he was out of his element and had kindly offered him a room in his apartment.

"Sorry I'm late." He sat down behind his desk.

Devlin said he had been out of town on one of his consulting jobs. His expertise brought his company lucrative contracts with foreign and domestic intelligence agencies.

"Stumpy gave me all the information on the case. He said you were following a lead and asked me to help you out. Any recent developments?"

He sat on the edge of his seat. "No, not yet." He wondered what details Stumpy had shared. The sheriff was skeptical, and dismissed most of his evidence as circumstantial.

"He seems to think you're on the wrong track, looking for the killer in New York. Was it the girlfriend who told you Matthew was here? Do you think she's reliable?"

He didn't answer.

Devlin leaned forward. "How are you feeling now? You weren't the same after the nasty head injury. I've been worried about you since that day I found you semi-conscious and hallucinating. You were in pretty bad shape. Any more episodes?"

He shook his head. "I'm ok."

"It's hard to get back on the job after an injury like yours. Let's hope you'll be well enough to come to work soon."

He shifted in his seat, his mind on the photograph.

"Maybe when you finish this case you'll be ready. And if it doesn't work out with Katya, you're welcome to move back in with me." It was obvious Stumpy had been gossiping about his shaky relationship with Katya.

A bell rang in the reception room. "Excuse me. I'm expecting a delivery. It might take 10 minutes."

Devlin left his phone on the desk. Roo stood, his legs trembling, and picked it up. It was the same one Devlin had been using last year, a J-Phone from Japan, the latest 2002 model, equipped with a camera. To his surprise, his boss had not changed the password, and he frantically began searching for Lucy's photograph.

He was overcome with a sharp pain in his head and dizziness, a recurring spell that previously had sent him to the hospital. A giant roar swelled his head and he saw flashes, like a reel of negative film, of a shadow in the forest. He struggled to keep focused, quickly going through the phone.

There were no photographs of Lucy. He knelt on the floor, relief flooding through him, and heard Devlin's steps outside the office door. The room spun around him. His legs and arms felt heavy; he slowly rose from the floor, wiped the phone with his jacket sleeve and put it back on the same spot, just as Devlin walked in.

Devlin was aware that he was sweating in distress. "Hey, are you all right?"

It was hard to breathe; the air was smothering. He wanted out, away from Devlin's gaze. "Yes, thanks. I have an appointment with Geoffrey Banks. Have to go."

Devlin insisted they schedule another meeting to discuss his new job, and he heard himself answer that he would call. Then he was out on the street, with no memory of how he made it to the elevator and through the lobby.

He staggered a few blocks and leaned against a building to recover and drink in the cold air. What the fuck was wrong with him? There was nothing on the phone. He had imagined the photograph. How could he have thought this? Devlin was in the clear and he was delusional, on the edge of crazy, and could not trust himself. He knew there was one person he could trust to help with the case.

Chapter 20

'COLDER THAN A witch's tit,' Stumpy's usual winter weather report came to mind. The temperature was near zero, the sky was overcast, threatening snow, and the streets seemed brutally cold without trees and bushes to soften them. Roo's boots smacked hard on the pavement as he walked from Devlin's office to the Business Library.

He crossed between columns of the grand neo-renaissance building and into the large, hi-tech room. The place was empty of researchers and the front desk was deserted, with no sign of Alice Jefferson Jones. He should have called, he thought, just as Alice came into the room. She wore beige slacks and a soft white sweater. Thin gold bracelets dangled on her delicate wrists as she raised her hand to greet him. A matching gold comb was planted in her hair. She peered at him through stylish, wire-rimmed glasses and broke into a wide smile, her blue eyes even more dazzling in contrast to her smooth, dark skin.

"Is it really you? You look better than when I last saw you." She gave him a hug, her arms not quite reaching around him, and led him into her office. It was as though they had never parted. They had an inexplicable tie to each other. He partly attributed this to their obsession with research, and their combined ability to make connections which often seemed farfetched to others.

He took off his jacket and sat down in the leather chair opposite her desk, filled with a display of her wedding pictures in silver frames. Several high-profile celebrities were among the guests, including a corporate executive, an NFL player and at least two senators.

"The wedding was ginormous. Daddy invited all of his many friends, and our relatives—even distant ones he claims are descendants and were slaves of Thomas Jefferson." She grimaced in embarrassment.

"Our engagement lasted three years. Daddy finally accepted Malcolm, even though he objected to giving his only child away to a Pilgrim descendant. Daddy is difficult, hung up on genealogy. Mother always says he's not a tolerant person, but a brilliant professor."

She sighed. "We managed to survive the celebration and have moved into an apartment on 78th and Park." It was hard for him to imagine her in any place but the library.

She went silent, discouraging more questions. Roo had never met her husband Malcolm Prescott, a Yale law graduate and a partner in a prestigious law firm. Alice didn't reveal many details about her personal life. The wedding pictures were an exception.

"How about you?" she said.

"I'm ok."

She gave him a penetrating look. There was no way he could explain his meltdown in Devlin's office. He wasn't even sure himself what had happened to him.

"Are you staying with Katya?"

"Yes."

"Hey, you look a little down. What's wrong? I know you didn't come here just to have a heart-to-heart."

"I'm on a case, looking for Matthew Knapp, accused of killing his grandparents on their farm near Paint Creek."

"So, you're working for Sheriff Stumpy again. I did read about the murders of those poor people, but only noticed because Paint Creek is your hometown."

"The Knapps were a nice old couple, pillars of the community. The whole town's in shock and terrified the killers will return. There is some evidence they were killed for drug money. Linny Brooks, Matthew's girlfriend, told me he had been working for a gang dealing drugs, but recently quit. We haven't been able, yet, to trace the distributors."

He showed her Matthew's photograph. "His prints were found in the house."

"And you think he might be somewhere in New York?"

He nodded. "Linny claimed that he received two letters from the post office. The second letter arrived a few days before she believes he left for the city."

"The post office; how strange is that? Who uses the post office these days for letters?"

"Linny said he was angry, and accused his grandparents of keeping secrets about his parents."

"That doesn't seem a very strong motive to commit murder."

"He told her he was going to meet a family friend in New York, and gave her a hotel address. I checked at the hotel, but he was gone. Dot said he had left in a hurry that same day after he found out two men were asking for him."

"Dot?"

For a moment a pink cloud of hair rose in front of him. "Yes, the hotel manager; an unusual woman."

"Wait. I think we need sustenance." She left the room for several minutes, and came back with coffee, bagels, and cream cheese. "I didn't have breakfast." She took a large bite of bagel. "Hmm. What else?"

"Betty Lou Cochran, the Knapps' neighbor, said that shortly before the murders he showed up at his grandparents' house and took a bunch of papers."

"Still doesn't seem reason enough to kill." She curled up in her large arm chair while he went over more background. "After the news reports he must know the police are looking for him," she said.

"The murders didn't get much coverage nationally. Right now, I have only circumstantial evidence, but believe he's innocent and there's not enough to charge him."

He stopped to spread some cream cheese on his second bagel. "Two facts make me think there is a motive other than drugs for the murders. One is the unidentified DNA evidence found at the farmhouse linking the killer to murder victims in my last two cases. Stumpy thinks it's more than one killer, but I have doubts. The Knapps could have been murdered by this same psychopath, still on the loose." He didn't need to name the victims in his previous cases, as she had read the files.

She stared at him speculatively.

"And there is a similarity between the brutal method used to kill the Knapps and that used on victims in my other two cases."

Alice said, "Those murders pointed to Russian criminals, but if I remember, their government refused to extradite them."

"Stumpy disagrees with my theory, and says there is no solid evidence, but put me on the case anyway."

She frowned. "I'm with Stumpy. It seems too much of a coincidence. Maybe you just have this impression from your last case. Russian thugs on the brain?"

He stiffened, insulted. She was questioning his judgement, but then he couldn't bring himself to tell her about his vision of the dark figure walking across the field swinging the knife; that would only convince her that he was subject to fits of craziness and needed a psychiatrist.

"If someone is after Matthew, wouldn't it be better for him to turn himself in rather than risk ending up dead, like his grandparents?" she said.

"Yes, if I'm right—" He hesitated, then said, "I thought you could help."

She broke into a smile. "I would love it."

They finished off the bagels and she went out to the main desk in the library, put up a sign, *Available tomorrow afternoon* and, asked her two assistants to fill in for her. Back in her office, she pulled her chair up to her computer.

"I'm ready for action. This is so different from when you were on the run from the police, using another identity; not really as exciting, but it will have to do."

"I found these photographs in the corncrib in the victims' barn." He was apologetic. "Stumpy didn't think they were relevant enough to be in the case file."

Alice grinned, showing teeth like little pearls. "A corncrib? The first time I met you, a raccoon had landed on your head. A raccoon! And now a corncrib?" she laughed. "Hard for me to believe. I'm a city girl."

She studied each photograph for several minutes. "These are old, very damaged, and will be difficult to restore. But hey, you're in luck. Part of my job is researching and restoring old photos. Not to brag, but I've become an expert. Two years ago, I enrolled in night classes for advanced restoration techniques and now I have an MA in fine arts. I can reconstruct even the most damaged photos and manuscripts, but it'll take me a couple of days."

"Thanks." He hesitated, looking down at the photographs. "There's something else. In 1974, Matthew's mother disappeared and left him with his grandparents."

She sat very still, in a momentary trance. "His mother disappeared? Tell me more."

"Stumpy says I'm on the wrong track, and it doesn't make sense, and I should drop it; but I looked up the unsolved case in the dead files. Julia Knapp was reported missing by a woman named Minna Johnson, according to the reception clerk at the Village Plaza Hotel, in New York."

Alice was the only person who wouldn't think he was crazy to pursue this. "I brought Julia's high school yearbook with me. Her photographs from 1966–68 are six years earlier than her disappearance, but that's all we have. And Linny gave me this." He took out Julia's large pink folder.

"It's kind of a scrapbook, with a lot of newspaper clippings, awards; mostly from high school. Julia was a gifted science student, and after graduating from Ohio State, won a scholarship to Imperial College in London."

Alice opened the year book. "This is history. Wow: beginning of hippiedom—bell bottoms, beads, and long hair."

"When Julia returned from London to the Knapp farm with Matthew, she told Mrs. Weeks, her high school friend, that she was waiting for Matthew's father, but wouldn't give any details. Mrs. Weeks suspected she was lying, that it was a one-night stand with a stranger."

Alice, stared with intensity into space for a long moment, then came to life. "Let's look for more detailed reports on Julia."

Roo contacted the Police Department's Missing Persons Clearinghouse. They waited for two hours while the division searched their archives, and came up with details on the case.

Detective Steve Payne, now deceased, was assigned to the investigation a year before his retirement, and had written two detailed reports. According to Payne, who interviewed the hotel receptionist Ronny Blake, Julia had checked into the hotel eleven days before vanishing.

Minna Johnson, a schoolteacher from Indiana who occupied the room across the hall from Julia Knapp, had become friendly with her, after they both checked in on June 1, 1974. According to Blake, they started up a conversation because Ms. Johnson was planning a trip to England. Since Ms. Knapp had lived in England, Ms. Johnson wanted to know what to expect. She told Blake she had recently received her passport and that this was the trip of a lifetime.

The two women planned to meet the evening of June 12 in the hotel lobby, before going to dinner. When she didn't show, Minna Johnson waited for several hours, then notified Blake, who was nervous about the crime that plagued the area, and called the police. Ms. Johnson told officers that Julia had been waiting for someone, but had no more information.

Her room was searched. All personal effects were gone. Her parents were notified, and the investigation continued for several months.

The second report stated that Minna Johnson returned to her home at 8 North Clark Street, Elkhart, Indiana, three days after Julia Knapp vanished. She died two weeks later of a heart attack.

"Hmm. Strange." Alice said, reading through the pages of the evidence file.

A small scrap of paper, a crumpled Manhattan tourist map, and a note from investigators had been copied and attached to the end of the last report.

This note and the map were later found underneath the lamp on the bedside table. The handwriting was identified as Julia Knapp's. The department failed to find any connection to the case.

Alice read the note aloud.

Alone, as before, in the universe
Without hope and without love!
—The Demon by Mikhail Lermontov

"This was written by the Russian poet in the 1800s. The Paint Creek library had one volume of Russian poetry."

She grinned at him, impressed. "Well, you definitely are a genius. It is probable that neither the detective nor relatives would know that Lermontov was a Russian poet. I certainly wouldn't." Alice stared out the window deep in thought. "Why would she leave a note like this? And why a quotation from a Russian poet that obviously not many would recognize?" Her eyes narrowed behind her glasses. "I have a crazy idea. Could it be that someone with the same name as the poet was meeting her?"

"She could have left this note as a clue, hoping that someone would find her," he said.

They began to check membership lists of Russian societies and organizations for a connection to Lermontov, scouring telephone directories, airport records, and car rentals, but found nothing related to that name. Several hours later, they returned to the report again and examined the map. It was creased at a point near the Hudson River, but this area had been searched thoroughly, without success.

"So, she could have been walking toward one of the docks and didn't need the map after her first day," Alice said. She typed quickly on the computer. "The docks at that time were located on the Hudson River between West 46th and West 54th Street."

"Let's try the name of a ship," Roo said.

They began looking through port records for ships sailing on that date from one of the piers.

Alice jumped up from her chair: her comb clattered to the floor. "Oh my God, a Russian ship called the *Lermontov* left the port of New York on June 12, 1974—the same day Julia disappeared. Its destination was Leningrad, now St. Petersburg, Russia. That couldn't be a coincidence."

They logged on to the Port Authority archives and examined the Lermontov shipping manifest which registered passengers and crew sailing that day.

"I don't believe it," she said. "A Minna Johnson is listed among the passengers."

They stared at each other.

Roo said, "Who was using this passport and identity? It couldn't be Minna Johnson unless there was another person with the same name."

He phoned the State Department Office of Law Enforcement Liaison, and requested passport records for Julia Knapp and Minna Johnson.

"I'll call Malcolm to let him know I'll be late," Alice said, putting the comb back in her hair.

It was early evening, and they were eating Chinese takeout when the information came in. The Passport Office had found records for Julia Knapp and Minna Johnson. In the '70s, many passports recorded only name, photo, and address, but in this instance, it was reported that Julia had traveled to the UK in 1972 and reentered the States in 1974. She had given her address as the Knapp farm.

Minna Johnson's passport, stamped in May, 1974, had shown up on the Lermontov ship's passenger list. They compared pictures on both passport records and were stunned by the discovery.

Both photographs were of Julia Knapp.

Alice said, "How terrible that she might have been taken away to Russia. I don't even want to imagine what happened to her."

Chapter 21

"MINNA JOHNSON'S PASSPORT must have been stolen from her home while she was in New York," Alice said.

"Yes, that's possible. They would have had to work fast; as soon as the two women met and became friendly," Roo said.

"Could it be that Minna didn't die of a heart attack, but was murdered before she could report her passport was missing?" Alice shuddered. "Is that too far out?"

"No, now that there is some evidence Julia was kidnapped. The forger had to be an expert to alter the passports in the short time the two women were acquainted. No one in Indiana would suspect Minna was murdered. Some poisons are disguised so that a victim displays symptoms of a heart attack. Potassium chloride is often used, and hard to detect."

Roo phoned Stumpy with their discovery, but the sheriff was unimpressed. He was grouchy and losing patience.

"No news here, just a lot of bullshit from Swenson. This information has nothing to do with the Knapp murders. I gave you free rein, but could you concentrate on locating the suspect, and not a missing person from the '70s? Call when you have something real to report."

They suspected that Julia was taken by force to Russia, and couldn't give up the idea that this was a Russian link to Matthew and the murders, but had nowhere to go with these tenuous clues.

Alice sat for a few moments, then jumped up and put on her coat. "I have to lock up. My assistants have been gone for over an hour. Malcolm will be picking me up soon. I'll have the results of the photographs in a couple of days."

She turned around at the door. "What about that old Russian guy, that professor?"

"I was thinking of him too. I'll look him up."

When Roo spoke to Linny again, she had not heard from Matthew, and was distraught. He walked uptown, thinking it seemed crazy to follow his wild hunch—that he would find Matthew somewhere in New York's crowded streets with only vague clues; like a missing person's report from the 1970s, and a shady hotel in Times Square. Nothing fit; there seemed no way to put this together.

Matthew had asked Dot for directions uptown It seemed farfetched, but there was a slim possibility he had gone to Kutusov's.

It was early evening, and the streets were teeming with people shopping and going home from work. In the dusk, the luxurious shops glittered with lights. He passed Saks Fifth Avenue, remembering his encounter in the cosmetics department, when he had saved Katya from a Russian thug. It was the beginning of their on-off relationship, which had changed and complicated his life. He had called her again, but there was no answer.

When he turned up at Kutusov's place on East 87th Street, he noticed that the door had been recently painted, and a polished brass sign, *Odessa Import Export, Ltd.*, had been added.

Before he could ring the doorbell, Kutusov's gravelly voice called out. "Mitya, who is there?" Mitya, a middle-aged, bald Russian with a curved mustache, opened the door. He wore a peasant smock, wide pantaloons, and red slippers. It was a mystery to Roo that the old Russian found servants willing to wear a costume like a character in a comic opera. Mitya smiled broadly and led him into the drawing room.

Kutusov extended a soft, manicured hand, with polished nails. A diamond-encrusted Rolex circled his wrist. "Ah, you've come again. Not surprised, yes, but not unhappy to see you. What is it can I do for you?"

The Russian was well into his seventies and had undergone a miraculous transformation. Roo had expected the usual wild hair, stubbly beard and the belly burgeoning under a stained shirt.

Kutusov was clean-shaven, slimmer, and looked years younger with a new slicked-back hair style, bereft of gray (if not examined too closely.) Roo suspected he was wearing a corset underneath his velvet trousers and smoking jacket.

The living room had been redecorated with oriental rugs, swooping curtains, and antique furniture in the Empire style. Large paintings of fierce Cossacks had been restored and again hung on the walls, and the latest issues of *Novoe Russkoe Slovo*, the Russian émigré newspaper, were stacked on the table. It was as though Kutusov and his apartment had been treated to a giant airbrush.

He read Roo's thoughts. "I have become very successful. Am still professor, but only sometimes lecture. Some very, very important new Russians need me even more. I am becoming one and only necessary middleman between certain important Russians and US politicians. These oligarchs—very, very rich—know value of my connections. Nothing illegal." He winked. "Arrange finances, visas; sometimes difficult. Difficult, but I know everyone worth knowing in my new import-export business.

"Come, come, Mitya." He snapped his fingers, waking his new servant from his slumbers on a chair by the door. "Bring us vodka and cigars. I deeply apologize. No bread and salt for traditional Russian welcome."

Mitya brought in a silver tray embossed with Russian imperial eagles, laden with vodka in tiny crystal glasses, and a humidor with cigars. *Pirozhki*, the delicious filled pastry from the White Guard Café, was stacked high on a plate.

"Take, take." Kutusov raised his hands in an imploring gesture.

Roo helped himself and stared at the saints looking down at them from the restored icon corner.

"But why? Why again you make me a visit?" The Russian looked up from bushy eyebrows.

"I'm hunting for this man, wanted for murder."

Kutusov stared at Matthew's photograph. He slumped down heavily, still gripping his *pirozhki*. "Am only precious go-between: have done nothing wrong. Needed to replenish—yes that is the word I think—replenish income." His eyes rolled in agitation. He lowered his voice. "I see a likeness, someone once I knew." He put his half-eaten pastry back on the tray.

"A likeness?" Roo said.

"Yes, yes. Now I recall. No, no." He shook his head, "Too dangerous. But could for a fee?"

"Rumors." His voice cracked and he looked wildly around the room. "Someone else hunting him. For sure, there could not be another murder after grandparents. Too much publicity." He frowned, stroking his chin, musing aloud. "Maybe could use kidnapping or disappearance?"

"Who told you this?"

"Dangerous rumor. I give example of bad happenings. My friend, Anatoly, did special work for one of powerful men in finance; was how you say, indiscreet. Ok? Kremlin didn't like. After, strangled, with his dog's leash, in Central Park. Of course, no proof it was not the dog." His body shook with hollow laughter at his macabre joke. Agitated, he deteriorated even more into half sentences. "Powerful man in Russia hunting him. I tell only you. Maybe has something he wants. Information? Very clever to hide." His chin waggled nervously.

"Where is he? You know where he is." Roo curbed the urge to punch him.

Kutusov shrugged his shoulders and held out his hand. "I risk life telling this to you. They are killers. That is all I can tell for now. But money needed: as they say, comes in handy."

Roo reluctantly took out his wallet and gave Kutusov two hundred dollars from his limited expense account.

The Russian frowned as he grabbed it. "Tiny, tiny. Not enough. But will see, maybe more rumors. Call back."

Chapter 22

ROO LEFT KUTUSOV'S and checked back at the Green Mountain Hotel. Dot Briscoe brightened when she saw him and leaned forward in a seductive pose. "There has been no sign of your Mr. Knapp. But the two uglies called in twice and asked questions about him; wanted to know where he had gone.

"I told them I didn't know anything about this Knapp and didn't mention your visit." She looked at him, her eyes glittering in an inviting way. "I'll let you know if Knapp returns, or if they come back. Perhaps you can stay longer next time, so we can become better acquainted." He thanked her, hurried out and found a bar close to Times Square and watched, with rising anger, Stoddard's fund-raising dinner at the Plaza.

The next day, on his way to meet Alice, his argument with Katya played in his head. She had come in breathless and excited after the campaign dinner and fell into his arms—he could still feel traces of her, small imprints caught up and entangled with him.

This morning they had sat in bed, and he kept his arms around her.

"I'm sorry you didn't come. Big's supporters were so enthusiastic. He's sure to win the primary."

"What's in it for you? I didn't know you were interested in politics."

Big, what a fucking stupid name he thought, but said, "Big is a ridiculous name."

She pushed him away. "I don't care if it sounds ridiculous to you. He is at least trying to do good for the disadvantaged, and I'm going to help him. I can't keep waiting for you to make up your mind about me. After everything that has happened to me in the past, nothing seems permanent. I can't put my trust in any man, even you. I have to be independent."

"So you've decided to attach yourself to Stoddard. Not exactly going out on your own."

"I'm not attached to him, only to his programs, and I'm only a volunteer. I need something to make my life meaningful after all my mistakes, including being with you." Her words were like a slap.

She broke into sobs and shut herself in the bathroom.

She was still in the bathroom when he left. Their argument filled him with regret and guilt, and he wondered how he could have said the things he did. He never liked to voice his thoughts to Katya; it always ended in a bad way;

Alice was waiting when he walked in. "I have some info on the photographs. Were you out last night at the dinner for Stoddard? It was a fantastic gala at the Plaza with VIPs, even the governor attending. Katya's picture with Stoddard was on the front page in all the papers. And they were featured on CNN. She looked great."

"Yeah, I saw it on TV."

"It's amazing. He has become so popular," she said, not intending to make him bristle. She changed the subject. "Did you have any luck with that old Russian?"

"Kutusov claims there are rumors that Matthew is in danger. Someone powerful, close to the Kremlin, is looking for him. I can't be sure Kutusov is telling the truth. There's no way to check on him and his sources. He claims to run an import-export business, but that's a front for trading information. And he always asks for a bribe."

Alice said, "At least there is some evidence that Matthew is innocent. I hate to think he's in some horrid place, hiding from killers."

She brought the photographs up on the screen. "I don't yet understand what these have to do with the Knapp murders. It's just weird that they would be hidden on a farm in Ohio. I did manage to restore three, and am still working on one. They're not perfect, but at least we can make out the subjects and surroundings.

"These three were taken with a Brownie Box Camera, manufactured in 1900 by Eastman Kodak; easy to operate. Seems strange now that a little cardboard box with a simple lens actually took 2 1/4-inch square pictures on a 117 roll of film."

Alice spoke in a professorial tone, "Judging from the subject matter, these are from Russia. Around 1904, the Brownie became a craze in that country. Even the Tsar and his family used these simple cameras and took scores of photos for their family albums. These first two pictures date from 1917–1918, during WWI, and the Russian Revolution."

In the first one, against a background of snow-capped mountains, a fierce looking man, mounted on a horse, stares at the camera. He wears an exotic costume: a high fur hat; a kaftan with elaborate braid on the cuffs; and wide trousers, tucked into high leather boots.

"He couldn't be a Knapp relative," Roo said, remembering Joseph's bib overalls, worn for all occasions.

"That's a Terek Cossack outfit, Caucasian national dress before the Revolution. Look at that amazing sheepskin hat and the brilliant decorations on the coat, like something out of a fairy tale." She stared dreamily for a moment, then brought herself up short with a jerk of her head.

"Let's go to the next. This is the same handsome fellow. I managed to define his features in both snapshots. He is on the left among this group of eight. It is a typical photo of the Cheka, the Russian secret police."

The old pictures only added to the mystery. Alice was right. They were out of place, foreign to the Midwest and an isolated farm.

"And this one?" he said. A woman in a glittering evening gown poses with two men in tuxedos at a table in a crowded ballroom. *Shanghai, Astor House Hotel, 15 Huangpu Road,* was written at the bottom of the heavily-creased, sepia photograph. *No. 12?* was scrawled in darker ink at the top margin of the picture.

"As you can see, this was taken with an Ikon Zeiss camera, and seems to have with no connection with the others. Again, no identification, only this number 12, with a question mark." Her forehead crinkled in a frown. "It's very strange. What could this mean? I think it was written later than the address."

"It could have been a message to someone," Roo said. They were both intrigued.

"I wonder if anyone ever received the message," Alice sighed, reflecting on this thought for a moment, then returned to the photograph.

"I couldn't find any information on the woman, but after searching through some old Soviet photographs, I did discover that one of the men in the picture was a Russian agent, named Borodin who was stationed in Beijing. He could have been on a mission. In the '20s and '30s, spies were everywhere in Shanghai."

"You're a genius at this."

She beamed. "Let's go on. This last photograph is in terrible shape." Two men stand near a railroad track and are barely visible in the crumpled photo.

"I'll let you know when I can make it out, but honestly, none of these seem to be going anywhere as evidence."

"Yeah, I know. Stumpy said from the beginning that I was off on a tangent."

They sat for a moment until she said, "Maybe Stumpy's right this time."

Disappointed, he left the library and walked downtown toward the gallery. There were no clues in the photographs to either the Knapp murders or to Matthew. If Kutusov was telling the truth, Knapp could end up at the morgue, in a drawer, with a toe tag.

Sachsenhausen, Germany: 1944

The Boy

Chapter 23

THE BOY STANDS in the midst of the hum and clatter of printing machines. The factory is clean and smells of ink. He cannot believe his eyes, as thousands of bank notes roll out. He tells himself it was luck that he escaped death by being chosen to work on this secret project.

He learns quickly; gobbles up instructions like the food he is given. His first job is inspecting water marks on bundles of paper ready for printing bank notes. He moves on to inspecting the printed notes, and then to the engraving room.

He is becoming an expert, a creature at beck and call.

To survive he will work for Germans, Russians, anyone. He concentrates on the job to escape the truth. When the secret project is finished, he will perish in this brutal world of SS guards and officers.

He is no longer able to cry. His face contorts in a grimace, almost a grin—grief. Will this be where he is found when he is no longer of use?

Moscow: Winter 2003

Chapter 24

THE GENERAL LINGERED at his office window, watching a few miserable-looking souls making their way across Lubyanka Square to the Metro. The fading light possessed an ominous quality that fit his mood. It was ironic that he had great power over the government's intelligence agencies, and yet his operation had failed.

He had sent his staff home early and was alone. For some years, it had been his habit to live mainly in his office, sleeping on the couch. He had continued his exhaustive search through mountains of obscure files and tapes for any clues to the Paper Man Dossier, but had found nothing.

Frustrated, he banged his fist on his desk, and winced at the pain. Blood oozed out from the wound, bringing back the memory of that unsuccessful mission long ago, outside Vienna. He and Kolya are running through the forest, escaping from vicious police dogs. Dodging the sweep of lights and machine gun bullets, they try to jump a wire fence, but he hangs there, caught, a target. Kolya runs back and pulls him off. His hand, hooked on the wire, is ripped open. He is carried. almost to the border, to an abandoned shed; its damp smell of decay suffused with fear.

His hand throbs with pain. There is blood everywhere. Kolya tears a strip of cloth from his shirt and bandages his hand in a tourniquet to keep him from bleeding to death.

As they hunker down, Kolya says in a low voice, "I've been thinking. We could get away from all this—stay in Switzerland. I would have money. You won't believe this, I know." Pasha wonders if he is delirious, dreaming. His friend smiles in his beguiling way at his astonishment.

"A joke," Kolya says, and laughs.

One of Kolya's stories buried deep in his memory, suddenly came alive, rushing through his head, shocking him with the realization that it could be true.

He went to the medicine chest in his bathroom, took out antiseptic and bandages, and dressed the cut, hardly noticing the pain. He could be attaching unwarranted significance to his friend's tale. Kolya often resorted to *vranye,* the Russian custom of fantastic exaggeration, sometimes as a joke or to make his exploits more dramatic or heroic.

Kolya knew that his family had been disgraced, but their identity, or why the authorities had denounced them as enemies of the revolution, remained a mystery. Kolya never suspected that Pasha was assigned to spy on him and, had taped many of their conversations. He occasionally informed on his friend with harmless information that would prove he was watching Kolya, but would get neither of them in trouble. He had never turned any of the tapes over to authorities.

That night, he dismissed his driver and drove his BMW to Rublevka, on the Rublyovo-Uspenslyae Road, leading west from Moscow to his old *dacha* in Barvikha, now surrounded by oligarchs' gigantic estates. He locked the car, clicked on his flashlight, and breathed in the cold clear air, redolent of pine and birch and the Moskva River.

His country place was small and unobtrusive, hidden by overgrown brush, and did not draw attention from the road. He had not used it since the '70s, and in those years of confusion and fear, he had stored many of his old tapes and documents in the garden shed.

Now he pushed aside the stiff bushes, coated with snow, to unlock the door. It was freezing in the main room of the *dacha*, but he did not light a fire in the *izba*, the tiled stove Sofka had built in the center of the room, and went immediately into the shed.

His heart pounded and on instinct, he drew his pistol and stared out the window of the shed at the path through the snow-covered trees. The sky was dark with snow clouds, and it was difficult to see, but there were no broken branches, crushed bushes, or footprints in the deep snow that would indicate surveillance.

He remembered placing some of his documents in a wooden box among the gardening tools. He shivered at the eerie shadows created by his flashlight. Someone could have stolen or tampered with the box without leaving a trace. He began pulling tools covered with dirt off the shelves, and found the box behind a stack of pots. Rotten from the damp, it disintegrated at his touch, scattering papers, an Aiwa cassette player/ recorder, and tapes, onto the floor.

He cursed softly as he picked up the material, brushing off the dark soil with fingers numb from cold, and placed it all on the work table. He stared at the contents with suspicion. His memory of that dark time seemed to have failed him. He had thought there were more tapes and documents, and became unsettled, uncertain whether he had heard Kolya's story, or dreamed it. He gathered up the contents into his briefcase and went back inside the *dacha*.

After he became a KGB officer he discovered that Aunt Sofka, his mother's friend, had left him the *dacha*, even though Lenin's decree on land had abolished private property. He suspected her connections with those in power had prevented the cottage from being confiscated by the state. From Bolshevik rule to the present, everyone knew that managing the right connections led to success in getting favors from the government.

He went back into the sitting room, a remnant of the tsarist period and unchanged from when Sofka had lived here. Her face rose in front of him as he gazed at the carved, Russian chairs with gilded swan arms; the icons on every wall; and the large sleigh bed used as a sofa. He reflected on how memories live on within the walls of houses.

He had spent several weeks here with Kolya in the summers, when they were off duty. Ghostly shadows from the past floated through the cobwebs and hovered in the beam of the flashlight. Vivid memory overtook him.

A cassette player, bought on the black market, blares out the Rolling Stones' "Jumpin' Jack Flash." He has returned from a swim in the river and finds Kolya and three young girls all naked, rolling around on the large sofa. Bottles of vodka are scattered on the floor. The girls are from a nearby village and eager to please for favors. One is moving in rhythm on top of Kolya.

He stares, frozen to the spot. Kolya, wildly drunk, takes turns with the girls, coaxing and taunting him to join in. "Pasha, Pasha, enjoy yourself." His heart thumping, he does what is expected and sinks down onto the couch into a suffocating mass of hot, sweaty flesh. One of the girls forces her breast into his mouth and straddles him. Repelled, he pushes her off, and gathering his clothes, runs from the room. Kolya chases after him, laughing and teasing.

He stood very still in the flickering light remembering his humiliation and the helpless fear that they were being watched. For days after he was sick, unable to eat, waiting to be arrested and questioned. Kolya scoffed at him for being so prim and cautious. Nothing came of it, but the fear had remained with him.

He left the *dacha* and drove carefully, taking a back route to Lubyanka Square; images of Kolya and the women at times blocking his vision and turning his stomach. A tape of that day could well be stored somewhere in old KGB files.

He checked in with the guard, rushed back into the safety of his office and removed a rare bottle of Chateau Lafitte Rothschild, 1961, from his temperature-controlled cabinet. He poured the wine, one of his few luxuries, into a crystal goblet.

Shivering from exposure to zero weather, and haunted by the images conjured at the *dacha*, he pulled his jacket around him. He did not wait for the wine to breathe, and drained his glass.

Kolya had told him this tale one night as they sat drinking together, which they often did when on assignment in Eastern Europe.

They were in Prague during Operation Progress, ordered by the KGB head, Andropov, during the Prague Spring uprising. The two were assigned a special mission, "administration of special tasks," a phrase used by the KGB to mean "hunt down and liquidate an enemy."

He and Kolya had picked up the popular dissident, known only as Jan, in a bar in a rundown part of the city, and efficiently completed the wet job, throwing his body into the River Vltava. The following evening they were relaxing in the safe house.

Earlier, Kolya had been with a woman he had picked up, and had come home slightly drunk. Pasha had been angry at him for being careless after the mission; another of his dangerous escapades that could end in death or prison.

He cradled his head in his hands, despairing how foolish he had been to protect Kolya and not report his stories. He had been unaware that the future could hold a trap; that the freakish coincidence of this dossier surfacing would put him in mortal danger.

He poured another glass, then clicked on the tape, *Prague— August 1968. Nicolae Andreyevich Platov-Kolya.*

He became again young Pasha, sitting close to Kolya, a thrill going through him at the accidental touch of his shoulder, and at his fine profile in silhouette against the street lights shining in the window. Even on the scratchy tape, Kolya's low, melodious voice moved him deeply, as it always had. He almost expected to turn and see him on the couch beside him.

Two years ago, in 1966, I was in Moscow, waiting for our next assignment, when I found a message printed in neat script on a piece of cardboard, in my uniform pocket. 'You must go to this place tonight at 11pm.' A crudely drawn map directed me to a spot near Prechistenka

Ulitza, the once-grand street lined with mansions of merchants and aristocrats.

I was suspicious, thinking it could be one of my enemies in the department trying to trap me into an indiscretion, possibly with a woman. Pasha, you know there are some who are jealous of my success in the fucking department.

He remembered then how his friend had laughed defiantly.

Then it occurred to me that one of my superiors from Department 7 was testing me. I was torn with indecision, but couldn't take the risk of ignoring the message and planned to say in defense that I was investigating for the department.

I walked cautiously toward the meeting place, practising proverka, (the dry-cleaning technique used to detect surveillance) and observed that I was not being followed.

The map showed a pereluk off Ulitsa Prechistenka. I arrived at this small alley in front of a wrecked mansion, partly demolished for new apartments. All that remained was a half-shell of the building hanging out over the street.

I walked through a collapsing doorway, weaving back and forth in the wind, and crossed over a huge gap between the sagging room and the ground. Not knowing what was ahead, I kept my hand on my pistol. The smell of mould and decay permeated the air. A hoarse croaking voice ordered me to enter.

I made my way into a broken piece of the old mansion, a precarious shell, which once might have been a small study or library for the aristocratic master of the house.

I was wary that I had made a mistake in finding the location. This man with the raw voice could be a vagrant, or a thief, who had taken shelter for the night. I took out my gun and waited in silence for the test, which only the ingenious Colonel Matsev, my superior, could have devised.

A cloud of cigarette smoke obscured the man's face. He was reclining in a tattered armchair and clutched a bottle of vodka in one large hand. The other held a cigarette between two dirt-caked fingers. He wore a shabby military jacket covered with medals. It was ripped near his chest and his huge shoulder bones protruded, exposing skin covered with violent red scabs. He was wrapped in a torn, dirty blanket.

I recoiled when the smoke cleared and revealed his face. He was ancient; long matted, white hair hung down to his shoulders. His face was creased with heavy folds and wrinkles, as though tracing what I imagined were terrible hardships. He leaned forward and handed me a number of documents. "Proof of who I am," he said, pointing to a photograph. He was still recognizable, posing with Beria, presenting him with a commendation for his bravery in weeding out enemies of the revolution. He stared at me and said, "Nicolae Andreyevich, I am your grandfather Timur Alexandrovich Platov. I needed to see you before I die."

Chapter 25

THE GENERAL TOOK a long drink, which soothed him while
the tape rolled.

> *I was shocked* and *found it hard to believe that this man was
> my grandfather, in spite of his documents. I could not be sure he was
> telling the truth. He said it was an accident of fate, a strange
> coincidence, which led to his life as a fugitive.*
>
> *He was told that I, his grandson, existed, and claimed that his old
> friend in high places granted him this favor to see me. Tears rolled
> down his cheeks. He staggered up to leave and said, "There is no time
> left. I have no permit to be in the city and if caught, I will be executed.
> I deserted our troops during the war to escape death from my enemy
> Bokov. After all these years, he is still hunting me. Remember—the
> information I have about him is dangerous."*

He jumped when he suddenly heard his own voice on the tape, *"What is it? What information? Is this true?"*

There was a wild laugh from Kolya. *"A fairy tale, only a joke. I knew you would believe me. You always do."*

The tape ended abruptly.

He remained in his chair, reviewing what he had heard. There was nothing in the tape about the contents of the Paper Man Dossier, and Kolya said the old man took the documents when he fled. But why tell this story? Was it to test his reaction and find out if Pasha was betraying him?

Shortly after that mission in Prague, Kolya became guarded and no longer confided in him. When he questioned him again about the incident, Kolya said he was not convinced this man was his grandfather, but someone who had been sent to trap him. He said the old man had rushed out of the room and had fallen on the street. When Kolya went after him he was gone, leaving large streaks of blood on the ground. He searched the area, but found no other trace of the man. He never heard from him again.

He had been deceived by his friend's previous comments about treasure, and living in Switzerland. For a moment he seized up, his chest constricting in pain at the realization that Kolya could have discovered he was spying on him and had searched the *dacha*. He did not know.

He went to sleep on his couch, falling into the dream that had haunted him since this threat of his extinction began. He is three and running through the rooms of the mansion, hunting for a safe place; but where to go? His bare feet patter on the polished wooden floors. Wild laughter and music stop him at an open door. In the room, blurred figures move about; men in uniform, clinking glasses.

Sofka's beautiful face and cloud of light hair hover above him. He cries out and runs toward her. He cannot see the shadowy faces of the men around her.

The next morning, he woke on the couch, with fading remnants of this recurrent dream, which had no ending. Valentina brought in his tea and fussed over his hand, applying ointment and another bandage.

Dima arrived with the daily reports, and the agenda for his next security council meeting. The aide stared at him with inquisitive, insect-like eyes. "Your car has been taken out."

"Yes. I went for a drive." He knew that Dima had checked the mileage and the GPS.

He did not like the aide's curious, sly look and dismissed him, then reviewed a tape from a surveillance camera in New York. A well-built man in his thirties, dressed in jeans and a ski jacket, is getting out of a cab in Soho and entering The Little Swan Gallery. He has been identified as Reuben Yoder, a deputy sheriff from the Midwest. The lawman is hunting for the murder suspect, Matthew Knapp.

His mood lifted. This Yoder could bring him closer to finding Knapp and the dossier. But he grimaced in disgust at his reasoning; his own men with all intelligence resources available, had not been able to locate Knapp.

Then something else in the written report caught his interest. Stoddard had become involved with a socialite, Katya Marston, once the mistress of the deceased oligarch Ostrikov, and recently the lover of Yoder. She was whispered about in social circles as unstable with a mysterious background, supposedly descended from an aristocratic Russian family. This knowledge might be of use in finding Knapp and the dossier.

He smiled, amused at how many Russians in this new era claimed to be descended from the nobility even though so few of the aristocrats had survived or remained in Russia during the revolution.

He fumed at his lack of success. The idiot banker was not taking the blackmail letter seriously, and was not cooperating. He suspected that Stoddard had discovered important details about the blackmailer, and the dossier, and was keeping the information to himself. He was infuriated at the banker's sign-off to his messages. "Fuck you."

Chapter 26

THE GENERAL FELT a twinge of anxiety as he stared for long moments at the swastika and the name *Bokov* on Kolya's interrogation folder. Was this a sign, some kind of message? Who was he? He had a vague impression he had seen or heard the name in the past, but couldn't recall. He had quickly covered the folder when Dima entered with the daily reports and the schedule for that day's meetings.

He had cancelled a dinner this evening with Yuri Sokolnik, an old acquaintance, at Aragavi, his favorite Georgian restaurant. Today he had no appetite for their special dishes of *khinkali* and the chopped salad, *pkhali*.

The restaurant had become shabby and was scheduled to close later this year, but it had once been an important gathering place for the KGB, a nostalgic reminder of the past. when he and Kolya dined there as young agents.

Dima stopped for a moment with a rare, apologetic expression because the operation in the US had failed. The General nodded and waited until he left the room, then placed the interrogation folder into his safe.

He was acting on his own now, without his aide's knowledge. Dima was useful, but not completely trustworthy, and there were pieces of information that must be kept from him.

He assumed that Bokov had been an intelligence officer, and began looking through numerous official directories stored on his bookshelf. He discovered a Colonel Ivan Bokov in a list of SMERSH officers, and was amused at the melodramatic acronym coined by Stalin, which meant "Death to Spies." SMERSH was formed during WWII to root out traitors.

He found Bokov's photograph on a page with those of other officials. His grim unsmiling features, a square head and full lips under his colonel's cap, were indistinguishable from any one of the typical officer pictures.

His biography was brief, customary for those out of favor. In 1917, he had been a member of the Cheka, the secret police, and had conducted several missions in China during 1920–1930. After joining SMERSH in WWII, he acted as a covert agent in Germany for the Fourth Department's counter-intelligence operations behind enemy lines. Bokov had been an assistant to Viktor Abumakov, head of SMERSH, until its end in 1946. After the war, Bokov worked in state security. His biography ended with his death in a hunting accident in the Caucasus in 1975.

This accident was shortly after Kolya had been arrested and executed, and when the Raven came under suspicion for his plot to overthrow the government. He frowned; the slight tic in his left eye became more pronounced. There must be some connection.

Something else disturbed him. He had searched for Kolya's interrogators, thinking one of them might still be alive, and was shocked to discover they had been liquidated for treason the same year of Kolya's execution. Their names had been redacted from the report.

This seemed more than a coincidence. His mind raced. He could only wildly guess at the Raven's motivation, but he sensed that the spy did not want this interrogation record to appear in an accessible, official file. He was certain that the Raven had concealed other incriminating documents. These would be difficult to locate, and he would not want Dima or any of his assistants, aware of his search.

He opened his gold cigarette case, a gift from the Raven, and took out another cigarette. Through the rings of smoke, the image of the old Bolshevik spy appeared before him.

He remembered thinking how lucky he and Kolya were, and how they had taken their elevated positions for granted. Both became members of the Communist Party, an honor given only to a few out of millions of Russians, and a requirement for advancement into privileged positions.

They both graduated with high honors and became officers in the KGB. Before the celebratory dinner, the two had met with the Raven in his study. Wide-eyed at the opulent surroundings, they were toasted with French champagne.

To their astonishment, the Raven confided in them and revealed his plot for a tsarist coup. His scheme, planned for years, was to replace the communist government with a new tsar, a member of the aristocracy that he would control.

Excited and filled with their own importance at being part of the conspiracy, they swore the loyalty oath. A year or so later, other young officers joined. Among those recruited were *besprizornye, the lost ones,* abandoned street children whom the Raven rescued and sent to military school. They followed him willingly, and became prominent officers and fellow conspirators.

The secret meetings were exhilarating, and afterward he and Kolya inevitably ended up at the Metropole Hotel, drinking and seducing more than one of the many whores permitted to frequent the bars and hotel rooms.

When the plot was discovered in 1977, the Raven was arrested for treason. Many of his followers were also arrested and shot in the Lubyanka basement. The Raven was sentenced to the Serbsky Institute, a prison disguised as a psychiatric hospital, and died in the same year by a fatal injection.

He escaped arrest by destroying evidence implicating him, and hiding his correspondence in his secret file at his *dacha*. Now the plot seemed so distant, and yet it had possessed some dangerous relevance that he couldn't yet comprehend. He pushed these thoughts aside and continued his daily routine; staring at the screen for reports, checking out the *New York Times* that Dima brought to him.

Stoddard was on the front cover. The headline read *Chance for Stoddard Victory in Primary.*

New York: Winter 2003

Big

Chapter 27

BRADY MEDFORD WAVED the latest press releases at Big. "New, very favorable poll numbers." He was smiling. "You're a hit. You're crushing the Senator. All good news."

There had been a rush to support him from additional large Republican donors, CEOs, and hedge fund managers. For some time, Big had been developing the image of a compassionate conservative. He had no real intention of carrying out the social programs he promised in his campaign speeches. After the election he would guarantee that his wealthy Wall Street friends, influential law firms and company lobbyists, who were large donors, would benefit.

After Brady left, Big hummed *My Way,* a song he identified with his success, while he opened his mail. Trembling, he tried to focus: The message was longer than usual.

You have refused to cooperate in finding the dossier or the blackmailer. There will be consequences if you keep information from me, and do not obey my commands.

You have met midwestern sheriff Roo Yoder, Katya Marston's lover.

Place the woman on your campaign staff. Find out what she knows about Yoder's hunt for Knapp. It should be easy to become intimate with her, knowing your proclivity to fuck anything in sight. Report back to me. I am sending someone, and I am watching your every move.

Chekhov, Чехов.

Stoddard had been feeling good until this message came. He had met Yoder, but was unaware that the deputy sheriff was looking for this Matthew Knapp. Why the fuck should he report any information that was advantageous to this Chekhov? There had been several messages, all of which he had ignored, but this one sent a spike of fear through his spine.

Always an optimist, he had been sure that the disturbing blackmail letter was a hoax from one of his political rivals. He had believed that no news from the Odessa group he had hired was good news, but danger from this Chekhov began to seem real. The deadline was approaching for his withdrawal from the senate primary. He broke into a sweat, rushed to his liquor cabinet, poured a large scotch and downed it.

What did he mean? *I am sending someone, and I am watching your every move.* Big could combat gossip, maybe even a compromising video tape, but this threat frightened him.

After his last campaign event in Brooklyn, a man had suddenly appeared near the front of the stage and crooked his hand like a gun aimed directly at Big's head, then vanished before he could be arrested. Reliving this menacing pantomime convinced him his life could be in danger from this unknown Russian. There was no way he could report this to the police. He picked up his phone and ordered his private security to beef up, immediately. Then it came to him—a terrible thought. Could someone he hired from The Odessa group be controlled by the Russian?

He had no choice and would try to accommodate this sinister figure. He would flatter Katya Marston, give her a position on the campaign, romance her, and then go after some trivial information to pass on to his tormenter. His mood lightened. It couldn't harm him; might even benefit him.

Roo

Chapter 28

IT WAS LATE evening when Roo returned to the apartment and found the note pinned to the refrigerator. *I've been appointed assistant to Big's campaign manager, Brady Medford. It was a wonderful surprise. Have gone upstate with the campaign. Will return in a week. Katya.*

The note was cold, without her usual sign off. She was still angry and had not forgiven him. He had phoned her earlier and left a message with a kind of apology that he would working late on the case, but she had not returned his call.

He shoved the note into his pocket and turned on the news. The networks were covering Stoddard's speech last night at Columbia. Cheers from a new student organization, *Progressives for Stoddard,* had filled the auditorium.

In the morning, he crossed Broad Street to Pearl on his way to meet Geoffrey Banks, and arrived at Kinks, a colonial building near the Fraunces Tavern. Geoffrey often said he wanted to change the name of the club but had been voted down by the majority of

members. Roo raised the polished door knocker, a brass likeness of
Bacchus, the god of wine. Ray the stern, elderly butler greeted him.

"I'm here to meet Geoffrey Banks."

"Please wait here while I check the appointment book." A few
minutes later, he returned and led Roo up the grand staircase into
the lounge, a paneled room lined with books and several racks of
newspapers and magazines.

Geoffrey was waiting for him. "Hey! Sit down."

He was dressed in a conservative suit and tie. "You look
surprised. My other persona, Jennifer Banks, doesn't appear these
days until after dark. And then I'm often too busy. I have a meeting
later this afternoon at the gallery with new customers."

Roo sank into a soft leather chair and looked out on the empty
street, half-expecting a horse and carriage to drive by. The room was
cozy with a log fire burning. Geoffrey ordered breakfast for them.

"You wanted to see me?"

"Yeah." The grin faded from Geoffrey's face. "It's about
Katya. I know she went upstate with the Stoddard campaign. I was
still at work in the gallery. She told me just as the car was picking her
up. I'm worried."

"She left a note that she would be back in a week."

"You know, I can't figure. It's only recently that Stoddard
became interested in her. He's attended any number of campaign
events, each time with a different woman dangling on his arm.
Before this, Katya was one of several young society women he was
recruiting for his campaign. It's a cynical attempt to get the college-
educated women's vote."

Geoffrey shook his head. "But he seems to have latched onto
her as the most important. I can understand that. A beautiful heiress

on the boards of charities would be helpful with his campaign. He's risking a scandal, although his wife Missy does shows up at a few events to make their marriage seem legit. But then voters these days don't seem to care about sex scandals."

They moved to a table by the fire and the waiter served omelets and toast. Geoffrey sat back in his chair, his mind still on Katya. "I can't believe she's going political, but I'm sure she has good intentions. She was on TV again this morning, with Stoddard and the other aides when they arrived in Albany. Still, it's strange she's become such an important part of the campaign when she has no experience. It has to be his attraction to her. I worry she could be eaten alive by those political sharks."

"What do you know about him?" Roo had lost his appetite and took only a few bites of his omelet.

Geoffrey paused and put his fork down. "Ivy League, son of a famous banker. His father was a WWII hero, and after the war he founded the Stoddard Bank. Big is highly regarded, a member of the exclusive Alfalfa Club, supposedly composed of the most important people in the country, who meet once a year. He recently became a government advisor on economic policy, but he resigned to run for senator.

"According to his news releases and interviews, this scion of the privileged has fashioned himself into a campaigner for the poor and the downtrodden. He says he wants to give something back." Geoffrey raised his hands in a parody of quotation marks. "A cliché, but people fall for it. Katya did. He's very smooth." There was a note of scorn in his voice.

"How did they meet?" Roo asked, as he pushed his plate aside.

"They were introduced by Ivan Murkovsky, a customer who lent some of his collection for our exhibition. He's an expatriate Russian, an investor with enormous amounts of money. Katya's very popular with the wealthy Russian crowd. They adore her."

His face darkened. "She has cachet, an A-lister in New York and UK society in spite of the scandal involving the oligarch, Ostrikov, the sleaze bag you brought to a bloody end on an oil derrick. Yikes! Sad to say, that makes her more interesting."

Roo winced at the sudden images of Katya and Ostrikov circling in his head.

"The society crowd was sympathetic and forgave her affair with the oligarch. They believed she was innocently taken in by him. Of course, I suspected all along that he was a dangerous criminal, but she never listens to me. Now, here we are again—another dubious adventure." Geoffrey was very protective of Katya, and always regarded her often-questionable adventures with appalled wonder.

"Do you think she's—" He wished he hadn't asked. It was not the first time.

Geoffrey shook his head.

"No, I don't think she would, and he probably won't even try to seduce her, at least not while he's being scrutinized by the press. He's rumored to have the morals of a goat, but has been careful these past two years with reporters on the prowl."

Geoffrey finished his breakfast before going on. "There was something she told me before leaving yesterday." He leaned forward. "Someone's blackmailing Stoddard with damaging information from a file called the Paper Man Dossier; demanding he withdraw from the race. She wouldn't tell me more.

"Before she joined the campaign, she had been invited to come to Stoddard's office. She accidentally walked into this meeting between him and two thugs. She said they were scary. After Big and the men left together, she noticed this letter on his desk.

"She didn't know if she should tell Stoddard that she had seen the letter, and wondered why he didn't go to the police. She was worried and went to see your old boss, Devlin, to ask his advice."

"Why Devlin.? Why didn't she tell me?"

Geoffrey shrugged his shoulders. "There's something else I don't like. Stoddard asked her a lot of questions about you. She thought he might want you to join the campaign."

He left Geoffrey and walked uptown toward the Business Library He was let down by Katya's behavior, and bewildered that she didn't trust him.

Four blocks from 34th Street, Roo noticed a man staring into the window of a sporting goods store. He wore a black jacket, and had dark, slicked-back hair. Two blocks further on, the man appeared again, this time lounging near a small vegetable market. Shocked that he was being tailed, Roo took a quick detour into an electronics store. From there, he could see the man lurking outside before disappearing from view. Roo bought three burner phones from a bored-looking clerk, then exited from the back of the store into a narrow alley. He moved cautiously down the next two blocks, catching sight of the man's reflection in a dress shop window, and decided then to walk on, past the library, rather than endanger Alice. Several blocks later, he ducked into a hardware store, then took a side street back to the library entrance. He crouched inside the entrance door, watching both ends of the street.

Chapter 29

ALICE RAN DOWN the library hall toward him, waving her arms in the air. "This is crazy. What I found!" she shouted, grabbing his hand and pulling him toward her office.

"Wait." He looked back out to the street. "Someone was following me."

She drew back from the door. "You have to be kidding. A man? Is he still out there?" Her voice quavered.

"I'm pretty sure I threw him off."

"That's a relief," she whispered. "Who could he be?"

Roo tried, but failed to hide his alarm. "I don't know, but I think it might be connected to my investigation. We have to be careful, but don't worry. I carry a weapon." That seemed to frighten her even more.

She closed the door to her office and locked it. He tossed off his jacket and sat down at the desk next to her. She was silent for a moment, recovering from the scare, then straightened her shoulders and opened her computer.

"This might be a clue, but, like the other photographs from the corncrib, there doesn't seem to be a direct connection to the murders." She brought up the damaged photo on the screen.

"This was taken with a Minox (Riga) sub-miniature, a classic spy camera, designed by Walter Zapp and manufactured at the VEP factory in Riga, Latvia, from 1937 to 1943.

"I discovered something else that's odd. This is not an ordinary photograph, but one of a micro-dot negative. The original photograph, taken sometime in 1944 or '45, is marked '1' and may be the first of a series. The negative was copied and photographed again, much later, in the 1970's. The number 0116 2385 2957 on the scrap of paper at the bottom was also added then."

Alice brought the restored photo into focus. Two men in uniform stand beside a large truck near a railroad track, with a shadowy building, like a barracks, behind them. The sign, *Sachsenhausen,* was now visible.

"*Sachsenhausen* was a Nazi concentration camp in Oranienburg, a town not far from Berlin," Alice said, her voice catching. "I have been working on this for hours and finally was able to get the two men in focus. Both are in SS uniforms, standing outside the camp. Any one of their officers could have taken this picture. Unfortunately for them, the Nazis photographed and filmed their deeds, even the darkest ones, believing they would glorify Hitler's Thousand Year Reich, which ended after 12 years. Their photographs and films only added to evidence incriminating them."

She caught her breath, glancing around, as though the horrors of the camps had filtered through the library window. An air of menace seemed to hang over the room. Looking even smaller and more vulnerable, Alice stabbed at the computer screen.

"I searched through all the photographs of SS officers, who were captured by the Allies. This man was Captain Bruno Melmer, the Nazi officer who collected gold stolen from concentration camp victims. His secret records of the gold were called the Melmer Files." She pointed again to the screen. "The officer with him is Lieutenant Manfred Weber, from the SS finance department."

She shuddered. "They ripped gold teeth from dying victims, stole their jewellery, and deposited the gold in the *Reichsbank* 'precious metals department.' The *Reichsbank* exchanged this stolen gold with the Swiss National Bank, for Swiss francs to finance the war. At that time, the gold may have been worth approximately $146 million, and today might be more than ten times that."

They read that the Melmer Files, along with other important SS documents, were found by American troops in 1945 and sent to the U.S. For some unknown reason, they were returned to Germany in 1948, and stored at the *Bank Deutscher Lander.*

"Would you believe this?" Alice said. "It was discovered in 1998 that the Melmer Files were missing. It is not known when they vanished or who was responsible."

Roo said, "This is a guess, but it could be that someone, maybe a former Nazi with an important position in post-war Germany, destroyed the Melmer Files because they contained incriminating evidence."

"There is more, but let's take a break and have lunch." Alice seemed to have recovered from her fear of someone stalking them. Roo ordered a pizza, unlocked the door, and checked out the street before taking it from the delivery man. They ate quickly in silence, trying to grasp the significance of their discovery.

Finally, Alice said, "I know this seems far-out, but there is more to this photograph. *Sachsenhausen* was also a Nazi counterfeiting and forgery center. The Nazi's planned to destroy the British and American economy by collapsing their currency. SS Major Krueger, head of the counterfeit operation, recruited prisoners, mainly Jewish, from *Auschwitz* and other concentration camps to forge British pounds, and later American dollars. The prisoners became expert at counterfeiting, also creating false passports and other documents for Nazi spies."

Alice went on again, as if she couldn't believe her own words.

"It was top secret; the threat of death hung over anyone who leaked information about the factory."

Her voice filled with anger and horror. "During the 1945 Allied invasion, the seriously ill forgers were murdered, but the majority survived. Some SS members attempted to hide the counterfeit money to use as bribes to escape. Since then, there have been more inquiries about the stolen gold, much of it dispersed into private Swiss bank accounts, some unclaimed since WWII."

Roo sat in silence, ruminating. He couldn't figure out how this photograph found in the corncrib linked the Knapp murders to the Melmer Files and the secret counterfeit operation. It seemed impossible to solve.

Alice said, "Are you ok? You don't seem yourself. Is it Katya? What's wrong? You're scowling."

"I don't want her to be around Stoddard. But anyway, his campaign might be over. He could withdraw."

"Why is that?" she said in surprise.

"Stoddard received a blackmail letter threatening him with scandal if he doesn't quit the race."

"That's curious. Wonder if the press will get hold of that."

It was late when he left the library, exiting from the back entrance. Alice waited inside the locked door for Malcolm to pick her up.

When he reached Linny, her voice was faint. She had heard from Matthew, but didn't know where he was. He told her he was leaving New York.

"If he calls again, tell him it's urgent to contact me. His life depends on it." He shivered, hunching into his ski jacket. In the shadows of the street light, he froze for a moment at the specter of the dark figure walking over the hill in Tecumseh County, swinging a knife. He ducked into an alleyway, listening for footsteps behind him, but there was nothing.

Sachsenhausen, Germany: 1945

The Boy

Chapter 30

LIEUTENANT WEBER CRASHES through the door of Block 19. His heavy face, distorted with fear, drips with sweat; his neck bulges over his collar. He is a large man, and his presence fills the shop with danger. He shouts like a maniac, cursing and threatening. The forgers stand paralyzed with fear while he beats one of them unconscious. They do not understand his command.

The Boy flees under the table during the beating and hides like a mouse. In a stream of screaming profanities, Weber gives an order, then thrusts the documents and the Zapp Kit, used to form microdots, at Elijah. He goes quickly about his work trying to appease the frantic man, knowing that after the task is finished they all might be shot.

The Boy watches as Elijah, using the Zapp kit, photographs the documents and develops the film. The camera shrinks the documents to fit onto a tiny square of cellophane, a microdot less than 1 millimeter in size.

Weber continues to shout, and holds a gun to Elijah's head. The forger remains calm and cuts around three sides of the microdot, then holds the cellophane while cutting the fourth side. Then he slits the edge of a postcard with a razor blade, inserts the microdot, and glues the opening.

When Elijah finishes, Weber kicks him to the floor. He grabs the postcard, and the paper documents, and rushes out. The Boy hears the roar of the truck, but he stays under the table, waiting for Weber to return and kill them.

The Boy knows that in his panic to escape, the Nazi wasn't aware that Elijah had made a duplicate of the microdot. Driven by fear, The Boy had seen and memorized the accounts. The swirl of numbers slides through his head. It is horrifying, all the gold, stolen from his parents, and his friends.

New York: Winter 2003

Roo

Chapter 31

ROO WAITED FOR Katya in the Oyster Bar at Grand Central Station, surveilling the spacious hall and looking up at the vaulted ceiling, decorated with tiles in a complicated herringbone pattern. He had checked out a number of ways to escape from the station, but in daylight it did not seem much of a risk, even if he suspected he was being tailed. He preferred beer, but had ordered a bottle of Sancerre, her favorite wine.

He had left the apartment that morning before Katya had returned from Stoddard's campaign trip, but she had agreed to meet him for lunch. When she walked in, he got up to hug her. She was distant, very cool, and kissed him lightly on the cheek, then broke away.

He wanted to make amends but didn't know how. Their arguments rang in his ears and filled up his head.

She sat down across the table from him.

He reached out and took her hand. "I missed you. And I apologize for what I said."

She smiled, but looked at him warily. He was about to say more, when the waiter came to take their order.

"I want to ask you something, and I hope you won't get angry," he said.

She looked away from him.

"Geoffrey told me that you saw a blackmail letter sent to Stoddard. Is it true?"

She paused, surprised at the question. "Yes." She lowered her voice so it could hardly be heard amid the echoes of passengers rushing to the trains.

"Can you tell me what was in it?"

"I don't think I should." Then she looked at him, and relented. "It was strange." She shuddered. "I interrupted a meeting. There were two men in the room with Big. They were frightening thugs."

"The letter was on the desk, and I accidentally glanced at it and couldn't help reading it. The handwriting was in large print, and there was no signature; only a number at the end."

She stopped for a moment, reconsidering her decision to confide in him. "The letter was really threatening. If Big does not withdraw from the senate race before March 15, this Paper Man file will be released to the public and cause a scandal."

"Were there any details on the contents of this dossier?"

She shook her head.

He paused while the waiter served the special seafood salads. He curbed his sudden impulse to warn her to stay away from Stoddard and his campaign, but knew she would take offense. He pushed his plate aside, trying to control his hatred of the man who had drawn her into this.

"What's he doing about it? Going to the police? Or will he withdraw from the race?"

"I don't know. I was too embarrassed to tell him I read the letter. I was afraid he would think I was spying on him."

"Geoffrey said you met with Devlin to ask his advice. Why didn't you tell me?"

She stirred uncomfortably and looked away into the cavernous hall.

"You were preoccupied with your case. And I know you dislike him. Besides, I was worried and thought Devlin, with his connections in intelligence, could help Big." Her voice faltered, as though she might cry.

He didn't press her or mention that he knew she had met with Devlin more than once.

"Why?" he said.

"Why, what?"

"Why are you involved in this; so concerned about Stoddard?"

"I know what you're thinking." Her eyes shot off golden sparks. "How could you? I'm not having an affair with him. Stoddard is giving me the chance to do something important. It's exciting. I work directly with Brady Medford, the campaign manager. He's connected with everyone at the Republican State Committee. It's a good group. We're all friends."

Roo felt a rush of anger. Being with him was not enough.

"What about Stoddard's wife?"

"She seems very nice. I've met her once. She doesn't like campaigning and isn't very involved. Why are you asking these questions, like I'm some kind of criminal?"

"Stay away from him."

She rose abruptly, knocking over a glass of water. "I have a meeting." The waiter came to mop up.

Her eyes glistened with tears. "Are you still coming with me tonight?" she asked in an unsteady voice, as she grabbed her coat and bag.

He caught her hand in a clumsy attempt to apologize. "I'll be there."

The waiter returned with the check and cleared their untouched plates, his chubby face quizzical. "Was something wrong with the lunch?"

Roo said, "No, everything was all right." He finished the wine.

Chapter 32

"WHAT IS THIS place?" Roo met Katya at the door of Tranquility Studio off Fifth Avenue in midtown.

"A surprise; something I've been wanting to experience with you. It's a sensory deprivation chamber; so relaxing. Shuts out the world. We're booked in at eight." She ducked her head, so that she wasn't facing him, anticipating his protests.

He had agreed to come to mollify her, because they were not getting along, and he had repeatedly declined to attend sessions at Solitude and Mind Peace, her exclusive retreat. She accused him of being stodgy; refusing to try anything new. It was one of their conflicts, another symbol of their differences.

He had visited the luxurious spa only once. It was equipped with private apartments, a pool, beauty salon, and massage room. Katya said the counselors were like family to her. A nice gray-haired lady named Jean, the mother substitute, took care of her personal needs.

He understood that she had been struggling to cope with her deep anxiety, but believed she was prey to these quacks. She claimed she was getting in touch with her inner self. He had trouble knowing what that meant, and why anyone would think they could discover what they already knew. Stumpy would say it was total bullshit and he agreed. He could see how people would start to imagine things, or make things up. It was bad enough to be reminded of the past and have the real, sordid images come back to haunt you.

He had met Gary Foster, her therapist from the spa, at the gallery. Foster was obese, had a high nervous laugh and wore little wire-rimmed glasses, reminding Roo of Santa Claus. Roo had checked on his credentials and discovered he had attended something called the "OM Institute," accredited but not well regarded, and then he had learned that Foster was the spa owner's nephew.

It was ten minutes before eight when they opened the door into a sleek, ultra-modern reception area and signed in. Their room was stylish, in white and pale gray, furnished with a comfortable couch and chairs; a shower, and glass doors which opened to two separate rooms, each with a pool, filled with Epsom Salts.

Katya said, "It's like the Dead Sea. These are pools rather than the more common pods. These have no enclosure and more room. I thought this would be easier for your first time."

Roo didn't think there would be a second time. After they showered, Katya insisted they wear no clothes, for a more genuine experience, even though they had separate rooms.

"Don't worry. It's all very private." She put her arms around him. "I'll be in the room next to you." She sighed, closed her eyes and kissed him. He held her for long moments, skin against skin, and wanted to forget about the pools and take her back to the apartment.

Katya had explained that music would play for 10 minutes at the beginning of the session. "Then you float for an hour in complete darkness and silence. Music plays again for the last 5 minutes. It clears your mind. It's magical."

This description of magic didn't relieve his doubts as he entered the shallow pool in a darkness so total he struggled to see his raised hand. After the piped-in, soothing music stopped, he tried to relax and float, but failed and stood upright, hating that he was so exposed and vulnerable.

A body brushed against him. Holy shit, someone was in here. Strong, muscular arms circled his ankles, drawing him down in the shallow pool. His head hit the bottom, and choking, he struggled up out of the water.

In desperation, Roo grabbed the attacker, punching him hard, until he released his grip. He staggered out and groped in the dark around the edge of the pool until he felt the latch on the door into Katya's pool. He ran into the room. She was gone. He pushed the security alarm and made it into the dressing room as the lights went on. He stopped, blinded by the light for a few moments. The dressing room was empty.

Frantic, afraid for her, he pulled on his clothes, picked up his bag and phone, and rushed to the reception desk.

"Someone attacked me. Did you see anyone coming in or out? My girlfriend, Katya Marston, was in the pool next to me. She's gone."

The receptionist, a blond young woman dressed in white said, "Security is checking."

He returned to the room, and ran into two security guards, who had found no trace of an intruder.

"You fucking think I'm making this up? I'm calling the police." The guards looked at each other like he was a crazy.

"Wait." The receptionist checked the appointment book. "You said Miss Marston? Oh gosh, I'm sorry. My mistake. I just took over. Miss Marston signed out several minutes ago. This is for you." She handed him a note.

Called to a campaign committee meeting. See you back at the apartment at 10.

"Again, I'm really sorry. I'm sure you can have a refund for another session," the receptionist said.

Then he realized someone had wanted to scare him, and keep him away from the dressing room. His clothes and backpack had been searched.

He pulled on his jacket and ran out of the building, shivering from the cold, his skin itching from the salt. Fear propelled him through Central Park among the trees. When he emerged from the park into the street, a large, black car was slowly following behind him, with two men walking beside its open back door.

The men jumped into the car and it picked up speed, coming toward him. He withdrew back into the park, and waited until the car passed. He crossed to Park then Madison Avenue, ducking into several doorways, watching them cruise the street, until he reached Kutusov's place.

He banged on the door. Mitya opened, and Roo rushed past him to the drawing room where Kutusov stood, his face under his bronzer, white with fear. Roo pushed him up against the wall.

"I think I am having a heart attack," Kutusov gasped.

He ignored this bid for sympathy. "Someone was following me. Who are they?"

"I am feeling great shock and surprise. How could I know?" He cocked his head to the side. "But possibility work for someone in Russia."

"Call your thugs off. Are they hunting Knapp?"

"The man named Knapp? Yes, they look for him."

"You know where he's gone." Roo let go of him, and he sank into a chair.

"It could happen they won't find him; but I not speak of that."

He waited, for a moment. breathing hard. "Need cash."

Roo took out his wallet and gave him one hundred dollars, all he could spare.

"This is nothing." he said.

"Is he still in New York?"

"Who knows? Nothing for sure. I heard spotted in JFK, and caput—he disappeared."

"Where?"

Disappointed at the amount, the old Russian shrugged. "No way to know. Out of country; maybe UK? Desperate man; hard to trace."

Roo ran down the street, watching for the car that had been following him; ready with an open door to some kind of hell. Rounding the corner, he pressed against the building into the shadows. An empty cab passed and he rushed out, hailed it, and headed to the gallery, He wanted an explanation from Katya—why she led him into that dark chamber, where he would be vulnerable, and then deserted him. He rushed through the closed gallery and took the elevator to the apartment. There was another note—*Sorry, I'll be late. Important meeting.*

He packed quickly, taking his keys and gun, leaving some of his clothes, so she would think he would return that night. He was furious at her treachery. Done with her. How could he believe a fucking thing she said?

London: Winter 2003

Roo

Chapter 33

"FROM THE STATES I see. A tourist?" Mr. Jenkins, the Beeton Hotel manager, an elderly man with a '40s-looking mustache, white hair, and tweed jacket, examined his passport and took details of his credit card.

Roo nodded. He was on a limited expense account after bribing Kutusov, and was using his credit card, hoping that Stumpy would reimburse him. On the advice of the taxi driver he had checked into this small hotel, in a cul-de-sac off Kensington High Street.

Jenkins pointed to a rack near the desk. "The tourist brochures will give you an idea of London attractions. You look tired. Jet lag?" He handed him a key. "Your room's on the third floor, on the right. Hope you enjoy your visit."

He dropped his bag in the room, took a shower and laid down the bed. He had acted on impulse in flying to London on the hunch that Matthew was here. All he had to go on was Kutusov's vague hint, Linny's message that Matthew was leaving New York, and Julia's university years in the city.

At the JFK Marriott Hotel, he had left phone messages for Stumpy and Katya, knowing his calls would be traced to New York. Then he contacted Alice, and late that night, she jumped out of a taxi at the hotel parking lot. She stood near him shivering in the heavy coat wrapped around her.

"Are you sure you want to go, to do this?" Her smooth forehead creased with worry. He nodded. Without another word, she grabbed his gun, tucked it in her handbag and jumped back into the cab.

After the long flight, he was exhausted but unable to sleep. Burning with anger at Katya, he went over everything that made him suspect she could be involved with the killers. Kutusov's voice ran in his head. "You will put it together—spotted at airport." He was still trying to put it together.

He sat on the bed and began going through Julia's folder. Her parents collected everything, and the many newspaper clippings praising her brilliance and school awards were records of her success. It seemed strange that the folder included all of the letters Julia received when she was in England. He sorted through the correspondence and began to read.

> *Dear Mama and Papa, Please forgive me for disobeying you, but I could not give up the opportunity to study in England. The scholarship to Imperial College, came as a surprise. The day I left, you said I was no longer your daughter and would never have a home with you. I hope you will forgive me and take me back into your hearts. I*

am progressing in my studies and may have a job with a research firm next year.

I have made friends with Lady Maisie Dunstable, a very nice English girl and had tea with her in her mews house in Kensington. I think you would like her. Please write to me.

He was nodding off when he came upon the party invitation from Lady Maisie Dunstable. *Hope you are able to attend. Love, Maisie.* There was an address: *14A Kynance Mews.*

Chapter 34

ROO SET OUT down Kensington Gore, conscious that "they" could be on to him. He didn't trust Kutusov. Despite the threat of being tailed, he took notice of London's gracious old buildings, a contrast to the slick high-rises of New York.

He passed landmarks noted on the hotel brochures: the Geographical Society; the layer-cake Albert Concert Hall; and the Albert Memorial, an ornate spire built in honor of Prince Albert, Queen Victoria's husband. Kensington Palace reclined at the edge of Kensington Gardens, a vast swath of beautiful park, the grass green in spite of the winter.

Winding through a series of streets lined with large, white porticoed houses, he found Lady Maisie's address off Gloucester Road. It led through a classical archway to the western side of Kynance Mews. Mews houses, according to the hotel booklet, were once stables for the horses and carriages belonging to the occupants of grand mansions, which still lined many streets in Kensington.

He rang the bell at 14 A. with nothing to go on but this old invitation. There might be no trace of Maisie Dunstable.

A dark-haired young woman answered the door.

"Deputy Sheriff Reuben Yoder." He cleared his throat. holding out his ID and badge. "I would like to speak to Lady Maisie Dunstable."

Her eyebrows arched in surprise. "You're from America." She was delicate, very slim, with abundant black, curly hair, warm brown eyes, and an infectious smile.

She laughed. "You mean my aunt. I am Lady Caroline. Wait, please."

He stood on the doorstep, studying the map and looking around the quiet mews at the archway, and the wall on one side of the alley, with stone steps climbing up to Christ Church and Eldon Road.

The young woman returned and opened the door wide.

"Come in." She directed him into a small square drawing room, its walls hung with large paintings in elaborate gold frames. He assumed the subjects were ancestors and stopped to look at one labeled *"Sir Richard Dunstable."*

"My father, in better days," she said, "Please sit down."

A baby grand piano faced the window, and two couches and a chair, covered in flowered chintz, were placed in front of a crackling fire.

He sat down just as Lady Maisie, a statuesque figure, made a dramatic entrance. She was in her seventies, tall and thin, and dressed in a flowing white silk kaftan. Her skin was smooth and youthful and her long, gray hair cascaded down her shoulders and back in unruly curls, reminding him of an aged hippie. He quickly stood up.

"This is Deputy Sheriff Reuben Yoder. He's arrived from New York, investigating a case, and would like to ask you some questions." Lady Caroline gave her Roo's badge.

Lady Maisie examined it carefully and then leveled her heavily made-up, brown eyes in a bemused gaze at him. "Hmm. Reuben Yoder." She turned abruptly.

"Caroline, could you please ask Smith for tea, and serve when it is ready?" Caroline left the room.

"Why are you here?" Lady Maisie sat with a flourish, her caftan floating around her.

He showed her Julia's letter. "I know that you were a friend of Julia Knapp's. I found your address on this party invitation."

She frowned. "These are Julia's personal items. How in the world did you come by them?"

"From her son, Matthew. There is a warrant out for his arrest, for the murders of Joseph and Maria Knapp, his grandparents."

She let out a cry and held her chest with long, thin hands, the fingers sparkling with diamond rings. "I had no idea Julia had a son."

"There is evidence he's hiding out somewhere in London," Roo said.

"What can I do? I am shattered." She waved her hands despairingly.

"Can you tell me what you know about Julia? It might help with his case."

She closed her eyes for a moment, regaining her composure. Her voice grew soft with remembrance. "Julia and I were students in aeronautical engineering at Imperial College. We studied advanced physics and mathematics, quite unusual in those days, for women."

She trilled with sudden laughter. "You wouldn't have believed we were future rocket scientists to look at us. We lot were serious, but also silly young girls who longed for romance."

Lady Caroline returned with tea and biscuits on a silver tray, and sat opposite them. Maisie poured the tea and Roo awkwardly balanced the china cup on his knee. He had missed breakfast, but restrained himself and ate only two biscuits.

Maisie's face took on a dreamy expression, and she seemed to forget that Roo was hunting for a murder suspect, the son of her old friend.

"Oh, those were my happiest days, when we were students. London was so alive. The best place to be for the young and hip. We grooved to the Beatles and the Rolling Stones, and shopped for clothes on Carnaby Street.

"We both had many boyfriends, but Julia fell desperately in love with one young man, whom she always met in secret. She was very discreet.

"At that time, there were large numbers of foreign students, mostly scientists, with special permission to attend graduate school. Very attractive, dare I say sexy? As you know, it was during the Cold War. In later years, I began to suspect some of them were spies."

She sat straight, indignant. "Julia told me she was involved with someone, but was closemouthed about him. I suppose it was not a coincidence that she fell in love. She was a naïve, young woman and he was—well, one doesn't know who he really was.

"Julia did confide that he had ended their relationship. She was broken-hearted. Shortly after that, about three weeks later, she returned home to America, without so much as a farewell. I was very hurt. We were such good friends; more like sisters.

"I wrote to her, but never received a reply, and did not hear from her again. Then the terrible news came of her disappearance, poor darling. The police informed me they found no trace of her." She trailed off mournfully.

Her face turned dark. "This episode in our lives was not totally on the up and up. A very strange business. She was vulnerable. We both were." She sniffed.

Caroline groaned softly, and rolled her eyes. "Oh Auntie, you know you're being dramatic. You read too many novels." She looked at her watch. "Excuse me, I must leave for the office, a business meeting."

"Business meeting. I think not," said Lady Maisie. "I suppose that Rupert Standish-Lyle is fetching you, as usual."

"Did you forget that you introduced us at one of your gatherings?"

Lady Maisie drew herself up indignantly. "I am not happy about that. He seems rather shifty. And I never know exactly what goes on with you at that Ikon company. These meetings occur at 1 p.m. every day. Do you arrive only for lunch? What is it you do, exactly?"

"We are flat-out busy, planning a reception at the Savoy, and I will be working late."

Roo took that to mean the interview was over and wrote down his new phone number on his card. "Thanks for your help. If you think of anything important, please contact me."

Lady Caroline showed him to the door. She was not classically beautiful, but very seductive. He was slightly dazzled by her sophistication.

She took his arm in hers and pressed against him, looked up at him, and whispered. "Perhaps we can meet again. Sometimes Auntie's mind wanders. I will go through her papers for anything that could be important to your case."

As he left and was going up the stone steps, a well-dressed man pulled up in a Porsche and got out of the car. He was holding a gun and walked the length of the mews, then placed the weapon in his shoulder holster, and rang Lady Maisie's bell. When Lady Caroline came out, he put his arm around her, escorted her to the car, and drove off.

Schlachtensee, Duppel Camp for Displaced Persons, Germany: 1945

The Boy

Chapter 35

THE BOY OPENS his eyes, peering from holes in the bandages that cover his head and extend to his body. He is lying in a hospital bed. There is a drone of voices as though he is under water. He battles up from the drowning noises into consciousness. A plump, middle-aged woman, dressed in white, her dull brown hair covered by a nurse's cap stands beside his bed. Luisa Kaplan, a nurse for the Swiss Red Cross, looks at him with pity and love. She speaks to him in German, the only language other than Czech, that he knows. Sometimes she speaks to him in English, which he is beginning to understand. A radio is playing softly in the background.

She props him up, his head lolling on the pillow like a limp doll's, and holds the part of his hand not covered by the bandages. "Listen to this song, *Someone to Watch Over Me.* My darling boy, I am watching over you. You are the son I always wanted."

A man in uniform stands near his bed. He is speaking in German to Luisa. He is blond and handsome. He smiles down at the boy, which fills him with terror. The Boy thinks it is one of the guards from *Auschwitz*.

"We know this patient was in the secret Nazi forgers' unit at *Sachsenhausen*," the man tells Luisa.

"We think he can give us some details about this man, Lieutenant Manfred Weber, first an aide to Captain Bruno Melmer, and then to *Reichsführer* Heinrich Himmler."

Luisa protests. "But he is in critical condition."

The man persists. "This will not take long. We need his cooperation. Let me give you the background, so you understand. It's very important to our country's defense."

"When the German surrender was near, Weber stole classified documents and photographs from the Berlin SS Economics and Administrative Main Office. He travelled to *Sachsenhausen* and ordered the forgers in the secret counterfeit unit to make a microdot of the stolen documents.

"Then Weber headed for Bern, Switzerland, taking a long route through the Bavarian Alps to avoid being caught by the Allied Forces. He carried the paper documents and the microdot copy, intending to use them as a bribe, to escape to South America.

"His charred body was found in a burned-out Mercedes truck, near the Swiss border crossing at the river Aare. Both the microdot and the paper documents were destroyed in the fire."

He stopped and asked for a drink of water. The Boy waited, knowing what was coming.

"During interrogation by OSS officers, Fredrich Bachman, a guard at *Sachsenhausen*, claimed that one of the expert forgers secretly made a duplicate of Weber's microdot, called the 'Paper Man Dossier.' If it still exists, the dossier would be a threat to our

national security. Bachman identified Elijah Aarons as the forger.
Aarons did not survive the prisoners' exit from the camp."

The man's face becomes a blur, and the boy sees the image of
Elijah beside him, joking, comforting him. Tears roll down inside
his bandages.

"Unfortunately, before his interrogation was completed,
Bachman killed himself. He had the mistaken idea he would be
handed over to the Russians.

"Now, may I speak to him?" He leans closer over The Boy, so
close he can feel the man's breath through his bandages.

Luisa whispers. "Go on. He's an American intelligence officer."

The man holds up the photograph of Weber. "Can you identify
this man?" The Boy does not answer.

"You have information about this dossier. Tell us what you
know. Where is it?" The Boy hears the growing menace in the
smooth voice.

Luisa interrupts. "He is only a boy, a mere child. How could he
know anything about this? I think he has fainted."

He closes his eyes. The man hovers over him. The man is right.
The Boy knows. The man never returns.

Moscow: Winter 2003

The General

Chapter 36

THE GENERAL PACED his office floor, staring in gloom at the photograph of Soviet Marshal Georgi Zhukov, famous commander in WWII. Zhukov had never failed in his mission to defeat the Nazi's.

His own mission, absurdly small in comparison, was a fuck-up. His agents had let him down. Deputy Sheriff Yoder had vanished from New York three days ago, and the blackmailer's deadline for release of this Paper Man Dossier was drawing near.

He stopped at the window overlooking *Detsky Mir*, the famous toy store. Recently he had begun to take walks past the shop, watching the children, and at these times, regretting that he had no family.

Kolya had also remained a bachelor, but that had not ruined his career. His friend refused to marry, saying it cramped his style. It was true that Kolya had multiple affairs, and was assigned, against the rules, to an overseas post when only married agents were sent to other countries. The organization thought nothing of killing or torturing, but they were prudish about divorce and affairs, a leftover from Stalin's reign.

He always strictly obeyed the rules, and for that reason took a calculated interest in Natasha Andreyev, a young secretary in the department, and often invited her to attend receptions. When she was killed in a car accident, he let the impression grow among his colleagues that he had been heartbroken by her death and there could be no other love. He realized, with some consternation, that soon after her death that he had no recollection of her appearance.

He occasionally escorted eligible women to important social and political gatherings and had casual affairs, but gradually became regarded as an ascetic dedicating his life to his work and the country.

Back at his desk, he unlocked the top drawer and picked up the photograph of Matthew Knapp, the man he must hunt down and destroy. His hand shook as he studied the picture. This was Kolya's son with the same large dark eyes. His face reminded him of a sculpture of Apollo he had seen in the Vatican Museum during one of his covert assignments.

When the photo first came to his attention, he was out for revenge. As the hunt for Matthew Knapp continued to fail, and the danger to his own survival intensified, he became obsessed with the picture and kept it near him. It was as though Kolya had come back to him.

Still, he mused, it had been wise not to marry. A family would have made him vulnerable to enemies, and he had made many over his years in the service. Kolya always joked that Pasha kept himself tightly buttoned up like his military tunic. It was true.

He had only faintly regretted his decision, until he saw the photograph, and began to wonder if the young man was anything like Kolya.

He closed the drawer on the photograph and called for his car and driver, and travelled to his mansion on Ulitsa Bolshaya Ordynka The mansion in the Zamoskvorechye Quarter was very grand, built in Empire style with high decorative ceilings, huge fireplaces, and rare antique furniture. It had belonged to Sofka, who managed, through her influence, to prevent it from being confiscated during the revolution. It had been left to him along with the *dacha*.

The mansion always reminded him of the empty, guarded life he had chosen, and he rattled around the rooms in a state of melancholy. He disliked the haunting images of living here with Sofka when he was a small child, watching her dress for grand dinners and parties at the Kremlin. Even now, her expensive Paris scent pervaded the rooms.

His attempts to investigate Sofka in his later years had uncovered only vague unproven stories. There were rumors of her reputation as a femme fatale during the revolution, so attractive and spell-binding to men that she had affairs with whomever had power in those turbulent times. She was said to have had the ear of Stalin when he became General Secretary.

He could never confirm any of these undocumented stories which may have been exaggerated, and always suspected she was a double agent, which could have been the reason for her sudden disappearance and death. The mystery surrounding Sofka had come back to haunt him.

Now, pacing through the mansion, he thought of his own possible demise; the reality of what could happen to him if his men failed to find and destroy the dossier. He would be exposed, like the *Rasputitsa*, the spring thaw, which brought rivers of water, uncovering the mud beneath the snow.

In these crucial days, his best strategy was to force Stoddard to question Katya Marston, and persuade her, using physical means if necessary, to reveal Yoder's location. This was a difficult task.

Stoddard was a victim of wishful thinking, with an exaggerated sense of his influence and power. The bastard even had the audacity to attempt to trace his messages, as though he were some common criminal.

He went to his desk for the latest report. Yoder had flown to London to search for Matthew Knapp. His agents had lost the lawman's trail after he left customs. But he was a powerful economic force in the UK. Expatriate Russians, opportunistic Englishmen, and Ikon Inc. employees were always eager to follow his orders, in exchange for their safety and their fortunes.

He studied the map showing the areas where they were searching for Yoder. With the intelligence resources available, he remained confident his men would find him.

He paused in front of a large mirror hanging in the drawing room. His impassive, neutral expression, cultivated since he was a small boy, remained the same if he were attending a party, witnessing torture or ordering a murder.

New York: Winter 2003

Big

Chapter 37

"SURELY YOU CAN tell me more about Yoder," Big said. He was dining with Katya Marston in The Forge, a small French bistro, chosen because he was sure no one would recognize them in this unobtrusive spot. The place was paneled with a small bar, and stained glass windows ensured privacy. It was cozy, with candles set out on checkered table cloths. He would have considered it romantic, but his focus was not in seduction. They had ordered *pot au feu*, a specialty, but neither seemed interested in eating.

After the waiter removed their plates, he positioned himself at the corner of the table, so that their knees were touching. "Come on, give me an idea of what Roo Yoder is like. He might be a good addition to the campaign."

She lowered her head, silent.

He moved closer, pressing against her leg. "You can tell me. Are you in love? Engaged? Where is he now?"

London: Winter 2003

Roo

Chapter 38

AGAINST HIS BETTER Judgement, Roo found himself on a bench in Kensington Gardens, next to Lady Caroline, who had telephoned him and suggested they meet.

She had been going through her aunt's papers, and hinted that she might have some information helpful to his investigation. He had no other choice, no other leads; but was intentionally late, and had surveyed the area to make sure no one was on his trail. He was on his guard, although it seemed unlikely that a killer would be stalking him in this civilized park, with children playing ball, people walking their dogs, jogging, or strolling hand-in-hand.

"Have you found anything that could help the case?" he said, eager to make this a short meeting.

"I think Aunt Maisie is making up this story of her days with her friend, but I'm still reading her papers and letters. I may have some details about her lover, but I need more time. I'm sorry to interrupt your work, but wanted you to know I am making progress."

She sighed, "Some days she is unwell, and she seems to have suffered hallucinations during this last year. Our family doctor has suggested a care home for her."

She shivered in the cold and moved closer to him. He did not try to stop her. She was wearing high heels and a black suit, trimmed with a fox fur, which accented her dark eyes and creamy complexion. Her hair was caught up severely by clips, but some curls worked their way out and fell by her cheeks in a becoming manner.

"I think I might be able to help you in another way. I have some connections." She moved even nearer to him; their shoulders were touching. He was mesmerized by her glamorous appearance, the faint smell of her perfume.

She said, "It is fascinating to be acquainted with an American like you—a lawman, a cowboy." He wanted to correct her, but she interrupted. "You are so very attractive."

He had no answer to this compliment.

"I can understand why you wouldn't be interested in me. I confess I haven't found anything yet for your case. I just wanted to see you again." She hunched in her jacket, looking like a little girl. There were sudden tears in her eyes. "My life has been difficult. I don't know why I am telling you this. Auntie has never been good to me. My mother died when I was twelve. My father gambled away his inheritance, and I was forced to move in with his sister, Maisie.

"And then I was left alone; no one paid any attention to me. Auntie Maisie was disappointed that I wasn't pretty. She said I had little prospect of marrying anyone rich, with my sharp nose. She said

I wasn't intelligent and made me leave school at sixteen, but I have tried to make myself attractive."

"I think you're very pretty." he said, dumfounded at his embarrassing comment; but she was very attractive and he was drawn to her. She wiped away her tears and grasped his hand.

"It would be wonderful if you decided to stay in London and forget about this case."

"I can't do that."

"So why not quit? It could be to your benefit. I have contacts; I could make it interesting in more than one way." She was looking into his eyes. He could not resist, and kissed her. This was not something he had planned. What was he doing? As he raised his head, Roo caught a glimpse of a man in a black overcoat, standing on the steps of the Albert Memorial looking toward them.

She closed her eyes for a moment and put her cheek next to his. He held her close. "I must go. I have so much preparation before the reception at the Savoy tonight."

He kissed her again, glancing over her shoulder. The man had turned his back and was looking toward the monument.

"I'll call if I have any information. I am still searching, but it may be a day or two. It's a rather tricky situation. I'm sorry I wasted your time." He was about to say she hadn't, when she hurried out to the street and stepped into a waiting car.

He slipped away into the trees, through Kensington Gardens, and crossed at Church Street, then ducked into St. Mary Abbots Church, and waited in a dark corner by the door. When he stepped out he pressed up against the end of the cloister near the flower market. The man was at the corner, looking in both directions before moving down the High Street.

It was still light when Roo made his way back through Kensington Gardens. To his surprise, he found himself captivated by Lady Caroline, and sympathetic to her description of neglect as a child. Weaving through bushes and trees, he went over her story. Could he believe her?

Chapter 39

ROO WAS DRESSED in his jacket and tie so he wouldn't stand out in the crowd as he watched for Lady Caroline from the outside corner of the Tea Shop. He was in the elegant Savoy lobby; its huge chandeliers sparkled, reflecting off the gleaming black and white tile floor. He could observe the party, undetected, from this partially-obscured spot. It was a risk to come here, but he wanted to check out the Ikon Company employees. Lady Caroline's meeting with him had ended with someone on his tail. It could have been a coincidence, but he began to suspect she had been sent to lure him into a trap.

Waiters were serving champagne and leading people to a reception room marked "Ikon Inc." A large photograph of the company chairman, General Pavel Romanovich Mikhailov, a stern looking Russian, hung over the entrance. In the center of the lobby a string quartet was playing Mozart, an amusing contrast to Roo's usual hangout at Shorty's Bar, which blared out shit-kicking country music.

Lady Caroline entered the lobby with the man he had seen stalking the mews with his gun. Roo knew it was Rupert Standish-Lyle. The couple were surrounded by a group of security men in evening suits.

Lady Caroline somehow caught a glimpse of Roo and stared in fright and astonishment as though he were an apparition. He froze, and moved out of sight, behind the door of the shop. She said something to Standish-Lyle before regaining her composure. Then he saw her speak to one of the security men, and recognized the battered face and the bulbous nose of the man who had trailed him from the steps of the Albert Memorial. After a quick glance in Roo's direction Lady Caroline had drifted away into the crowd slowly filing into the party room.

Standish-Lyle raised his champagne glass and waved to several acquaintances, and then took out his phone. The man who had tailed him in the park broke away and joined two others.

After the call, Standish-Lyle nodded to the three men. They were weaving their way through the lobby toward him. He looked around for an escape, not believing this was happening in a hotel. It was unreal, like a scene in a B-movie.

He began to walk fast, then to run, and reached the hotel fire exit, broke the lock on the handle, and raced down to the Embankment. He glanced back in the growing darkness. They were following, picking up the pace. His heart pumping, he dashed ahead of them several yards and hid in a clump of bushes near the river, then dove into the icy Thames, under the Hungerford Bridge.

Grasping a railing, he rose up to take a breath. The men had stopped, looking around, cursing and panting before they ran on.

Gasping from the cold, he dipped back into the water, holding his breath, then came again to the surface. He heard them in the distance, shouting to each other, and saw them retracing their steps.

Soaking wet and freezing, his jacket clinging to him, he swam to the shore and clambered out, his boots sloshing, He avoided the street lights, taking alleyways and lost his way several times before getting back to his hotel. There was no one at the reception desk to notice the flood of water he left on the stairs.

Shivering uncontrollably, he peeled off his clothes and took a hot shower. His time now was limited. For a moment, he saw the huge picture of the Russian General looming over the Icon reception entrance. Roo knew instinctively that he was the powerful Russian who was hunting him, and would eventually track him down—and try to kill him.

Chapter 40

THE NEXT MORNING, Roo went out the hotel's service door and scaled the high fence into an alley, taking small back streets to Kynance Mews.

He waited on the stone steps that led to the church. On schedule Standish-Lyle drove up, and Lady Caroline came out of the house and got into the car, laughing, unfazed about the scene at the Savoy last night.

He rushed down the steps and rang the bell. After peering through the keyhole, Lady Maisie opened the door. She was trembling. Her hair flew around her face, like a Medusa he'd once seen in an art book.

"Oh, my God, I am so relieved you came. Someone is after me. I think they want to kill me. There was a man stalking the house, walking by my front door. Caroline didn't believe me and threatened to call the doctor."

"I no longer trust my niece. I haven't for quite some time. She tells people that I am gaga, and has talked to our family lawyers and the health authorities about putting me away in an insane asylum." She let out an outraged shriek.

"I have given her a home all these years, and have been good to her, except for my comment, only once, about her sharp-looking nose. She wants this house and my small inheritance. She will do anything to get rid of me."

Lady Maisie rushed over to the window. "I don't know when she'll return, but it won't be soon. She often comes back very late at night." She hunched up in her wool caftan, embroidered with colorful peacocks.

"Please sit down. Forgive my bad manners." She took a huge swallow of whiskey from her glass.

"Whiskey for you?"

He nodded. She poured a large one for him and went on.

"Caroline has become very involved with Rupert Standish-Lyle, a questionable character, an aristocrat, one of our own, but I don't think he will marry her. He runs with a bad crowd; *nouveau riche Russians,* some of them gangsters, whom I consider very dangerous. He's in business with them and makes a bundle of money. He has no scruples. His grandparents, who were great friends of mine, would not have approved."

She perched on the edge of the sofa, like a wild bird about to fly. "I think I am in danger for my foolish actions long ago. I didn't tell you everything because I am afraid of Caroline.

"In the '70s, I was a victim of a honey trap, lured by a spy into giving him classified information." She sighed. "I have not spoken of it for years in fear that I could be arrested for espionage." Roo thought she seemed an unlikely spy.

"After Julia and I received our degrees, we were hired by Lockheed-Thorn EMI Defense Electronics, a high-security firm. Julia had decided to stay in England. I didn't know her real reason then.

"Everything changed for me after I met Daniel Berger, a student from Eastern Europe, in one of my classes, and fell desperately in love with him." She slumped down on the sofa and lowered her head. "I confess, I did give him data from the company. He said it was for a special project.

"And then one evening, my life tumbled into ruin. I returned to the classroom to pick up a notebook I had forgotten. I looked on with horror, seeing first Julia's raised skirt, and then Daniel on top of her on the lecturer's desk. The noises!" she shuddered. "I never recovered from the shock. The realization came to me soon after that he was making love to me only because I was giving him information."

She broke into sobs. "I loved him so. I was heartbroken."

Roo sat like a stone at the wild outburst, not knowing how to comfort her.

"I never saw him again." She grew quiet, and held her long, slender hands, several rings gleaming, in front of her in a beseeching gesture. "I wanted to confront him. We had always met for our assignations at a small hotel in Bayswater. But I found the address he had given to the college and went round to the building, only to discover that the porter had never heard of him."

Her eyes narrowed. "Julia must have known where he lived. Their secret trysts had to take place somewhere."

She had calmed down and mused, while pouring another drink. "Daniel was charming and very handsome, but he was not as you say, on the level with either of us. Even when I told Julia I knew about their affair and that he had seduced me as well, she didn't believe me. She was starry-eyed, and said they were going to be married.

"I suspected that Daniel Berger was a cover name, and the bastard was a spy posing as a student. I was broken, shattered, devastated; I quit my job and entered a convalescent hospital in Switzerland.

"During my recuperation, a very frightening man came to visit. He knew of my unwise behavior involving Daniel, and tried to blackmail me into working for him. I refused, but ever since I have lived in fear of being exposed as a spy and sent to prison. My only excuse was that I couldn't resist him." She sighed, wiping her tears with a lace handkerchief. Her handsome features seemed sharper, constricted with grief.

"Wait, wait. I kept a photograph of my lover." Suddenly animated, she jumped up from edge of the sofa, and took out an album from her antique desk, quickly leafing through until she found the page. "I thought about destroying it, but just couldn't."

"Here we are in Kensington Gardens, not far from the college. It was one day after classes were over. I took this picture of him with the Albert Memorial in the background. He was so charming, so handsome."

Roo carefully put his glass down on the table. The large man, dark blond with bony, high cheekbones and large, staring eyes could have been Matthew. He was stunned. Daniel Berger was Matthew's father. She poured each of them another drink.

"This could be very dangerous." Her voice was filled with drama. "Two days ago, a man with a foreign accent came here. I should never have let him in, but he said he was a friend of Caroline's. He was very uncivilized and demanded to know if I had seen Matthew Knapp. I pretended complete ignorance. I think he was the villain outside the house early this morning.

"You might think I've gone 'round the bend' and need to be put away, but this is all true. All true," she repeated.

"Has Matthew been here?"

"Yes, yes. I'm very sorry that I lied to you. Wasn't positive I could trust you. He came here before you. Caroline was out, and of course, I didn't tell her. I was shocked, as I had not heard of the murders, and had no connection with the Knapps, but believed Matthew when he said he was Julia and Daniel's son. How could I not? He is the image of Daniel."

She took a long drink. "He asked many questions about his mother and father, and I answered as best I could. He said he was in danger because he had found some documents at his grandparents' farm. He believes his parents might still be alive and has set out to find them. He also knows that you are looking for him, and mentioned someone named Linny in that regard. He wants to meet with you."

"You mean he'll give himself up and come back to the States?"

"I didn't say that," she snapped. "He has the need to explain. He had nothing to do with the murders. I feel sorry for him; so frightened, on the run, yet determined. He will set up a meeting." Her eyes were bright with excitement.

Roo didn't have to warn her to be careful. He glanced at the gun, not completely hidden behind the music stand on the grand piano.

"It's a Winchester rifle for hunting deer, but will do as well for an intruder. I'm a crack shot."

He left Lady Maisie, who bolted her door after him, and walked to the Imperial College Archive Office. Showing his badge, he checked records for Daniel Berger. He was born in Prague and registered at the College as an exchange student from The Czech Technical University in Prague (CTU). Roo was aware that in the '70s, Czechoslovakia was part of the Communist block controlled by Russia. All of Berger's information could be false; a legend for a spy.

If Lady Maisie's account was true, it was only part of a complicated story connected to Matthew and the Paper Man Dossier.

A picture formed in his mind; Julia alone and pregnant, waiting in desperation in a shabby hotel room. Daniel could have promised to meet her in New York and never showed, leaving her defenseless to have their son Matthew, and fend for herself. But Roo sensed this might have been an intense love affair. Was it possible Berger had been desperate to be with Julia and escape from his life as a spy?

Chapter 41

ROO WAS PACKING his bag when his phone rang.

"It's Lady Maisie," she whispered. "Meet at the Churchill Pub. Kensington Church Street, 8 p.m. Get there early and wait. If you are not on time, he will leave."

He put cash on the bed to pay for the room and went out the back alley, walking at a fast pace, stopping in two different shops to check if he was being tailed. As he approached the pub with its colorful sign of Winston Churchill, he passed a homeless man crouched in a doorway.

The Churchill's exterior was covered with plants and greenery which seem to have sprouted from its walls. Inside, it was decorated with the owner's many collections, a riot of miscellany; tea pots, pottery, framed photographs, and portraits of Churchill.

There was no sign of Matthew in the dimly-lit room.

He ordered a pint and found a quiet booth by a small window. It was past eight and Knapp still had not appeared. Uneasy he watched a group of businessmen gather at the bar, and was getting up to leave when there was a tap on the window. Matthew was staring at him from the street.

Roo stood by the door to block his entrance from sight of the bar until he slipped in among the crowd and sat down in the booth. He was carrying a plastic shopping bag, and placed it on the seat. Underneath his hooded sweatshirt, his face was strained and dirty. Roo held out his badge.

He said, "I remember you from high school—the quarterback. Look, I haven't got much time."

Roo shoved his pint over to Matthew and ordered another one from the noisy bar.

"Thanks," He gulped half of it down.

"I'm taking you back to Paint Creek. It will be safer for you."

"You know I didn't do it. I loved my grandparents." His bloodshot eyes were milky with tears.

"I believe you. I'll see to it you won't be charged."

He spoke in a loud angry voice, covered by the talk and laughter from the men at the bar. "But I have what the killers are looking for. When I discovered the Paper Man Dossier, it was too late. They were after me. I knew that even if I gave up the dossier, they would kill me." Roo pushed his pint over, and Matthew finished it before going on.

"I tried to find every document hidden at the farmhouse that endangered my grandparents. They were terrified. I'm sorry now that I was furious, because they resisted. Now I know they wanted to protect me. They had scattered all the evidence, trying to hide it from the killers. I wasn't able to find everything. I would be dead if a friend in New York hadn't helped me to escape."

Before Roo could ask, he said, "I can't tell you; too dangerous for him. I've been sleeping rough on the street here. They weren't able to find me."

He pushed the bag across the seat. "This is the dossier, what they are after, why they murdered my grandparents. It's all there. Use it to expose the killers, even if I don't make it. Linny said I could trust you. I am leaving here tonight."

"Where?"

He didn't answer the question. "I want to find out what happened to my parents."

Roo said, "I don't think that's a good idea."

He shook his head. "I think they might be alive. I know they loved each other. I found more papers at the farmhouse. Linny has kept them for me."

Matthew stood up, looking around the room.

"Don't do this." Roo gripped his arm. "You're under arrest." He sounded ridiculous.

Matthew shook him off and ran outside. Roo went after him, but he was not fast enough. Two men had appeared out of a side street, and were holding Matthew down. Roo made a mad rush at them, knocking them off balance, and crashed down on the pavement, dazed by the fall. When he came to, Matthew was gone. The scuffle had brought people out of the pub.

Two of the businessmen helped him to his feet.

"Are you all right? You've had a right bad knock," one of them said. "They ran that way." He pointed toward Campden Street. "Should we call an ambulance, or the police?"

"No, no, thank you. I'm a law officer." Brushing off the dirt, he staggered inside, picked up the plastic bag and his backpack and began to run. At the end of Campden Street, the thugs were dragging Matthew along the pavement as though he were drunk.

He followed them to Notting Hill and a gated road, leading to Palace Gardens Terrace and a large mansion. He stopped in amazement. Holy Shit! It was the Russian Embassy. Matthew and the two men had disappeared. He hid in a small space behind the compound entrance. A light came on in a basement room, and a short time later an SUV with a diplomatic license plate pulled into the side entrance. A figure wrapped in bandages was carried out of the compound on a stretcher and lifted inside. He was helpless, and couldn't even be sure it was Matthew.

A guard was patrolling near the entrance to the compound. Roo stepped into the shadows and crept away from the booth at the embassy gate, down to Kensington High Street, then onto Church Street.

His head splitting with pain, he took a back route through a maze of streets until he reached Lady Maisie's. The house was in total darkness. He knocked softly. "It's Roo Yoder." After several minutes, Maisie, carrying a flashlight, opened the door. She was dressed in her robe and nightgown, her wild hair pressed down by a large net. She recoiled at the bruises on his face. "Oh, dear god. What happened to you?"

"Matthew has been kidnapped. Do you know where he was taken?"

"Oh, no! He was planning to leave, I don't know to where. Best not to come here again." She was trembling, and looked over her shoulder.

"Wait, please." It was Lady Caroline, in the shadows of the hall.

Lady Maisie said, "Oh dear, I am so sorry. She overheard me when I phoned you. I could do nothing to stop them."

"You're working for those killers." He braced for her to signal them.

She was weeping. "Yes, I was waiting for the phone call, so I could tell them where to find you. I need the money. I didn't know you were going to get hurt. They didn't tell me that. I have to get away. Please, please take me with you." She gripped his arm. He pulled her off and brushed past, running into the street.

Moscow: March 2003

The General

Chapter 42

HE SPENT THE evening wandering aimlessly through the
mansion, eventually stopping at Sofka's bedroom. He had not
entered the room since she was taken away. He sank down on the
gilt chair at her large vanity table, shaken by the sudden memory of
Sofka in her lace negligée, reclining in the vast bed, drinking tea, and
reading the morning papers.

Numerous silver-topped jars, engraved cosmetic bottles, and a
heavy bronze casket remained in place, as though any minute she
would walk in the room to make up her face in the large vanity
mirror. The casket, once owned by a Byzantine emperor, always
fascinated him as a child. She had kept her letters and documents
inside this ancient box. He raised the lid, knowing the men who
arrested her would have searched the room and removed the
papers.

On impulse, he ran his hands over the figures portraying
Odysseus in the Trojan War. Then he gazed at his reflection, and

quite suddenly, his recurrent dream came alive in the mirror. He is a tiny boy running, his bare feet padding through the giant hall of the mansion. Dwarfed by enormous rooms crowded with furniture, and figures from paintings staring at him, his pale eyes dart, searching for her. He hears frightening voices, shouting, and opens a door. Sofka is lying in bed with two men. He runs to her, his arms out to embrace her. She rises up and comes toward him, flushed, her hair flowing around her, and slaps him in the face, so hard he falls back. She looms over him, her large, full body like a menacing goddess.

"You must never tell what you have seen. Those you have seen. People will die. You will die."

He gasped, even now, breathless at the deep, buried hurt; how he cried, running in terror from the room. He had witnessed the alarm in her eyes. the fear in the slap that changed his life.

This unexpected ending to his dream was so intense that he saw every detail. Always before, deep in his subconscious, the men's faces were shadows eluding him, but now they became clear. He stared in shock of recognition, of what he had blocked from his mind. Bokov and the Raven slowly faded from the mirror.

With grief filling his heart, he struggled up from the chair and stumbled, catching his foot in a small crevasse in the floor underneath the dressing table. He easily pried open the flapping, loose floorboard and found a cardboard box.

That night he went through Sofka's documents from 1918 to 1948, the year she was taken away. He read the two short notes placed first in the box.

Bokov is our enemy. We must find the all the evidence against him before we strike. We must locate Timur and the dossier.

The Raven.

Dearest, I can only hope you find this. They will be coming for me. You and your friend, Timur, will be next. Bokov ordered my arrest. Take care of Pasha. He will be alone.
　　Sofka

He had tears in his eyes; she was speaking of him.

Several other letters made it clear that the two men had been her lovers. The Raven had many affairs, so he was not surprised at that. Comrades during the revolution and rivals for Sofka, Bokov and the Raven became political enemies. This old Bolshevik conflict had continued into the '70s, long after Sofka was gone.

Now he knew the mystery which had tormented him. It became clear that both men, in a struggle for survival, were hunting the dossier. The Raven arranged for Bokov's death, disguising it as a hunting accident to prevent exposure of his long-planned tsarist coup. He then hid Kolya's interrogation in the desk in the Lubyanka basement.

Riffling through the contents of the box, he found a photograph, taken sometime in 1944 or 1945, marked *Series 2: evidence against Bokov.* The number *0116 2385 2957* was written at the bottom.

Sofka's phrases from her letters ran through his head when he returned to his office the next morning, in a state of sorrow. It was long ago, but Sofka's treatment of him—her slap—had broken his heart and changed his life. He managed, with practiced discipline, to shrug off his melancholy by concentrating on the latest report.

His men had captured Matthew Knapp, but Yoder had escaped with the dossier. He waited, but in the next two days there was no news of Yoder. He was sure the bastard, Stoddard, was holding out on him.

The old photograph found with Sofka's letters would not force Stoddard to give him crucial information on Yoder. So far, nothing had moved the stupid bastard, not even his subtle threats of violence. Time was running out. A coil of fear wound through his body like an electric wire. He must make the threat real. He would order direct action.

New York: March 2003

Roo

Chapter 43

ROO KEPT WATCH out the back window as the cab rolled into Manhattan from JFK. He touched his forehead, bruised and throbbing from hitting the pavement in the fight outside the Churchill Pub. He should have arrested Matthew and forced him to go back to Ohio.

During the flight he had put ice on the wound, and drank to numb the pain, but couldn't erase the image of Matthew being dragged through the streets. Over the Atlantic, the plane's engine droned failure. Then its melancholy sound hummed "loneliness," and a sudden longing for Katya crept over him. He needed to see her, to hold her. He sat awake in the darkness, thinking of her.

As soon as he landed, he contacted Stumpy. The sheriff was furious that he had gone to the UK without notifying him, but Roo persuaded him to place an official call to London to report the incident at the Russian embassy.

He worried about Lady Maisie and used his burner phone to try to contact her. It was a relief to hear her rasping voice. She had called the police who were checking the area.

"I didn't tell them everything; only reported that someone was stalking the house. Caroline has gone. I don't know where. She moved out after I called the police." Lady Maisie was worried about Matthew, and upset that Roo had no news of him. "He could be in a prison cell in Siberia," she said in a dramatic voice before hanging up.

Aware that he might be followed, Roo had checked into the Marriott and waited until 11 p.m. to meet Alice. He paced back and forth in the hotel room and finally decided to phone Katya, but there was no answer.

The cab dropped him three blocks from the Business Library and he sheltered in doorways until he reached 34th Street. Alice was waiting at the delivery entrance, shivering from the cold blasts of air, her tiny hands dangling a large flashlight. She led him into her office, closed the blinds, turned on the lights, and threw off her coat. She was dressed in a light beige track suit, and sneakers to match, which made her seem even more fragile.

"I was returning from the gym when you called. It's less crowded at night and Malcolm is working late."

She stared, her eyes wide. "Oh my God, you look awful. What happened in London?"

"Matthew sent me a message that he wanted to meet, and we were ambushed by two thugs." He didn't mention Caroline and her treachery, another one of his stupid failures.

"I can't be completely sure I wasn't followed." He sank into the chair across from her, worn out from lack of sleep.

"They could come here." She opened her handbag, and handed over his glock. "You might need this."

"Yeah, thanks, for keeping it."

She stared out the window before closing the curtain. "Where is he?"

Roo couldn't look at her. "He wouldn't leave with me; said he was looking for his parents. The killers caught up with him and dragged him along on the street, like he was drunk. They disappeared into the Russian Embassy. After about thirty minutes a bandaged body was lifted by stretcher into a car."

She drew in her breath. "Oh, how terrible. Are you sure it was him?"

"'I think it had to be Matthew. I couldn't save him. Several guards surrounded the car and made it impossible to attack." His voice faded.

"I arrived this afternoon and contacted Stumpy who notified the London police. Matthew gave me this bag before he was taken away, and asked me to hand over the dossier to the press."

He removed the battered cardboard folder from the shopping bag and placed it on her desk.

"I can't believe it. Is this really the Paper Man Dossier?" Her head bent over the papers.

"Yes, when I started the murder investigation, I never thought it would come to this."

"I don't believe it. Some of these are Melmer accounts," she said in a hushed voice. She went on reading, quickly flipping through pages. "How strange. They're written in both German and English."

She looked up, her voice tinged with excitement. "There are receipts to the *Reichsbank* from SS Finance for gold deposits from *Auschwitz* and other concentration camps." She turned to the next pages.

"These accounts were missing from the Melmer Files found at the *Reichsbank* by Allies in 1945, and used in Melmer's trial. They were stolen before the war ended, and copied in the dossier before the remainder of the documents came into Allied hands," Alice said.

They came to a separate folder and stared in amazement. *Reichsführer of the Schutzstaffel Heinrich Himmler: Classified*

Chapter 44

HIMMLER. THE NAME rattled in his head. He was haunted by the picture of the small man with the receding chin and little wire-rimmed glasses, a mass murderer.

After they had found the photograph of the three men, Alice said, "I think the SS officer is Himmler. I have seen pictures of him, and even now he scares me. Anyone who has studied WWII would know this monster."

She went back to the computer and found another picture of Himmler. "I am positive that he is the one in the SS uniform." Her voice trembled. "He was Hitler's interior minister, head of the Gestapo, and in charge of the concentration camps. In 1943 he oversaw what the Nazis' called 'the final solution'; the plan to exterminate all the Jews, and many others who were not Aryan."

Spooked, she peered out the window into the back street, and then came back to look again at the photograph. She took a deep breath. "I can't believe this. I think the officer in the American uniform could be Stoddard's father."

"As of yesterday, Big is still in the race. He has shown no sign of quitting. The primary is in a week; on the 15th. He must be worried, but it could be that he doesn't know what's in the dossier."

"And Katya?"

"She's still working on his campaign."

Alice brought up a recent New York Times article. "I remember now. After Big announced he was running for the Senate, the paper featured his father, Frank Stoddard II, describing his heroism in WWII."

She clicked on to a series of old photographs. "I've found the identity of the other man, a Russian officer named Bokov."

The photograph in the dossier was accompanied by written accounts, revealing that some of the victims' gold was not deposited as expected in the *Reichsbank*, but siphoned off by Himmler and the other two men in the photograph.

They delved into the US National Archives and Records Administration, searching for documents from two years before the war ended, and found a 1943 *Aide-mémoire* from the US State Department.

This document reported that in 1943 Himmler attempted to bargain with the allies, using his Swedish masseur as contact. His plan was to negotiate a surrender, remove Hitler, and become head of a new Nazi government. The Allied governments were ignorant of his attempt, earlier that year, at a secret deal with Stoddard and Bokov.

Alice said, "Hmm. these are receipts for the stolen money, deposited in Swiss bank accounts. Himmler gave millions to these two men, as bribes, to influence their governments to permit him to take over from Hitler. In the end, none of his deals worked. He was captured by the British and committed suicide."

Roo said, "It looks like one numbered account remained uncollected. It could still be there."

"So Stoddard's father set up his bank with the proceeds of gold stolen from holocaust victims, and bribes from Himmler. The dates of his travels in Germany after WWII, and the launching of his bank, point to that conclusion."

Roo said, "And the timing of Frank Stoddard's trips to Germany after the war, suggests he stole the Melmer Files from the bank and destroyed them, believing the evidence incriminating him was still part of their contents. It was later discovered that the copy with the important, incriminating proof of his guilt existed in this Paper Man Dossier."

"This will be the end of Big's campaign," Alice said.

It was 3 a.m. when Alice let him out the back door. His head was spinning from his fall at the pub, and lack of sleep. Alice placed the dossier in the plastic bag into the library safe. When he protested, she held him off. "No one would think of looking there."

Still aware that he might have been followed, he made his way back by taxi to the airport hotel. He couldn't go back to Katya's apartment. They might look for him there, and she would be in danger. He had tried to call her several times, but there was no answer.

Alice's words seemed to hang in the air, as he hurried back to his hotel room. When he went public with the dossier, "the shit would hit the fan," as Stumpy would say. He was not unhappy that it would be over for Stoddard, and Matthew would be vindicated.

He fell into bed, but couldn't sleep, unable to erase his last sight of Matthew. Roo believed he was still alive. He would start tomorrow to find some trace of him. He picked up his phone, longing to hear Katya's voice, but then thought better of it, and hung up.

New York: March 2003

Big

Chapter 45

BIG HAD PLACED an offer to buy a Washington DC residence in the Kalorama District, and was browsing through the description of the mansion, suitable for the parties and receptions he was anticipating as senator. The polls were now projecting a win for him in the primary, and to his surprise, in the general election. He was as good as in.

It was late in the evening and he was alone, except for the security guard at the corporate entrance. He put down the brochure to check his mail and froze at the message slowly appearing on the screen.

You have been holding out on me. You have screwed me around for the last time. Now you will believe me.

Knapp has been captured in London. Yoder is on the run with the dossier. Katya Marston knows where he hides.

You could be saved if you flush him out. I will take care of him.
If you follow my orders, there will be no need for a useless killing. This
is your last chance. There is a gift package waiting for you.
Chekhov, Чехов.

He went to look for the "gift," and found a brown package, addressed to him. He guessed it might be the civics award for his good works with the homeless, and removed the brown wrapping, thinking it was a shame he had not been able to attend the ceremony. It would have been great publicity, he mused, as he tore off the gold paper from the elegantly-wrapped package and opened the lid of the plastic box.

He shrieked and drew back, gagging and sobbing. He crawled to the bathroom and threw up, then dragged his limp body back into the office. Shaking uncontrollably, he shoved the box into a desk drawer. Feeling faint, he collapsed on the floor, with one thought piercing his fog of terror.

He had been an idiot, believing he could bargain with this Chekhov, and if his Odessa group found and destroyed the dossier, there would be no evidence that it had ever existed, and the man stalking him would disappear. But this Russian was intent on killing both Knapp and Yoder, and anyone else who had knowledge of the dossier. To his terror that included him. He writhed in agony. He would be eliminated. Even his hired men would be helpless to save him. Didn't they call it "liquidation?"

A humming ran through his head as he checked into the Plaza later that evening. He wore a hat pulled low over his face, and was relieved that no one, not even the receptionist, had recognized him. He lay on the bed in his room, drinking scotch from the bottle, trying to drive out the horror of the severed hand, in a claw of pain, caked in blood, cushioned in gold velvet. An encrusted finger pointed to a note: *Hand, arm, head?*

Death solves all problems—no man, no problem. Rybakov.

The low humming in his head was incessant. He had called his office, and left a message with Lily that he was ill and would not be in for the next two days. Alarm filled him; he might not act fast enough. He had been in some dicey fixes before, but nothing like this. No one of influence could help.

Hung over and in a terrible state, he forced himself to return to the office two days later, and pretended nothing was wrong; "a bout of flu," he told Lily. He was still panicked and overcome with fear three nights later when he picked up Katya from Solitude and Mind Peace Retreat. He had controlled his shaking voice and phoned her at the spa, asking if they could discuss some campaign ideas. He assumed that if he were more aggressive, and tried forcibly to seduce her, she would be willing like most women, to do anything for him.

He sent his driver home and took the elevator to the parking garage to avoid the press. He'd had no previous success questioning Katya Marston and thought he had been too subtle. There had been a problem all along, he realized; either she didn't get it, or she was stalling.

He had tried to appear kind and affectionate to gain her trust, but still she pretended ignorance. Surely the bitch knew where the country hick was hiding out. He screamed, a high, animal sound. The image of the bloody claw, suddenly popped up in front of him and he swerved nearly hitting a car on the other side of the road.

This was the bitch's fault, and he would settle things with her after this was over, after the election.

Katya came out from the retreat, smiling, slightly puzzled. She was dressed in a suit and high heels, her long, blond hair curling around her shoulders.

"Sorry to disturb you, but it's urgent. I had to see you. We have to do more work on my speech before the primary. I need your suggestions." He tried to keep his voice on an even keel.

"How's my girl? Such a great campaigner," he said in a hearty manner. He put his hand on her knee as he drove off. "There will be an important job for you after the election. You're too valuable to give up."

He pulled into his private garage, and with his arm firmly around her, escorted her to the elevator. He turned on the lights in his office and led her over to the couch. "The latest polls show I'm running ahead of Conrad in the primary and ahead of the Democrats in the general. Let's have a drink to celebrate." He took out a bottle of wine and poured both of them a glass.

"That's wonderful. How can I help?" She liked him; he could tell.

"You are so beautiful," he said, not answering, and forgetting his intent to be subtle. The humming noise in his head grew louder. He kissed her, hard. She jerked away in shock.

"Listen to me. You have to help me. Brady told me you saw the blackmail letter. What reporter did you leak this to?" He growled.

"I would never do that."

"Your boyfriend, Yoder, is involved. The deadline to comply with the letter is next week. This could ruin my career, my reputation."

Trembling, Katya moved to the edge of the couch and tried to get up. He pulled her back and patted her knee again. Then he leaned over and pressed against her, holding her down.

"You have nothing to worry about. Just tell me where Yoder's hiding out in London, and everything will be ok." He saw her eyes flicker with surprise and fear.

"He's in London? I didn't know. I don't know where he is. What will happen to him?"

He didn't believe her, and didn't bother to answer her. He was in a panic, and felt something go loose inside him.

"You bitch. You're lying. You know where he is." He gripped her arms hard. Tears of pain filled her eyes.

"Tell me now, and this will be over." He had gone over the edge and couldn't stop, ripping her blouse and pulling up her skirt.

She jumped up and scrambled for the door, but he caught her, squeezing her chest. "You do know. Tell me where he is, or I'll hurt you more."

He twisted her arm behind her back. She screamed, and kicked him in the crotch. He let out an animal howl, bending over. She ran from the office, and down the fire stairs.

His fury grew at the stab in his groin. He would beat her, smash in her face. He didn't wait for the pain to ease, but raced after her onto the stairs. His gold pen dropped out of his pocket and clattered down the steps in front of him. Catching up with her, he leapt, reached out, and grabbed her by the hair.

Katya pulled away, screaming. He teetered, his arms flapping out like a large, disoriented bird, and lost his balance. His foot rolled on the pen—disbelief, amazement shot through him. This could not be happening, not to Big, always the lucky one. He fell forward and tumbled over, his head bumping down three flights of concrete steps. He never heard her screams.

New York: March 2003

Chapter 46

THE NEXT MORNING Roo woke early in the airport hotel, with the roar of planes taking off as though he were underneath the wheels. He made a cup of coffee while dressing, and turned on the TV.

Stunned, he turned up the volume. Big Stoddard had died last night from a fall down the fire stairs at his office. The death appeared to be accidental, but police were not ruling out foul play. He jerked, spilling his coffee, at the next announcement. *"Socialite Katya Marston, who was at the scene of the accident, is being held for questioning."*

Holy shit! This was a nightmare; it could not be true. He turned to another channel only to find the same report, with vivid speculation on Big and Katya's relationship. He sat motionless, unable to comprehend something he could never have imagined. Then anger ripped through him. What was she doing in his office at night?

He tried again to reach her, but her phone was disconnected. He hurried to the gallery, hoping she had been released and was in the apartment and he could see her, talk to her.

The large sign in the gallery window, *"Closed Until Further Notice,"* did not deter reporters, TV cameras, and the curious gathered near the entrance. He went around to the back alley and knocked. Geoffrey, trapped in the shuttered gallery, unlocked the door.

"Christ! What happened to you?" he said, looking at the bruises on Roo's face.

"I ran into some thugs. Do you think I can see her? Where is she?"

Geoffrey was reading the newspaper and occasionally looking through the blinds at the growing crowd in front of the gallery. "She's no longer in police custody, but didn't come back here. I don't know where she is. My God, I can't believe it. Hey, I'm sorry."

He avoided looking at Geoffrey and walked away into the gallery, studying one of the remaining landscape paintings not yet removed from the exhibit.

He wanted to see her, hear her explanation, and save her from this mess. She wasn't capable of murder.

"I shouldn't tell you, but she called me last night, crying, and asked me to get her a lawyer. She sounded near breakdown. She's being released today, but is still a suspect and not permitted to travel."

Geoffrey held up the paper. "Did you see this? It's really awful. After Stoddard's fall, she phoned emergency. When the police arrived, she was at the foot of the steps, her top ripped off. She was sobbing and trying to revive him. The police found clumps of her hair in Stoddard's fist. There are reports that they were having an affair and were arguing. I know that's not true. It was an accident."

Roo felt a tremor run through his guts. Something was breaking apart inside him. "I have to go."

He wandered out onto Spring Street, pushing through the crowd, bumping hard into a couple. The man cursed and swung his arm at him, but Roo hardly noticed.

Chapter 47

ALICE WAS WAITING with the usual bagels and cream cheese when he arrived at the library. Surprised when he turned it down, she looked at him with sympathy, but said nothing about Katya. He tried not to think about it, and to go on with the search for Matthew. The London police and the FBI International Operations Division had nothing to report.

He sent Stumpy his official account of the investigation, which angered the sheriff again. He detailed his trip to London, and Matthew's disappearance, but his explanation did not sit well with Stumpy, who was yelling over the phone. "You went to London without telling me, and came back without him?"

Stumpy said Roo had no real proof that Matthew had been kidnapped and taken to Russia. He was still dealing with folks in Paint Creek, who believed Matthew was a suspect and demanded that he "face the music." Stumpy was getting a lot of heat from the mayor who wanted his head on a plate.

The sheriff asked if Roo's relationship with Katya had ended now that she was involved with Stoddard's death. "There's a lot of rumor around that she had something to do with the Knapp murders." Roo had nothing to add. "I don't know. I haven't spoken to her."

Stumpy said, "I heard this Stoddard had hired some thugs from the Odessa group. What have you got yourself mixed up in?" After this question, the sheriff had hung up.

Alice said, "Have you seen her?"

"No, she's in hiding. Geoffrey says she is in misery, humiliated."

"Hiding even from you?"

"Yes, especially from me. I'm not sure why." After a few moments of uncomfortable silence, he went back to work.

He contacted the State Department Office of Law Enforcement Liaison, requesting passport records for Matthew Knapp. He sent a photograph of Matthew, his personal details and approximate dates of when he might have left the country for the UK. There was no record of any passport in Matthew's name, but there was one issued to a Henry Lewis, which matched Matthew's details and photograph.

"Henry Lewis traveled to the UK at about the same time as Matthew. This has to be Matthew, using a fake passport," Alice said.

Roo said, "The UK National Document Fraud Unit reported the arrival of Henry Lewis in the UK, but there is no record of his movements after that."

He looked out the window. Light snow was falling. A dark shadow fell on the pavement.

"Did you see that?" Alice shuddered.

Chapter 48

BIG'S DEATH WAS ruled accidental. Katya was cleared by her phone messages calling emergency and the position of Stoddard's body on the steps.

She kept her head down and cried during the inquest. Roo tried to talk to her, but she turned away, and was hurried out with her lawyer to avoid him and the crowd of TV reporters.

While searching Big's office, detectives found the box with the severed hand. Roo told Alice the police record read like a horror story. Officers checked hospital emergency rooms on the dates surrounding Stoddard's death and discovered a report on a homeless man, bleeding out on the street. He was taken to Brooklyn Hospital Center and, when he regained consciousness, was terrified and incoherent. He didn't know his own name, and howled that while he was begging for money, a monster wearing rubber gloves attacked him with a knife. The monster sliced off his hand and was going to kill him, but ran off when he began screaming for help. Until they connected the man to the severed hand, the doctors had thought he was having delirium tremens.

During the investigation, NYPD Detectives discovered the email messages between Big Stoddard and General Pavel Romanovich Mikhailov, further implicating the General in the Knapp murders.

Then the investigation had taken a surprising turn. a series of coincidences that seemed at first to have no connection with the Knapp murders. Suspicious activity was uncovered at the Stoddard Bank. Law enforcement's Bank Fraud unit had turned their attention to General Mikhailov's business dealings and those of other high-ranking Russian officials.

The General, the wealthy oligarch and most influential of the *siloviki,* head of the listed Ikon Company, was suspected of laundering money outside Russia by parking it in secret accounts. Roo believed there was enough evidence to request his extradition for the Knapp murders.

The Russian government claimed they had no knowledge of these accounts. The bank fraud investigation would continue for months. If there was proof of illegal activity, economic sanctions would be imposed on oligarchs connected to the Kremlin.

Roo was intrigued by the freak coincidence. Both Stoddard and General Mikhailov were hunting the Paper Man Dossier. Stoddard was desperate to avoid scandal and a withdrawal from politics. Roo believed the Russian had feared Stoddard's exposure would bring about this investigation into his illegal business deals, and lead to the identity of the sleeper agent in his network who killed for him. He knew he was next on the Russian hitlist.

Bensonhurst, Brooklyn: March 2003

Chapter 49

ROO TOOK THE subway to Bensonhurst, and made his way in the fog past Devlin's apartment building. The street lights cast grotesque shadows, and he kept watch while walking in the dark alleys. It seemed exaggerated, but he sensed the killer could be on his trail.

Scenes of Katya with Big played in front of him as he walked toward Dino's, the neighborhood Italian restaurant. Although she had been cleared at the inquest, he questioned her motive for being with Stoddard that night.

As he approached Dino's, he saw Devlin near the window in one of the restaurant's large booths. He was nursing a drink and seemed far away in thought. The cop's thin face, which always reminded him of a tortured saint, seemed wary, on the lookout.

Roo had shrugged off his suspicions of his old boss. He reasoned that he had been delusional, suffering from his head injury, when he imagined Lucy's photograph appeared on Devlin's camera.

At their last meeting in his new office, Devlin had said he had rented an apartment in midtown, and soon after would be moving to Europe, where a lot of his business contacts were these days. Roo had trouble reconciling the change in him, trying to imagine the cop living in Europe, or even in Manhattan.

Devlin's face lit up when Roo entered the restaurant. He was wearing one of his well-tailored suits, and had come from a business meeting, although he wouldn't say more.

"Great to see you. Let's have a drink and order."

Roo had his usual spaghetti with meatballs.

"Make that the same and add a bottle of your house red. This is like old times. I heard you were in the UK and made contact with Matthew Knapp, who somehow escaped. Still on the run? Any news of him?"

"Not yet. He's innocent of his grandparents' murders. He was torn up by their deaths, and surrendered the dossier to me, claiming that a Russian had been hunting him for it. I believe he was kidnapped and taken to Russia, on orders from General Mikhailov Do you think their government would agree to extradite him?"

They waited while Dino, who welcomed them back, served the food himself. Then Devlin said, "I've been reading the newspaper accounts. As we both know, the Russians don't have an extradition treaty with the US. It would be more likely our government would request extradition for financial fraud. I'll talk to my contacts, but it probably will be futile." Devlin said.

"I know. Thanks."

They fell into silence, and were finishing their meal, when he summoned up the courage to discuss Katya. "I'm worried about her. She won't let me see her."

"It was bad luck that she became involved with Big Stoddard. He had a reputation with women before his campaign began, but his team managed to effectively hide it."

"I know she came to you for help."

"Yes, she was very upset. She told me about the blackmail letter and asked my advice. She was worried the story would leak and Big might blame her. I'm sorry now, but perhaps wrongly advised her to keep quiet about it; that it could get her in trouble."

Devlin drained his glass before going on. "But then, what else did she know about Stoddard's activities? Her motives seem suspect. Could they have been having an affair? What were the circumstances that led to his death? That severed hand was the worst thing I've ever seen."

This struck him to the heart. "I don't believe that." Roo was outraged at his comment about Katya.

"And I suppose you know I've been consulting Stumpy. He still suspects Matthew might have been involved in some way in the murders. And of course, the guy disappeared. I hope you're not assuming Knapp is completely innocent before you have all the evidence."

He tried to control his rising anger.

Devlin pressed on. "Even if he told you he was innocent, you don't know the truth. He could have been on drugs that night and with the killers. From the evidence, the grisly scene looked like crazed addicts killed his grandparents. He could have been faking his feelings about them. It seems too easy to blame this on the Russians."

Roo had nothing to say to him as they left the restaurant. His old boss knew he was angry.

"Hey, no hard feelings. I was asking what any detective on the case would. Let me know if you find anything."

Moscow: March 2003

The General

Chapter 50

FEAR OF THE shadows from the window had crept over him with the report of Big Stoddard's death.

He had not figured on the strange events, based only on chance, that had taken place—the major finding the interrogation file and attempting to defect; the blackmail letter to Stoddard from a mysterious source; and the death of the banker. Now Yoder had the dossier, which would be made public.

Destroying the dossier would have protected him and his wealth, and given him power to survive in luxury anywhere in the world. What is it they say in America? "Money talks."

The nervous twitch under his left eye became more pronounced as he tried to control his fear. He smoked a cigarette, and then another.

It was midmorning and there were no meetings scheduled for that day. While Dima hovered around his desk, the General asked Valentina to notify his driver that he wanted to travel to his *dacha* late this evening, and might be staying for a few days. She nodded briskly and said it would do him good to get away. After she brought his tea, he asked not to be disturbed, and locked his door.

He opened the safe and removed Kolya's interrogation file and Sofka's papers, then called his private courier to send them to his safe house. He reached in another compartment for cash in American dollars, and one of his false identities, which he had kept because he had never left his own survival to chance.

He searched in the bottom drawer of his closet and found the workman's clothes and shoes he had worn long ago, as a disguise when he was working undercover. Valentina had wanted to throw them out, but he had refused, and, joking, said they might go in a museum someday. There had been no change in his weight over the years, and they fit as they had when he was a young man.

Before he stripped and dressed again, he concealed the money and the fake ID into a belt around his waist. He packed a few old clothes in a bag and left his Mauser and holster in his safe. Dizzy with fear, but determined, he was taking his first perilous step toward freedom, and against state authority.

At dusk, a workman carrying a tattered bag walked swiftly across Lubyanka Square to the Metro, heading to Belorjsskaya Station on the Koltsevaya line.

***

Larnaca, Cyprus

Larnaca Airport was packed with Russian vacationers, seeking the sun. The man was simply dressed in workman's clothes and carried a small bag. He calmly surveyed the crowd with his sharp, pale eyes before going through customs.

Then he made his way toward the airport exit, searching for the driver who would take him to a private office where his banker would meet him in absolute secrecy. It must be done in person.

As yet, US investigators had failed to locate his Archangel account, well-hidden in the shadow banking system. Finding the account would be a long arduous task, which he hoped would take months, or even years.

Before Stoddard's unforeseeable death, he had ordered that Matthew be taken to a safe house, then to his yacht registered to a Romanian shipping company. It was anchored at the harbour in Cyprus and scheduled to sail to the UK the next day. He had contacted Oleg, head of his private ops group and tied to the mafia, to handle the rescue. It would be the last time he could issue orders before he was hunted down.

He also had transferred many of his relevant documents directly to Matthew. When he was kidnapped, Matthew had not been told the fate of his parents, and still believed they could be alive. Soon the General would face him, and explain what had happened to his father. He would tell him the truth.

During his useless struggle with Big Stoddard, and his failed attempts to find the dossier, he had begun to think that all his efforts, all the scheming he had done in the past, to get to the top, were a waste. He felt tired and drained, wanting to sink into some semblance of comfort, and to have a connection with another human who was not just part of his intelligence machine.

Finally, he was forced to face the painful truth. Kolya had attempted to defect only because he was in love. After years of ordering torture and death without compassion, he had realized he had no one to love, or to love him. Only fear of his enemies had driven him, left him wasted. Then he had made the fateful decision to rescue Matthew, the flesh and blood of Kolya, the only person he had ever loved. Now Matthew was all he had, and he would be his forever.

His last chance to escape with Matthew depended on Oleg, and the agent in place in the US. He had cleaned up before he left; two of his agents who knew about the dossier were eliminated, the only men spared were Dima and the Priest.

If Stoddard could be discredited, he might avoid detection. It was a risk, but the Priest would find and liquidate Yoder, and the one other source of evidence in the US.

Perhaps it was his subconscious that prompted his use of Chekhov in the messages to Stoddard. The writer's stories and plays were about the truth, and the sense of what is important in life. His quote, *"Life is not given twice,"* inspired him to take the risk with Matthew.

As he waited on a bench near the exit, his thoughts strayed back to Kolya, and his selection by the Raven. When the Raven had chosen him and Kolya, he had been plotting since 1918 to overthrow the communist government and place an aristocrat, or a descendant from the tsar's family on the throne. Was this why he picked Kolya? His friend's background had never been disclosed.

Impatient, he walked toward the door. The driver was still not at the appointed place. He stopped in alarm at this absence. Clammy sweat poured from his body.

A tiny, smiling man dressed in an immaculate uniform pushed out of the crowd toward him. Dima and his men had come to take him away. He would never see Matthew, never know him, and he thought how easily one fades into nothing after death. There would be no memory of him.

He sees again the nightmare which has always tormented him, waking him in terror throughout his life. He is back in Moscow, in a meeting. His former colleagues are shouting, accusing him. A plastic bag is shoved over his head before he is led to his death.

New York: March 2003

Roo

Chapter 51

THE "SHIT DID hit the fan" when the Paper Man Dossier was made public. Alice gave a copy to a friend who worked for the NY Times. The newspaper conducted a thorough check of the evidence before publishing the dossier two weeks later.

The Stoddard family was permanently disgraced. Frank Stoddard's medals for his valor fighting in WWII were removed from the bank's office, and he was posthumously given a dishonorable discharge. In the next months, the bank offered reparations to the holocaust victims, a last attempt to try to save the Stoddard reputation.

When the money laundering investigation began, the bank's stock had already reached a disastrous low, and threatened the stability of other financial institutions. Investors began withdrawing their deposits. The Federal Reserve announced they were stepping in to prevent the bank from failing and causing panic on Wall Street.

The day after the dossier became sensational news, Alice had come in from the library reading room holding several newspapers. With a quick glance at Roo, she hid them under some books she was carrying.

"What is that?"

"I hoped you wouldn't see it."

Alice surrendered the paper, with the front page interview, and the photograph of the widow, Missy Stoddard, and her two daughters in her Manhattan apartment. Missy, an attractive Park Avenue matron, was wearing a black long-sleeved dress; her dark hair was drawn back with a clip. She claimed Big was ignorant of his father's betrayal and his deal with the Nazis, and had only hired the Odessa Group to protect the family. She accused Katya of breaking up their marriage.

"This was our home before the affair and poor Big's death. It was very difficult for him. He was lured into a relationship with her and was determined to break it off. She became difficult and abusive, and threatened to go to the newspapers with lies. Before he died, he said he suspected her of being a Russian spy."

New York: March 2003

The Boy

Chapter 52

"PERFECTION!" HE EXCLAIMS aloud to himself and flexes his long sensitive fingers, his hands still smooth, in spite of age. He places them out in front of him, admiring them. They are still like a young boy's; the only undamaged part of his misshapen body that can still perform, always ready for his work. Yes, his hands are the beautiful part of him—they saved him.

His work occupies his mind, and only when he stops, the jagged fragments of the past intrude like pieces of broken glass, wounding him.

Each day he quickly eats his take-out meal from the café, a tiny hole-in-the-wall, several blocks away from the boardwalk. Marta, the nice woman behind the counter, always has the same food waiting for him. He can walk only a few steps without feeling his body give way, but it is easy to get to the café in his wheelchair.

Then he waits for Dot to check on him before he closes up the shop, locks the door for the night, and wheels through the hall to his room. Before he knows it, he falls into sleep and travels back to the camp and his lucky escape. Even in old age, he dreams he is The Boy in the book, waiting for the Golem.

The Golem holds a gun; his muddy face looks down at him, and then he is lifted up and rides on the giant's strong back. The Golem is running, then ducking into the forest away from the bombs. He stops, and gently places The Boy on the floor of a shed in the bombed-out train station. They wait until the explosions cease. Then, with enormous hands, he again lifts The Boy onto his back and hurries on. The Boy teeters on the edge of consciousness, and falls into blackness. When he wakes in a hospital bed, the man is gone, as though he had conjured him, as though he were the imaginary Golem in the book.

He does not remember how he arrived at this workshop. Only faint, ghostly scenes float by. Luisa speaks Russian to a man in a dark military tunic and high leather boots. His hypnotic, deep blue eyes stare down at him. Luisa leans over, whispering that an important person connected to the US government has sponsored him. Closing his eyes to blazing spotlights, he is carried on a stretcher through a long hall with many rooms and corridors. Metal doors clang shut behind him. He hears the roar of engines before he falls into black. When he regains consciousness, he finds that he has been wheeled into this warehouse filled with forgery equipment.

He suspected, but did not know, who this sponsor could be. He was always afraid and never asked questions. He once overheard Luisa say that the organization believed no one would ever suspect a cripple.

He always did the bidding of his mysterious patrons and was known for being discreet, often overhearing their conversations. Agents, intelligence officials, and shadowy figures from every country on the edge of the law came to him in secrecy for his expertise in forging visas, identity cards and passports, assured that all would be confidential.

In 1974 he worked at breakneck speed to alter the passports of Julia Knapp and Minna Johnson. He heard the agents speak of Julia's kidnapping, and the attempted defection of Nicholae Platov, a.k.a. Daniel Berger. Then he discovered, to his shock, that Nicolae was the grandson of Timur Platov; the man the Paper Man had finally identified as his savior. He did not learn until it was too late that Nicolae and Julia had a son named Matthew.

When Luisa died, he was broken and alone with no one to care for him. He feared he would die from neglect. Two months after her death, a new woman came into his life, requesting forged documents for someone in her department. Was it a coincidence or something planned? He did not know.

Hannah Winthrop was plain, with stringy hair and dowdy clothes. Her red nose gleamed without makeup. Soon after her first visit, she arrived at the warehouse in great distress. She had quit her high-security job, and was frightened and on the run from her company.

After he created her new documents, she became Dot Briscoe and gave up her identity as Hannah Winthrop. She altered her appearance and her personality, in complete denial of her background which had only brought her grief. She said she had devised a new career as a hotel manager. She vowed to always protect him.

New York: March 2003

Roo

Chapter 53

ROO WAS IN the library with Alice Jefferson Jones when Devlin called. As predicted, the Russians had refused to extradite the General.

Later that day, Ikon, Inc. announced General Mikhailov's retirement as chairman and CEO. He also had stepped down from his role as top advisor to Russia's intelligence committee.

Ikon stated that he had been in ill health for some time. The investigation of his finances by US authorities on money laundering charges had hardly begun, and Roo knew his retirement was the Russian government's attempt to avoid a potential scandal. Whatever torture or punishment the man would inevitably receive seemed justified for ordering the Knapp murders.

Alice broke into his thoughts. "I guess you haven't been able to talk to Katya."

He shook his head.

She looked apologetic. "There's another story in the 'Times' today, but I don't think you should read it."

He read it anyway. It was a feature on Katya, with the headline *The Party Girl*, detailing her background and sexual adventures in London and New York. Was this the woman he knew? Everything he thought about her seemed pointless after this. He threw the paper in the waste basket and tried to block out any thought of her so he could concentrate on the case.

He went back to his conversation with Devlin who suspected Matthew had written the blackmail letter to Stoddard, and re-examined the letter in the police department's evidence file. There was no signature, only a number at the end of the page. The number flashed in front of him, and suddenly he saw the tattoo on the man's arm. It had seemed so unlikely but he had received a forged passport from this man who was near death. The scene clicked in his mind and came together like a mosaic: the forged passports of Julia Knapp, Minna Johnson and Matthew; the counterfeit workshop at *Sachsenhausen*; the photographs of the Nazis Melmer and Weber at the concentration camp. He had not thought it possible, not in his wildest imagination that the forger, who was frail and old, would be capable of this. And why now, after all these years?

He put on his ski jacket and ball cap.

"Where are you going?" Alice said, "It's snowing out there."

Little Odessa, Brooklyn: March 2003

The Paper Man

Chapter 54

ONCE HE WAS Jacob Kohn, The Boy in the Book, but that person no longer existed. The prisoners in the forgery workshop had named him the Paper Man because his first job as the youngest worker was to handle the printed papers, drying them on a rack. He closed his eyes, and the room, smelling of ink, appeared in front of him. It was stacked with wooden crates, full of paper waiting for watermark inspection, and tables piled with bank notes.

He had planned to forge documents for the rest of his life in this Brooklyn workshop, a safe refuge from the dangerous outside world.

The newspaper article profiling Big Stoddard and his father, Frank, changed all that. Something broke inside him, a tear through the fog of his memory, bringing with it a rush of fierce hatred.

The recent newspaper photograph of Frank Stoddard came alive in front of him, and he was back in his hospital bed. He awoke to the smooth, handsome face with eyes like stone; the man in uniform leaning over him, terrifying him with questions about the counterfeit factory and the dossier.

This same man, Major General Francis Stoddard, lauded as an American hero, was a traitor to his country who had schemed with the mass murderer, Himmler. Frank Stoddard had a perfect life after the war, profiting from the torture and murder of holocaust victims. His death earlier this year had not diminished the forger's obsession with taking revenge on the family.

The Paper Man's eyes misted with pure hate. The devil's son, Big, had been a candidate for US Senate. He had vowed that he would not permit this indignity, which dishonored all who died in the camps. He had always hidden in fear, avoiding the truth. This time he had taken on the responsibility of making the monsters pay for their evil, and had found the courage to step into the real world and face his enemy.

He thought of that day when he had fled into, the forest carrying the Paper Man Dossier. The dossier's numbered accounts and plans, records of pure evil, were stored in his mind. He had believed his evidence, committed to memory, could bring about an investigation, and the end of Big's campaign and his bank.

After Dot sent his blackmail letter, demanding that Stoddard withdraw from the primary, he had heard the story about the identity of this Matthew Knapp, wrote twice to the young man, warning him he would be the target of ruthless killers.

When they met, he had not expected Matthew, with his high cheekbones, light hair, and large frame, to look so much like the Russian, Timur, who had rescued him. The young man was frightened and in danger. The Paper Man knew he was responsible, and had forged a passport and visas for Matthew, under the name Henry Lewis.

Now, after Big Stoddard's death and the release of the dossier to the newspapers, the Paper Man sits in his wheelchair, finished with his work of the day. He contemplates the results of his revenge.

Although the banker's destruction was his desire, he didn't foresee the unintended consequences. To his profound sorrow, his blackmail letter set in motion the tragedy in the Midwest farmhouse.

It is late and the Paper Man peers out the small warehouse window into darkness relieved only by the distant street lights. The snow has turned to a cold rain. He shudders, he does not like the rain. It takes him back to standing in the *Appelplatz* in the early morning dark, waiting for the *Aufstehen*, the roll call, and watching his father being dragged away.

He hears a clicking sound. Someone is breaking the locks. The door opens. He turns in his wheelchair to look up at the intruder. "I knew you would come for me. You are one of the Devils."

Chapter 55

ROO WAS CHOKING and out of breath from running when he reached the warehouse in Little Odessa. The door was open. The strange, cracked cry of the Paper Man, and a low guttural voice, echoed through the vast room.

The Paper Man sat in his wheelchair in the middle of a plastic sheet spread on the floor, facing a shadowy figure who held a large knife to his throat. A growl came from him. "I am the Slayer of Souls; the Priest. You have been useful, but I cannot let you live. You must be sacrificed."

The killer raised his head toward the ceiling and cried, "Last day of last days. Final sin. Final redemption." Roo jumped him from behind, and slipped on the sheet and fell. He grappled for the knife, and threw the monster back on the floor. He rose, howling, and came at Roo again. Huge, dark wrinkles ran down his cheeks like rivulets from a bloody stream. His eyes, like fiery coals bore down on Roo. His black shirt was open; a large hammered cross swung on his bare chest.

Roo shouted, "No! No!" Pain shot through his chest. There was an eerie ringing in his ears, the sound overcome by the loud whirr of the wheel chair moving toward him. He heard the Paper Man cry out for the Golem to rescue him.

New York: March 2003

Chapter 56

ROO WOKE WITH the sound of the wheelchair still whirring in his head. Devlin's gruesome face loomed above the hospital bed, and the cry from the Paper Man rang in his ears. His first thought was that he had been an idiot; not identifying the old man who had once made a fake passport for him. He had believed Devlin, who had told him the forger had died. It had not occurred to him that the counterfeiter could have been the real Paper Man who had written the blackmail letter, until he remembered the prison number tattooed on the man's arm.

Alice was sitting at his bedside. He had been in Mt. Sinai hospital for four days, recovering from a knife wound in his chest, and an injury to his hand from the Paper Man's wheelchair.

"Oh!" Her glasses steamed from tears dripping down her cheeks. "I'm so glad you're ok. I'm still in shock that Devlin was the murderer." She trembled. "It's horrifying, what he did to the

Knapps. That monster could have killed you any time before you rescued the Paper Man, but how could we know?"

"What is a Golem?" he asked Alice.

"After you muttered that yesterday, I thought you had gone off your head, but then I did some research. You won't believe this, but the Golem is a giant monster, created from clay, by a rabbi, to save the Jews from a pogrom in 16th century Prague. According to legend, the Golem was kept chained in the old Prague synagogue, and could only be released if the Jewish people were in danger.

"It seems from reports that Jacob Kohn, who insists on being called the 'Paper Man,' was calling out for this Golem when a patrolman noticed the door to the warehouse was open and heard his screams," she said, with a quizzical look on her fac.

She drew her chair closer to his bed. Her sharp eyes seemed to probe into his thoughts. "I think he wanted to believe that the Golem would save him. You know, we all have devices to escape our traumas. I think yours are silence and denial," she said in a crisp voice.

Alice's visits were a painful reminder of his separation from Katya. He had heard nothing from her, even though the attack and Devlin's death were reported on TV and in the newspapers. Alice was right; he couldn't reach out to Katya.

He was released from the hospital after five days, and the following week attended the inquest into Devlin's death. He was astonished when Dot Briscoe, a macabre study in pink, pushed the Paper Man in his wheelchair into the courtroom and identified herself as his nurse. People stared, wide-eyed, at Dot. It was difficult to reconcile her appearance with her stated role as nurse.

At the inquest opening, the Paper Man, who looked slightly bewildered when he was identified as Jacob Kohn, stated that Roo had saved his life, and that he had not been injured in the attack.

The jury was shocked by the photographs of Devlin's mashed in face, with wheelchair tire marks visible, but concluded after the coroner's report and Roo's testimony, that the Paper Man was innocent of murder. They were convinced his wheelchair had spun out of control during Devlin's knife attack.

Roo had some doubt that the Paper Man was telling the truth, but asked himself, who wouldn't believe this elderly, crippled, holocaust survivor with a number tattooed on his arm? The sympathetic jury listened attentively when he turned his shattered face toward them and rattled out his testimony, choking at times on the words.

The police had found Devlin's secret apartment, and the photographs, with notes celebrating the murders he'd committed as "the Priest, the Slayer of Souls." The grisly evidence proved that he had killed the Knapps at General Mikhailov's orders. The press did not print the gory photograph, nor those of Devlin's death.

But another shocking story came to light. Devlin had taken the identity of a soldier who had died in Vietnam, and had become a sleeper agent, disguised an American cop. Roo found it hard to face up to the truth about the real Devlin. Someone he had thought was a mentor and friend had been plotting against him, and intended to kill him. He remembered the mysterious trips his former boss had taken, and his thorough knowledge of the case, now all too late to save the Knapps. The brilliant craziness of the killer was chilling. According to his deranged jottings, in his early years in Siberia,

Devlin had bee initiated into the *Khlyst* Cult. Their main tenet; one had to sin to be saved.

He wondered if his vision of the figure with the knife walking across the hill in Tecumseh County had been a sign, a warning. He had not trusted his instincts and believed he was the crazy one, imagining the photograph on Devlin's phone, of Lucy posing minutes before her brutal murder.

He reflected on the strange events surrounding the case, mystified at the randomness, the interconnected stories, and the series of bizarre coincidences.

After the inquest Dot had taken the Paper Man back to his home. Roo didn't think the frail old man would continue his work after his counterfeiting activities were made public. He was exonerated from any crime, when it was learned that at age 12 he had been a prisoner in *Auschwitz*. He survived only because he was chosen to be trained as a forger, at the secret Nazi counterfeit group at *Sachsenhausen*.

Roo went to the warehouse to check on the Paper Man. He rang the bell, and after 10 minutes, Dot, in another version of her pink outfit, came to the door. "He is very ill, and doesn't want to speak to anyone. There is nothing to explain. He thanks you for saving his life. Don't call again."

Tecumseh County: Spring 2003

Chapter 57

ROO KNOCKED AT the door of Linny's apartment, and she answered after he identified himself. He was surprised at her put-together appearance. Her pale hair was caught up in a ponytail. She was wearing jeans, a white shirt, and an expensive weed jacket. But it was more than that. She seemed confident and happy.

He hated to tell her why he had come.

"Hi," she said, smiling, but backing away.

"I'm sorry. Matthew is still missing. I've done as much as I could. Authorities have not found a trace of him. There is no way of knowing—" He stopped short. "I tried to call you several times."

"Oh, I'm sorry." She turned red. "I should have called you before now. He's alive."

He stepped back, off balance for a moment. "How do you know?"

"I couldn't believe it. He phoned from Cyprus, and said he was leaving there. I told him that they had caught the murderer and he was free, but he says that he can't come back because the killers are after him."

She hesitated, then went on. "A week after the call, he sent money to my post office address. It was a lot of cash, hidden in boxes of candy, and passed through customs as a gift."

Roo realized Matthew had used the numbered Swiss bank account on the photograph to collect the money. Although a numbered account adds a layer of some secrecy, he was lucky he had not been identified as yet.

"I don't know where he is now—There was no return address. The package was postmarked from Switzerland."

She looked embarrassed, and her voice faltered. "There's something else. I didn't give you all the documents that Matthew left with me. I didn't completely trust you, or the sheriff."

She went to a small kitchen drawer and brought out a heavy envelope. "Matthew asked me to keep this safe for when he could return. The killers could identify him with these documents."

She guessed, looking at his face, what he was thinking. "I don't have to keep the money. Would you arrest me for that?"

"I have no reason to." He had decided he would not report this. It might help the killers locate Matthew, if he sent more money.

She looked at her watch. He saw that it was new. "Sorry, I have to go. I have a job at the library, thanks to Fiona."

"I'll give you a lift."

"After tomorrow it will be easy to get to work." She climbed into his truck, still holding the envelope. "I'm moving into a new apartment with two other roommates. It's walking distance."

Her voice quivered, and her eyes brimmed with tears. "If Matthew returns we could maybe have a normal life. He asked me to wait for him. I am saving most of the money. I know he'll come back. I'm frightened after all that has happened. Could you keep this for me?"

New York: Spring 2003

Chapter 58

1974

My dearest Julia, These fragments were torn from my grandfather's journal. Keep these records of family history safe. I have translated them in the event I need to establish my identity. I will return for you. Love forever, Kolya

"SO, THESE DOCUMENTS tell the last of the stories connected with the Paper Man Dossier," Alice said.

Roo had returned to New York and was sitting with Alice Jefferson Jones in Bryant Park cafe behind the Main Public Library. They were ending lunch with chocolate brownies, which neither could resist.

Timur's crumpled and soiled papers, along with the English version, were arranged in order on the table. Alice had contacted a Russian friend on the Columbia faculty, who authenticated the translation. Over the last two days, they had been sorting through the documents, searching for some clue to finding Matthew.

"All we know so far is that we think he's alive," Roo said. "Linny is sure of it."

Bright sun shone through the budding trees, but the early spring air was chilly, and he was bundled up in his old ski jacket. Alice was wrapped in a white, cashmere coat, over a silvery gown. A small tiara with diamonds poked through her hair. She was attending a dinner and ball that evening and didn't want to waste time changing clothes before Malcolm's car arrived to pick her up. Roo thought she looked spectacular, as did some others who admired her from their tables. It was as though a princess had materialized in the park. Her life of balls, receptions, and exclusive dinners seemed foreign to her research at the library.

Alice put on her glasses, and studied the photographs found in the Knapp barn: the man on horseback with the Caucasus mountains behind him, and his group photo with Cheka comrades.

"This is Timur Alexandrovich Platov, grandfather of Kolya, Nicolae Platov. Would you believe it? He is Matthew's Russian great-grandfather? What a surprise it must have been for Matthew to find these documents and photos from faraway Russia, hidden in a barn in the Midwest."

Roo said, "Timur had to be on the run when he ripped out these pages."

1968

For Nicholae Andreivich Platov, Kolya, my grandson.
Soon I will meet with you for the first and last time.
We are the only survivors of our family, erased from history by Stalin
and his followers. I give what is left of my journal to you.

This is my story.

1917

I was born a Terek Cossack, in the North Caucasus mountains near
Chechnya. When the revolution began, I became a committed
Bolshevik, rebelling against my family, who were loyal to the Tsar,
and abandoning my studies at the tsar's military academy. I was a
true believer and worshipped Lenin, inspired by his vision of the way
forward to a glorious future.

1918

After Leon Trotsky signed the peace treaty at Brest-Litovsk, ending
our part in "The Great War," Civil War raged between our
Bolshevik government and those Tsarist and foreign interventionists
who opposed us.

I was trained as a Cheka agent and assigned to the headquarters
in Pyatigorsk, one of the spa towns in the North Caucasus. Spies
were everywhere, and my job was to hunt them down. We searched
homes of aristocrats, tsarist officers, and the wealthy who had fled from
Moscow and Petersburg, confiscating their money, jewels, and weapons.
We posted a list of enemies to be kidnapped or killed if they did not
pay ransom.

Later I was appointed leader of the prodotriad, in charge of requisitioning food supplies from the Kulaks. I eagerly followed Lenin's orders and took great satisfaction in punishing these bandits for hiding food. We liquidated the worst of them. Kulak 'fist' was the name we gave these hoarders, bloodsuckers.

"Look at this." Roo held out a creased soiled leaflet.

Comrades! The kulak uprising in your five districts must be crushed without pity … You must make examples of these people.

> **(1) Hang (I mean hang publicly, so that people see it) at least 100 kulaks, rich bastards, and known bloodsuckers.**
> **(2) Publish their names.**
> **(3) Seize all their grain.**
> **(4) Single out the hostages per my instructions in yesterday's telegram.**

Do all this so that for miles around people see it all, understand it, tremble, and tell themselves that we are killing the bloodthirsty kulaks and that we will continue to do so …

Yours, Lenin.
P.S. Find tougher people

Chapter 59

ALICE SHUDDERED, AND turned to the next pages. "This part seems to be a love story; a relief from all that savagery."

1918–1919

Pyatigorsk: I was a boevik, the name for a true warrior, a hit with the women and with the men I commanded. Dedicated to the class war, I prided myself on my toughness and was without sympathy or mercy.

But life took me on a different path when I met Irina and love found me forever. All the women I had known faded into nothing next to her.

I first saw her while riding on horseback through the Pyatigorsk market. She was dressed in a worn, faded safaran, the long peasant dress, but I was attracted to her bright blue eyes and beautiful Russian face. Her light brown hair shimmered with streaks of gold in the sunlight. Her shy smile filled me in that instant with desire.

She trembled with fear when I dismounted and introduced myself. I assumed she would be flattered by my attention. You might not believe it when you see me in my present state, but I was handsome then, well-built and much admired in my Cheka leather coat and polished boots, a Mauser pistol in my holster, and my kinzal at my side.

She resisted me at first, but I did not give up. Every day when I was free from duty I waited for her at the market. After I persisted for some time, she lost some of her shyness and began to talk to me, to trust me.

She said her parents were dead, and she lived a distance from the town, with relatives named Orgulov, who were prosperous farmers. I was surprised that she spoke Russian with an accent, and was vague about her background, although I pressed her for details. I wanted to believe her story, and knew as a Cheka agent that I could be taking a risk, but I was trapped by an overwhelming desire. I did not care; I only wanted to possess her.

The fateful day she did not appear at the market, I rode on horseback toward the farmhouse, and found her bathing in a small hidden inlet of the Podkumok River. She was beautiful, like a goddess coming out of the water. I called to her, and she yielded to me. We laid together in an abandoned hut, her arms wrapped around me, clinging to me and begging me to save her. I vowed to protect her.

Our passion incontrollable, we continued to meet in secret in the hut in the forest. There was risk from bandits and dispossessed kulaks roaming in the forest, but even more danger of being discovered by Cheka comrades. Our son, Andrei, was born toward the end of the year, and without our attending, was christened as a member of the Orgulov family in the local church.

Commissar Mironov at Cheka Headquarters had become suspicious of my constant visits to this village and household. I was unaware that we were being watched.

Soon after Andrei was born, I was ordered to conduct a raid on a kulak village a great distance from Pyatigorsk. Before I left, I met her in the forest; I did not know this would be our farewell.

We danced like enchanted creatures of the forest. I opened my arms to her, and we raced in a circle around the trees in a wild ecstasy before falling together. This was the last time I was happy; my last memory of Irina. After I returned from the raid, I rushed to see her. The Orgulov farmhouse had been razed to the ground. There was no trace of Irina and Andrei.

Stunned with grief, I stared, unbelieving at the charred ruins. An old man, bundled in rags, appeared from a dugout shed on a path next to the ruin, and stood close to me, He whispered that the Orgulovs had been shot and pointed to the place in the farmyard where they had been buried by neighbors. He claimed a woman had been taken away on horseback by some important man. Siberia, they said. When I asked about my son, he shook his head and said he knew nothing about a child. Fearful, and unwilling to say more, he hobbled away.

I searched for Irina and Andrei everywhere, not believing they were dead. My frantic efforts were noticed by the authorities, who discovered that Irina was not a member of the Orgulov family. Her identity was unknown.

I was brought before the investigative commission of the Revolutionary Tribunal, accused of betraying the revolution by consorting with an enemy, a spy. My outstanding work for the Cheka spared me from harsh punishment, but I was demoted and remained under suspicion. My career as one of the young, leading Bolsheviks was over. I was never cleared of the accusations.

In 1921, The Bolshevik government was victorious in the civil war. I should have been triumphant and happy, but I no longer cared. I was consumed with my search for Irina and Andrei.

Chapter 60

1936–1938

Caucasus: The Purge Order, which brought the Red Terror to the country, came from Stalin. His aim was to wipe out the Old Bolsheviks, and others in the government who opposed him and his plans. The mass murders opened the way for him to become dictator. The mark on my record gave the secret police—death squads under Yezhov, the head of the NKVD—an excuse to kill all my family in the Caucasus.

I too was listed among those early Bolsheviks to be eliminated and escaped to the Caucasus, with my comrade, Peter von Krantz, a.k.a. the Raven, who had many supporters in the area. He had begun planning to topple the government. We survived through the Raven's ingenuity. I remained in the Caucasus and secretly worked to end Stalin's rule. I was disillusioned and no longer believed.

It was fortunate that in the confusion of the revolution, some of the files for the Caucasus Cheka were incomplete, and there was no record of my true identity on police registers. I was free, after the great terror ran its course.

Chapter 61

THEY WERE SILENT, thinking of the numbers who were killed, just to make up quotas during the terror. Then Roo said, "The papers skip to nine years after the purge. We don't know anything about his life until 1945."

February 1945
My involvement with the Paper Man dossier was an accident of fate. When WWII began, I was conscripted into the intelligence section in the army, and my fluency in German led to my post to the special unit SMERSH, acronym for "Death to Spies." My orders were to advance into enemy territory in front of our troops, and kill traitors in the front lines.

During the Red Army's invasion of Germany, I was assigned to the forward units of General Zhukov's First Belorussian Front. That evening and the following day, exhausted, my face and body filthy with mud from combat, I was searching the area when I heard screaming and crying, and came upon this boy.

He had been caught escaping from Sachsenhausen and was being brutally kicked and beaten by a Nazi guard. I felt outrage, even though I had killed many, without caring. I shot the bastard Nazi.

The boy was severely injured, and begged me to save him and the other prisoners. Before losing consciousness, he gave me a pouch he had been hiding under his coat. To my surprise, I discovered the pouch was filled with teeth. Accepting this from the boy put me on a course that led to disaster. I carried him a long distance back toward our advancing army, and left him with a hospital unit.

Although it seemed incredible, I suspected some information must be hidden in the teeth, and examined each one. It took me some time before I discovered the microdot embedded on one of them.

As an intelligence officer, I had been trained to work with microfilm and microdots. When I opened the microdot, using the equipment at headquarters, I found the Paper Man Dossier. It contained classified SS-listed accounts of gold stolen from concentration camp victims. The files were printed in English and German, which struck me as unusual.

Then I discovered there was something extremely dangerous in the documents: a conspiracy, a deal to make Reichsführer Heinrich Himmler the new ruler of the Third Reich. To my shock, I recognized one of the names in the conspiracy, a Colonel Ivan Bokov. He was an important member of SMERSH, under Beria's former deputy, Victor Semonovich Abakumov.

There were photographs of the three, Reichsführer Heinrich Himmler, Major General Francis Stoddard, an American, and the

Russian, Colonel Ivan Bokov. This was more evidence that Colonel Ivan Bokov was a traitor.

Alarmed by this information, I worked in secret and made a hard copy of the dossier with the negatives of the microdot, which included photographs, more records, and a bank account number. I should have been aware that I was under surveillance, like every soul in the country.

My room was searched. They discovered the bag of teeth and were fooled by it. Alert to the danger, I deserted my unit and went into hiding, and was hunted ceaselessly by Bokov's men, My fate was to become one of the many vagrants wandering in the ruins of the country. I remain a fugitive to this day.

Chapter 62

1947

Khabarovsk: I fled with the Paper Man Dossier to Moscow, and at Yaroslavskaya Station, caught the Trans-Siberian Railway hiding in one of the freight cars.

I arrived at, Khabarovsk, close to the Chinese border suffering from starvation, and begged for food at the station. A sympathetic babushka gave me bread and a kopek, which I spent on drink. I wandered, staggering and falling, through the forest to a settlement too small to have a name, and fell on the doorstep of Varvara, a poor old widow. She offered me work in exchange for a room once used as a stable, and one meal a day. That night, I crept out and buried the dossier in a wooden box, in Varvara's back garden.

I formed a desperate plan, to use the dossier to barter with Bokov's enemies, to find Irina and Andrei, and escape across the. border. I attempted to contact comrades I knew from the past revolutionary days, but was unsuccessful. They had never returned from the war.

My one consolation was a rough tavern in one of the old wooden houses, where cheap vodka was available. I swept the floor and did odd jobs for a drink. I often stayed until late at night, nursing my ration. The aged bar owner was friendly, but, fearing discovery, I kept to myself.

The stranger who walked in was a surprise, as no one came to this desolate place. He was dressed in worn clothes and high boots. His hair was cropped close around his handsome face, and his large, dark eyes gave him away. I was overjoyed. The Raven had come to save me. I asked how he found me. He didn't answer, but then his vast secret network must still have been in place.

He sat down and ordered a drink. "I heard that Bokov is looking for you. You have a dossier, some evidence that he is a traitor?"

"Yes," I said. I did not know how he received the information, but realized he was aware of Bokov's many interrogations.

"Bokov was involved in a conspiracy with a Nazi leader. He is a traitor. It will mean his death. I will bring the evidence to you. I am here because an old man who witnessed the killings and fire at the Orgulov farmhouse, told me that a woman was carried off to Siberia. I know it was foolish but I hoped to find some trace of Irina and my son."

He ordered me another drink. "I have bad news. I received information that your son, Andrei, and his wife, Vera, perished in a camp during the war."

I cried aloud and he tried to comfort me and said their child—you, Kolya—had survived. Then he took from his pack a photograph of a young woman believed to be Irina. He had bought it from an impoverished Russian, a waiter at the Astor House Hotel in Shanghai. Although years have passed, I believe that the woman is

*Irina, but have only this photograph to prove her existence. I never
found her.*

*That night I returned to Varvara's and dug up the papers,
intending them for the Raven. When I arrived the next evening at the
meeting place by the Khabarovsk Station, police were everywhere. I fled
with the dossier.*

*I suffer great hardship as a beggar and have hidden from Bokov
and his men for many years. Still the traitor has not given up. You
must be wary of him, although he is old now and has gone out of favor,
and is no longer as powerful. Bokov and the Raven are bitter enemies.
Both still search for the dossier. I give it to you now in hopes that The
Raven will be saved.*

Roo said, "We don't know what happened to Timur after this
meeting, He could have gone on to try to find Irina, but then he
somehow gets to Moscow in 1968 for the meeting with his
grandson Kolya."

"Kolya must have become aware that he was being followed by
Bokov, still out there in 1974, hunting the dossier, to save himself
and expose the Raven's coup. And this is how the poor guy ends
up," Alice said.

Roo continued. "The dossier became dangerous again when
The Paper Man sent Stoddard the blackmail letter. The coincidences
are mind boggling." They sat for a few minutes in silence.

"And Matthew is the fourth generation of his family to be
hunted down for the dossier," she said.

"When I met Matthew at the pub, he insisted his parents were
in love. I wasn't sure I believed that, until now."

"I know it sounds soppy and exaggerated, but to me, this complicated story with all its twists and turns is really about love. There is another love story here, but I don't know the ending." Alice said.

Roo turned away, knowing what she meant.

"Please don't be angry. I know I shouldn't interfere, but I've been in touch with Katya. As you know, we were always friendly, and she trusts me. She has not gone to Europe, but is in seclusion. I've convinced her to see you; told her that you are not disgusted or angry." She looked at him. "Is this true?"

He could not answer.

"Why did you come back, then? I thought it was to try to see Katya."

He had come back and had moved to a small hotel near midtown, living without her, and at this point, without a chance of seeing her.

She said, "You know, after we learned that the General used Chekhov as his signature on emails to Stoddard, I began reading about the author. One of his quotations remains with me.

To fear love is to fear life, and those who fear life are already three parts dead."

Chapter 63

ROO THOUGHT OVER what Alice had said, and in spite of Stumpy's protests, stayed in New York, determined to see Katya. He assured the sheriff he was still working Matthew's case.

The State Department investigated Matthew's possible entry into Russia using the passport of "Henry Lewis," with no results. His last contact was with Linny, but she had not heard from him since the call from Cyprus. He had just simply disappeared.

There was more bad publicity for Katya. She had been cleared of being an accessory to Stoddard's death, but was humiliated and disgraced by the scandal, and incessantly hounded by reporters. One headline, *A Fistful of Hair*, seemed a permanent reminder. The media couldn't get enough of the scandal.

Alice told him that Katya had been living upstate, but was back in New York City, and was staying at the townhouse spa. "She usually goes out very early in the morning, to avoid the press."

The next day Roo was at the townhouse at 7 a.m., and waited across the street near a newsstand. To his astonishment, Lady Caroline was on the cover of Vogue's spring issue. The feature article described her as the aristocratic new wife of a 75 year-old Russian billionaire, coping with running five houses and a yacht. At least she hadn't ended up in the morgue, which had been a possibility. An opportunist, she had ditched Rupert, who may well have ended up in a mortuary, and quickly latched on to her new source of income. It made him uncomfortable to compare her attraction to powerful magnates with Katya's past behavior.

Yet when he saw her come out of the building, he rushed down the street toward her, grabbed her arm, turned her around to face him and hugged her tightly.

"Oh, it's you?" Her eyes sparkled with tears. He waited for her to tell him to go away. Instead, she curled her body into his, and they walked down the street to a diner which opened early. They sat in the back, hoping to avoid any reporters. He stared, drinking in her loveliness.

"Why did you come after me, or even want to see me? I feel so humiliated. I was trying to make it easy for you to go away."

After they ordered breakfast he was silent for a while, then said, "Why did you get mixed up with him?"

"I can't explain it. I admit I was attracted to Big, and I was angry with you. And it was exciting to be part of the campaign, doing good. He promised to contribute to my charities and help publicize them. I thought he was a good person, and didn't realize that he had hired me to get to you. I was stupid, and believed it was because I was talented, and could help the campaign." She turned away for a moment before going on.

"He would take me out to dinner and then eventually began to question me about you, about the case. I had nothing to tell him. You had disappeared. You never told me anything. How could I know? But he didn't believe me." Roo hated it that he had made her vulnerable.

He couldn't help himself; had to know. "What happened that night?" Images of her torn blouse, her shoes left in the office, and her hair clutched in Big's fist, rose in front of him.

She took a deep breath. "He picked me up at the spa and said he had some special work for me. Somehow, he found out that I saw the blackmail letter. He seemed different, almost hostile, and said you had the dossier. He kept threatening me, asking where you were. I didn't know."

She trembled, and moved away from him. "I was really scared. He shouted that I was a liar, and, and grabbed me, ripping my clothes and hurting me. I thought he was going to rape me. I kicked him and he went after me like he was going to kill me. I just ran—and then."

She began to weep. "I didn't mean for him to die. It was terrible, and all my fault. And then I didn't know about Devlin, and had thought he would help me when I went to him and told him about the letter. He was a killer, a beast."

Roo moved close beside her and took her in his arms. He realized he had to accept her weaknesses, just as she did his inability to speak about his feelings, his need for privacy, and his obsession with whatever case he was on. She was always tolerant and forgiving in spite of her waywardness, getting into trouble, and always seeking attention.

He held her more tightly, thinking that it was all right that they couldn't finally settle into each other; that it was "on-again, off-again," as Ben said. Maybe that was the nature of their relationship and neither of them really wanted to be like Ben and Fiona. Maybe this suited them.

The words from *Birches* filled his head as he kissed her. He wasn't sure he believed the last lines but hoped they were true.

> *May no fate wilfully misunderstand me*
> *And half grant what I wish and snatch me away*
> *Not to return. Earth's the right place for love:*
> *I don't know where it's likely to go better.*

Epilogue
New York: Spring 2003

Chapter 64

ROO PULLED ON his jeans and a sweatshirt and crept out of bed, not wanting to disturb Katya. She woke up, screaming, and couldn't sleep the rest of the night, tormented by nightmares of Abigail, her guardian, warning her that the killers were coming to get her.

She remained distraught over facing the press, but Geoffrey had convinced her that public interest in the scandal would fade, and they could reopen the gallery next month with an exhibition of American primitives. He had been successful in canvasing for loans and sales, mainly in the US. "No more Russians," he said.

Roo went into the kitchen and ate a bowl of cornflakes while reviewing the surprising turn of events since he had discovered that Devlin was the psychopath killer.

Last week Ikon Inc, had announced that General Mikhailov had died of heart failure. Funeral services would be held with full honors in a closed-casket ceremony, in the historic House of the Unions, where Joseph Stalin had lain in state in 1953.

The investigation into the General's finances and his connections to the Kremlin was stalled. Then yesterday, the federal investigators cancelled the probe, citing lack of evidence. Roo was outraged and disappointed. This had not turned out the way he wanted. There would be no sanctions on the Russians. The oligarch had been intent on killing him and Matthew, and he was certain another murderous figure would soon replace him.

After it was discovered that Devlin was the killer, the Knapp tragedy gradually began to fade in importance from the Paint Creek community. Matthew was no longer a murder suspect, but Roo hadn't given up on finding him, and had received news yesterday that he was alive. Linny had phoned, and said Matt had contacted her from Budapest. He was safe, but still in hiding, and couldn't return home and that he was searching for his Russian relatives.

Roo took the elevator downstairs to the gallery, past the ladders and equipment for installing the exhibition and went into the office where Katya stored the Blood Archive, the Romanov documents collected by her mother.

He sensed he was missing something, even though the Knapp case was solved. He wondered in frustration whether he would ever know what really happened in the past. Letters from witnesses, photographs, and other documents could only partially recreate events from earlier times. Timur's excerpts from his journal turned his mind to the Raven, a.k.a. Peter von Krantz. The spy had been a mysterious figure in Russia during the Revolution, through WWII and the Cold War, until his death in 1977.

Roo remained intrigued by the Raven, a lingering shadow behind each of his cases, and whose clandestine operations were inextricably tied to the last Tsar and his family. Circumstantial evidence in the Blood Archive indicated that the Raven could have been involved in rescuing the Romanov children.

Although it was generally accepted that the Romanov bodies had been found, some skeptics questioned the DNA results, believing the test samples were extracted from earlier Romanovs buried in St. Petersburg's Ss. Peter and Paul Cathedral.

He went into the files and opened the thumb drive, which led him back to the Russian revolution and the imprisonment of the Tsar and his family in Ekaterinburg, where they were photographed and identified like common criminals.

The Cheka identity cards, mug shots taken in 1918 by their Cheka captors, Vasily Pankratov and Alexandr Nikolsky, came up on the screen. There was a number for each card above the photos: Tsarevich Alexei, identified as Citizen Alexei Nikolaievich Romanov and the number 29-34-08. Number 29-34-09 belonged to one of his sisters, Grand Duchess Anastasia Nikolaievna Romanova. The third card, noted as added later, number 29-34-10 was that of another sister, Grand Duchess Maria Nikolaievna Romanova. On his last case, Roo had found the number 29-34-11, on the back of the photo of the girl believed to be Tatiana. Grand Duchess Olga was the only Romanov duchess not accounted for in the identity cards.

He knew this was probably crazy, but he opened the Knapp case file and examined the photograph found in the Knapp barn. A woman in a glittering evening dress poses at a table in a crowded ballroom, with two men in tuxedos. *Shanghai, Astor House Hotel* was printed at the top of the creased, sepia photograph. His eyes rested on *No. 12?* scrawled at the top margin of the picture.

He was stunned. How had he missed significance of *No. 12?* ? He would never know who wrote this message or who received it.

He could only guess that it was someone who wanted to identify the young woman.

Then, he detected a slight mark—a small, crossed line on the woman's forearm—which was raised over the table. He scrambled around in the desk drawer, and picked up a magnifying glass to study it more closely.

He and Alice had thought it was a flaw in the photograph, but he saw now that it seemed to be a bent cross, tattooed in fine lines. It was a swastika, called at that time in history the "Heart of Buddha," and later adopted by the Nazis.

Before the revolution, the swastika was a favorite sign of the last Russian Empress Alexandra Feodorovna; a symbol of happiness. She placed it everywhere she could, scratching it in the windows of the Ipatiev House while the royal family were prisoners.

Roo went over it all again, thinking that if the children had survived they would have been scattered to the wind; hidden. What was the mystery still remaining?

Timur did not mention this swastika or the No. 12? in his description of Irina. Was he trying to hide her identity? Was there enough circumstantial evidence to believe it was possible? It suddenly flashed through his mind; Matthew might be searching for traces of her, his great grandmother. Could this be the last photograph of Grand Duchess Olga?

The noisy morning traffic on the street outside the gallery faded. The years slid away, and for a moment he saw them together, whirling, dancing in the forest, Timur and the mysterious young woman.

Biographies of Historical Figures
The Paper Man Dossier

Yuri Andropov: (1914–1984) Leader of the Soviet Union from 1982 to 1984. He was head of the KGB, Russia's State Security Service from 1967 to 1982 and known for his ruthlessness in putting down the Hungarian uprising in 1956, and for the brutality of his agents. He died of ill health in Moscow and was buried in the Kremlin wall.

Lavrenty Beria: (1899–1953) Chief of Soviet Security and Secret Police, NKVD during World War II. Deputy Premier of USSR from 1946 to 1953. In August 1920, he was Managing Director of the Central Committee of the Azerbaijan Communist Party. The following year, he became Deputy Chief of the Secret Operations Department of the Azerbaijan Cheka. During Stalin's purge (1937–38) he and his organization tortured and killed many of the dictator's political enemies. After Stalin's death in March 1953, he made a grab for power but was arrested by a group led by

Khrushchev, Molotov, and Malenkov. He was executed, cremated, and buried in an unmarked grave in a forest near Moscow.

Mikhail Markovich Borodin: (1884–1951) born Mikhail Markovich Gruzenberg; a Bolshevik revolutionary and Communist International agent. He was an advisor to Sun Yat-sen and the Kuomintang (KMT) in China during the 1920s. After a 1927 purge of Communists from the Kuomintang, he fled China and returned to the Soviet Union in 1927.

Leonid Brezhnev: (1906–1982) Leader of the Soviet Union. General Secretary of the Central Committee of the Communist Party of the Soviet Union from 1964 until his death. He succeeded Khrushchev and ruled over a period of economic stagnation. He died of a heart attack and was buried in the Kremlin Wall.

Felix Dzerzhinsky: (1877–1926) First head of the Cheka, the Bolshevik secret police, established in 1917. He organized the reign of Red Terror to keep the Bolsheviks in power. Known as "Iron Felix" for the Cheka's merciless torture and mass executions without trial, he died of a heart attack in Moscow and was buried in the Kremlin Wall.

Reich Leader (*Reichsführer*) Heinrich Himmler: (1900–1945) head of the Nazi Party from 1929 until 1945. He was the second most powerful man after Adolf Hitler in the Third Reich during WWII. He was the key Nazi official responsible for conceiving and overseeing implementation of the Final Solution, the Nazi plan to murder the Jews of Europe. Himmler attempted to go into hiding, but was detained and arrested by British forces once his identity became known. While in British custody, he committed suicide on 23 May, 1945.

Nikita Khrushchev: (1894–1971) Leader of the Soviet Union from 1953 to 1964 during the Cold War. He is known for his denunciation of Stalin's purge in his famous Secret Speech, resulting in the return of Chechens and other exiled groups to their home countries. He supported the early Soviet space program and attempted agricultural reforms. His reign at the height of the Cold War resulted in the erection of the Berlin Wall in 1961, and the Cuban Missile Crisis in 1962. Removed from power in 1964 by party colleagues, he was succeeded by Leonid Brezhnev. He died of a heart attack in Moscow and was denied a state funeral and burial in the Kremlin Wall. He was buried in the Novodevichy Cemetery in Moscow.

Major Bernhard Krueger: (1904–1989) A member of the SS during WWII. He was in charge of a counterfeiting operation to collapse the currencies of Britain and the US. Operation Bernhard, named after Krueger, conducted the operation from a secret factory at *Sachsenhausen* Concentration Camp. In the 1950s, he went before a denazification court, where inmates under his charge at *Sachsenhausen* provided statements that resulted in his acquittal. He eventually worked for the company that had produced the special paper for the Operation Bernhard forgeries. He died in 1989.

Vladimir Lenin: (1870–1924) born Vladimir Ilyich Ulyanov; Leader of the October Bolshevik Revolution in 1917. He was the head of the Bolshevik Russian government from 1922 to 1924. Once in power, he began to confiscate all private property, and ended Russia's part in WWI. He founded the Cheka and instituted the Red Terror, to eliminate opposition and consolidate power. He died after a third stroke at his estate at Gorki, outside Moscow. His body was embalmed and placed on exhibition in Lenin's Mausoleum in Moscow, on January 27, 1924 where it remains today.

Captain Bruno Melmer: (1909–1982) A member of the SS during WWII. He was responsible for transfers of valuables and gold from the Nazi concentration camps to an SS account at the Reichsbank, between May 20, 1943 and April 2, 1945. He was taken prisoner at the end of the war and sentenced on November 2, 1948 to three years in prison.

Vladimir Putin: (1952–) Current President of Russia. A KGB officer for sixteen years, he became Acting President after Yeltsin's resignation in 1999, and then Prime Minister. He was President from 2000 to 2012. After a change in election laws, he ran for a third term in 2012 and was re-elected President for a six-year term. Putin won the 2018 presidential election with more than 76% of the vote. His fourth term will last until 2024.

Joseph Stalin: (1878–1953) born Iosif Dzhugashvil; All-powerful Dictator of the Soviet Union from 1941 to 1953. He was General Secretary of the Central Committee from 1922 to 1953, and led the Soviet Union during WWII. He began his revolutionary career in Tiflis, moving to Baku in 1907–1908. He was a member of the Bolshevik party and an early agitator in Baku, fomenting strikes among oil workers, conducting robberies and extortion. He took part in the Bolshevik revolution and was named Commissar of Nationalities in the new government. As General Secretary of the party, he consolidated power after the death of Lenin in 1924, and thereafter, ruled by fear. He forced Russia to become an industrialized country and began an agricultural program, which resulted in famine in 1932–1933. During his repressive regime, millions of people were sent to the Gulag. In the Great Purge (1937–1938) he eliminated his enemies and old Bolsheviks who were major figures of the revolution on the pretext of rooting out enemies of the government. Thousands were executed. Officially Stalin died four days after a massive stroke, but rumors abound that he might have been murdered by warfarin, a tasteless rat poison, possibly added to his wine by Beria or Khrushchev. His body was embalmed and exhibited in Lenin's tomb. On 31 October 1961, it was removed from the mausoleum and buried in the Kremlin Wall.

Leon Trotsky: (1879–1940) born Lev Bronstein People's Commissar of Military and Naval Affairs. He was the founder and first leader of the Red Army and a chief architect of the Bolshevik victory in the Russian Civil War. A member of the first Politburo, and effective rival to Stalin, he was removed from power in 1927 and deported from the Soviet Union in 1929. While in exile in Mexico, he actively opposed Stalin and was assassinated by Ramon Mercador, a Soviet agent.

Nikolai Ivanovich Yezhov: (1895–1940) He was head of the NKVD from 1936 to 1938, during the height of the Great Purge and organized mass arrests, torture, and executions during the Great Purge. He fell from Stalin's favor and was arrested. He was executed in 1940 along with others who were blamed for the Purge.

Important Dates
Paper Man Dossier

1914–1918: World War I

1917: February to October: Russian Revolution, tsarist government toppled. Tsar abdicates and is imprisoned.

1917, December 15: Russia exits World War I.

1918, July 16–17: Reported murder of the Romanov family.

1918–1922: Russian Civil War between Reds, Bolshevik government, and the Whites, including tsarists, foreign interventionists, and others who opposed them.

1936–1938: Great Purge (Great Terror) conducted by Stalin to eliminate his opponents.

1939–1945: World War II

August 13, 1961–November 9, 1989: Berlin Wall

January 5, 1968–August 21, 1968: Prague Spring

December 26, 1991: End of Soviet Union. Boris Yeltsin became
    president of the newly independent Russian state, the Russian
    Federation. Sell-off of Russia's resources begins.

August 1999: Boris Yeltsin appointed Vladimir Putin Prime Minister.

May 7, 2012: Putin inaugurated President of The Russian Federation.

Made in the USA
Middletown, DE
08 November 2023